Scions of Belhaven, Book One

ROOTS IN INK

Ariella Monti

sweet
magnolia
media

Cover Design: Amanda Hawkins, Eternal Geekery Design
Editing: Jenny Sliger, Owl Eyes Proofs and Edits
Diversity Consultant: Ruthie Bowles, No Market for That Book

3nd edition 2026
Paperback ISBN 979-8-9920601-2-6
Ebook ISBN 979-8-9920601-3-3

Series: Scions of Belhaven
Reading order: 1st
Adult Fiction – Romance – Contemporary/Modern Fantasy

To the storytellers

BEFORE WE GET STARTED

Recommended Reading Order

Roots in Ink
Bound by Ink: A Scions of Belhaven Novella

Roots in Ink is the first novel in the Scions of Belhaven series. Chronologically, the events of the primary storyline occur after *Bound by Ink*, but based on beta reader feedback, I recommend reading *Roots in Ink* first.

Read with Care

Roots in Ink is a fantasy romance in a contemporary setting. While it has a happy ending, this book contains dark themes, discussions, and events. It is not intended for readers under 18 and contains the following elements:

Explicit descriptions of sexual intimacy
Intimate partner violence (verbal and emotional)
Death
Blood
Ritualistic self-harm

Struggles with mental illness and severe depression
Violent government regimes (violence is off page)
Misogyny
Suicidal ideation (implied)
Physical violence
Alcohol consumption
Cigarette smoking
Parental abandonment (off page)
Animals in peril (but unharmed)
Dog attack (Non-fatal human injury)
Explicit swearing

Mental Illness and Intimate Partner Violence

Roots in Ink is a fictional story about imaginary people who live in a magical world that doesn't exist. But it deals with the very real challenges of mental illness and touches on intimate partner violence.
You are real and you exist.
If you're struggling with depression, emotional distress, alcohol or drug use, or just need to talk to someone, please reach out to the suicide and crisis lifeline at 988 or 988lifeline.org.
You deserve to be in a healthy relationship. If you aren't and you need assistance, contact the National Domestic Violence Hotline at 1.800.799.SAFE (7233) or visit thehotline.org/get-help/

ADHD Friendly Formatting

You may notice that the print edition of this book looks a bit different from other books.

The typeface doesn't have those little curls on the ends (called serifs) and the size is a bit bigger. There's more white space on the page and paragraphs are shorter. There's also a bit more space between each line.

These subtle changes are meant to make the text more accessible for neurodivergent readers—like myself. Traditional formatting can make it harder for people with ADHD, dyslexia, and autism to process the information on the page. Many neurodivergent readers have already found ways to accommodate for these challenges, but I wanted my books to have the accommodations built in.

PROLOGUE

Belhaven Island, Ascaria; about 65 years ago

Rose DiMarco had no reason to trust Victor Yates with her family's most valuable objects, but it'd become too dangerous to keep them in her possession, and she was out of options. Georgia Katz's death sent a tidal wave of fear over Belhaven Island's remaining Amora and even the loudest rebels quieted their opposition. The Commarasi government used the young woman to send a message and with a new life growing inside her, Rose felt she had no choice but to listen.

Rose shifted her weight from one foot then the other as she nervously twisted a lock of her hair that came loose from her side comb. Aside from a flattened dirt trail, the back entrance to Yates Manor remained wooded and wild, reminiscent of the island village's earliest days. The same couldn't be said for the rest of the sprawling property.

Smoldering tobacco floated in the air, and Rose glanced at her husband Sam expecting to find him with a lit cigarette. But his empty hands were deep in his jacket pockets, and his lips were pressed in a firm line as he stared into the darkness beyond the trees.

"What if Victor is setting us up?" Rose whispered. "What's stopping him from turning us in and throwing these things into a fire?"

Sam sighed and rubbed his stubbled cheek with a dirt-stained hand.

"Nothing," replied a disembodied voice. "But if I were, why would I wake up before the rooster's crow to meet you here when I could just make a call?"

Victor Yates' stocky form materialized from the shadows. The darkness around him faded as he took a drag of his cigarette.

Rose's temper flared with the man's flagrant use of his ancestral magic while everyone else used theirs in fear. Likely sensing her rage, Sam put a firm hand on her shoulder. A grounding reminder to keep control of her explosive emotions.

She answered his question with several of her own. "Why do it then? Why risk your life to preserve our family's history? Your wealth and influence will only get you so far."

Victor stepped closer. The shadows trailed behind him until darkness circled the threesome and the heavy pickup truck Sam borrowed from his boss, the manor's caretaker.

"It's what my ancestors would have done."

"Your ancestors are the reason why we have to hide." Rose seethed through gritted teeth. "They destroyed the village, cleared the land of everything the Goddesses gave us, and built that monstrosity on the ashes."

Sam grabbed her hand and gave it an urgent squeeze. "Rosie, please."

"No, Sam. She's right." Victor stared into Rose's dark hazel eyes and despite her discomfort, she refused to look away.

With a smirk, Victor stepped forward to the side of the truck, stopping at the tailgate. Rose ran to Victor's side, not yet ready for him to get close to the old box that held her family's history and their secrets.

"Long before my great-grandparents aligned themselves with the Commarasi, the Yates family guarded our people from evils beyond this realm." Victor began calmly. "For centuries, they fought beings both human and magical that sought to do us harm. I don't know why the protectors became the aggressors, but I'm done being a traitor."

Rose searched his face for anything that would give her confidence in his words. When she couldn't look at him any longer, she trained her eyes toward the pile of blankets and Sam's work supplies that hid all that her family had left.

Victor gripped the latch of the tailgate. "You either trust me to keep your relics safe or you don't."

"That's the problem, Victor. I need to trust you, but I don't."

The corners of his mouth lifted into a faint smile as though he were amused by the dilemma. "It's now or never, Rose. What'll it be?

CHAPTER I

EMMA

Belhaven Island, Ascaria; present day

Waves of magic flowed off the smooth planes of the gemstone necklace and into Emma DiMarco's fingertips. She admired the delicate iron details in the incandescent light that dripped from dusty fixtures.

The weak magic was familiar; like a scent that triggered a memory. The longer she held the necklace, the more she struggled to grasp the memory that remained painfully out of reach. Wanting an end to the distressing sensation, Emma slid the jewels back into their leather pouch. She sat back on her heels and ran her fingers over the detailed workmanship. The initials '*SC*' burned into the soft leather were the only clues as to whom this functional work of art once belonged.

Emma had few theories for how the necklace and the chest that held it ended up in the deep, dark corners of the Belhaven Art and History Museum basement. She picked up the notebook beside her, but with her pen on the page, she hesitated. She always made notes about the items she found in the basement, but the vast majority of those items weren't imbued with magic.

Magical items are illegal. Whoever hid the enchanted piece of jewelry did so despite the risks. They were either very brave or very stupid, or like anyone who still practiced magic, a little bit of both. She'd have to be extra careful with this piece. With a heavy sigh, she returned the notebook to its spot beside her. It wasn't worth it.

Turning her attention back to the weathered wooden chest, Emma carefully pulled back a scratchy wool blanket to expose a small stack of leather-bound books spread evenly along the bottom.

"Oh, hello." She picked one from the pile. "What stories do you have for me?"

With gentle hands, she turned a few fragile pages of a ledger. Black ink flowed over the delicate paper, creating a gentle stream of prose that worked its way around soft sketches of flowers and birds. Emma itched to continue leafing through the handwritten tome, but the magic in this part of the basement buzzed around her. The constant hum was sending her over her sensory threshold.

The underground floor had more twists, turns, and secret rooms than the sprawling estate that housed the museum above. There weren't any written records of it, but the older folks on the island agree that the space existed long before the construction of the mansion in the late 1800s.

Even without the anecdotes, Emma knew the museum's basement and the tunnels that fanned out beyond it were connected to Belhaven Island's magical history. She always felt something stir inside her when she sat within the thick stone walls. The sensation was equal parts comforting and terrifying. The untrained earth magic she carried within her veins reached out to it like tree roots seeking water. It was a thirst she had no desire to quench, however, and the possibility of connecting with ancient magic filled her with dread.

It was only after she loaded the trunk and its contents onto a cart that she felt the aches from sitting on a cold, hard floor for three hours. She moved through the winding hallway, the magical buzz easing with every step closer to the elevator.

When the doors opened on the second floor, she heaved a breath of relief.

On the way to her office at the end of the hall, Emma saw museum volunteer Mabel Turner refilling a flier display near the conference room. Mabel stopped her task to greet Emma with a hello and a wide smile that deepened the wrinkles around her mouth and friendly brown eyes.

"Find anything good today?" As she spoke, Mabel adjusted the clip holding the tight ringlets of her gray hair away from her oval face.

Emma stepped closer and spoke with her voice low. "I think I found a set of Amoran diaries that escaped the burnings."

Mabel's eyes widened, and she leaned in closer. The softness of Mabel's magic radiating from her light, freckled skin was an antidote to the lingering heaviness in Emma's body.

"Are you sure?" Mabel whispered. "There are so few primary sources left from that time. They would be extremely valuable."

Emma nodded. "I need to examine them in better light."

Mabel slid a finger slowly along the grain of the chest's wooden lid. "White oak," she murmured. Her expression turned curious. "There's old magic in this chest. I can feel it. Just barely."

Mabel pulled her hand back. Mabel's reaction struck Emma as odd, but she knew the old woman well enough that Mabel would never admit something spooked her.

"Is Judy in her office?" Emma asked. "I need to tell her about this."

Mabel's smile turned wicked, and her eyes brightened with mischievous glee.

"Last I saw her, she was giving a tour to the new caretaker. Have you met him yet?"

Emma narrowed her eyes. "I haven't. Why? What do you know?"

Mabel shrugged innocently. "You were down in the basement for a long time. You should get some sunshine on your skin. See the view. Your eyes will thank you."

This was more like the Mabel she knew, Emma thought.

Mabel shooed her away and Emma moved on, pushing the cart into her office. After three hours in darkness, it took her eyes a few moments to adjust to the flood of light that poured in from the open windows. It was an unseasonably warm day for early March and the breeze from Belhaven Sound floated through the room.

She stopped at the window overlooking the wide expanse of water, losing herself and time in the process. Mabel was right. Emma needed some fresh air and time outside.

She locked the diaries and the necklace inside a refrigerator-sized cabinet, grabbed her light jacket, and made her way out the door.

The sun and salty air hit her olive skin and shook loose the cobwebs that took up residence in her head over the past few days. One hundred acres of museum property lay ahead of her, much of it visually boring. While the wooded edges of the sprawling estate were slowly starting to come alive with the warmth of early spring, before her lay a field of dead grass stretching from the nineteenth century building to the sandy shores of the sound.

In the spring and summer, it was a flat field of green, completely uniform in color and shade. Any errant flower that dared to poke through the monoculture carpet was punished with weedkiller. For what they spent on irrigation to keep the sprawling lawn's deep green color, the museum could offer free art classes to every child in Belhaven.

At least that's what the new guy's landscape renovation proposal claimed. He used the cost savings to justify ripping it out.

Luke? Leo? Logan?

She didn't remember his name, but she did remember the proposal he submitted as part of his application. Pages of native plant suggestions, complete with hand-drawn illustrations of how each planting area would look when the flowers, trees, and shrubs grew to fill in the gaps. Oaks and maples towering over long benches for needed rest while traversing walking paths. Tall grasses with deep roots to hold the soil in place could bring back the fireflies seldom seen on summer nights.

Rain capture and greywater irrigation systems would save even more money. How much? Emma couldn't remember. She was too stunned by it all.

Any qualified landscape designer could walk onto the museum property and make it look less boring and stay within budget. But LukeLeoLogan clearly had a deep understanding and love for the natural world that rivaled her own. It was the sexiest project proposal she'd ever read.

There was no doubt that his proposal was far superior than the others, but the ease with which he sailed through the application process gave her pause. The financial breakdown that accompanied the proposal was $25,000 over budget. It was the most expensive proposal the board of directors reviewed.

Emma couldn't decipher the complicated spreadsheet, but the financial director said the proposed changes would save the museum oodles of money in the long term. The museum's board of directors weren't known for spending money to save money. Over-budget proposals usually went straight into the reject pile, but LukeLeoLogan got an interview and a job offer. Emma—and the financial director for that matter—had no idea how he did it.

Magic?

Enforcement had gotten a little lax, but practicing magic still came with a life sentence of forced labor at best. The last time someone allegedly used magic to influence a hiring committee, their execution aired live on every government media channel. Emma didn't think being a museum caretaker on a small island was worth the risk, but maybe LukeLeoLogan had his reasons.

Her walk took her through the forested bluffs that ran along the shoreline. The sun sat high and light bounced off the calm water. A week of rain and clouds felt like an eternity, and the sun returned just as the darkness began to affect Emma's mood.

Evidence of rough tides streaked across the sand, and the gulls squabbled loudly over the scraps. Clear skies meant she could finally see the blurred lines and blended colors that made up the coastline of Valen, the mainland to the island's north. The incessant buzzing that haunted her in the basement finally vanished.

Her makeshift walking trail connected to a gravel access road better suited to heavy maintenance vehicles than a casual stroll. At a fork, she took the road that would loop back toward the museum instead of taking her deeper into the estate. It also passed by the carriage house that served as LukeLeoLogan's new office. And his new home.

The property caretaker was the only position that seemed to remain relatively unchanged since the bankrupt

Yates heirs turned the estate over to a fledgling historical society for good publicity in the early 1990s. The man overseeing the property lived with his family in a small, but functional, apartment on the second floor of the maintenance building. The most recent one finally retired after forty years and a hip replacement.

From behind the trees, the imposing building looked more like a fortress than a garage. Terracotta roof tiles and vivid emerald moss fused to thick stone walls softened its appearance.

Conversation emanated from the parking pad in front of the building. Voices often got picked up by the sea winds, but there was no mistaking the expressive voice of her boss, Museum Director Judy Baudin. The striking woman was speaking animatedly with a man Emma didn't recognize. Given the circumstances, she assumed this was the infamous new property manager.

The man leaned in, giving Judy his full attention. And when he spoke, it was with his whole body. The clipboard in one hand didn't stop him from making wide arcs with his long arm. After several expressive gestures, he stilled to adjust the band of a large silver watch, its face flashing when it caught the sunlight. The sleeves of his collared shirt were rolled up to the middle of his toned forearms, exposing black ink that snaked over his sun-darkened white skin.

"Emma!" Judy summoned her with a wave, her bangle bracelets clicking lightly.

Emma caught a bit of their conversation as she walked over.

"I'm just so excited to have a space where we can start having some outdoor classes and activities," Judy continued as she wiped her glasses with a small cloth she pulled from her pocket.

"I'm glad you're excited about it," the man said. "The nature classroom was my favorite part of the design."

Judy gently brushed her long box braids over her shoulder and smiled when Emma stepped closer to the pair. Standing next to the tall woman, Emma could smell the sea breeze swirling with the scent of cocoa butter that danced off Judy's deep amber skin.

"Emma, this is Liam Doran. Our new property manager."

Liam.

Not Luke, Leo, or Logan.

Liam's lips curled up into a smile, but his eyes fell on Emma with an intensity that made her heart pound and her stomach twist. His cream-white shirt deepened the icy blue of his hooded eyes. The sun against his face highlighted the red in his short chestnut beard that softened the angles of his jaw. A gust of wind came off the water blowing his hair over his forehead and in front of his eyes. Emma bit her lower lip to hide a smile as he ran his fingers through his shaggy locks a few times to brush it out of his face. It fell lazily until it found its way back to its natural part.

Please throw me up against a wall and tear me in half.

The thought flashed like lightning and was just as ferocious. Emma was so distracted by her body's response that she barely heard what Judy said after his name.

Liam reached out his hand and Emma caught another glimpse of the tattoo on the inside of his forearm. His eyes still locked on hers, he licked his lips when she took his hand.

"Nice to meet you, Liam." Electricity pulsed through her body with the touch of his rough skin against hers.

It wasn't magic that got him the job, she realized. It was pure sex. And a stellar resume. And an impeccably researched and designed project proposal.

But most definitely sex.

"Yeah, you too." His hand lingered for a bit before releasing his grip.

Judy placed a grounding hand on Emma's shoulder. "Emma is our collections researcher and handles some of our publicity."

"That's just a nice way of saying that I write press releases and post pictures on social media."

"Well, I don't know anything about social media, but spreadsheets are my specialty." Liam smiled, causing little wrinkles in the corners of his expressive eyes.

"I'm sure you'll learn a lot from her." Judy winked. "There will be many opportunities for you to collaborate and publicize the progress of the redesign."

Liam nodded, his eyes never leaving Emma's. He put his hands in his pockets and leaned in a bit.

"I hope so. I'd love to learn all about you ... your job. The social media and the collections." His cheeks flushed, and he awkwardly tried to share his eye contact with Judy. "I'd love to learn all about it."

Emma pressed her lips together to stifle her laughter. Under that gorgeous exterior, Liam was probably just as awkward as she was. "I totally got what you meant. I'm sure we can come up with a few ideas."

Like tying me to your bed.

Emma looked away and tried to quietly exhale a breath in hopes it would dispel all the sexually intrusive thoughts about her new coworker. She always felt her emotions deeply and instantaneous physical attraction wasn't unusual for her. Usually, though, Emma had to interact with a person for more than five minutes before considering rope play.

Judy's voice broke through the tension. "Liam, why don't you go inside and poke around the office? I just have to check in with Emma about something and I'll be right in."

The lightness in Emma's chest instantly turned into a stone of anxiety.

Was she getting fired? Did Judy know all the dirty things she was thinking about Liam?

"Emma, you're not in trouble," she said once Liam disappeared behind the door. Judy's sympathetic brown eyes fell on her. "You've got that look on your face like you're convinced I'm about to fire you."

Emma sighed with relief. "I didn't choose the anxious life. The anxious life chose me."

Judy laughed but pressed her hands to her temples with a shake of her head. "I'm definitely not firing you. I got another status survey for you this morning."

Emma groaned and rolled her eyes. The surveys from the Ascarian government security offices were sent to employers at unpredictable intervals, but this was Emma's third in the past year.

"I know," Judy said with equal annoyance. "I'd like to tell you that they stop eventually, but the museum board got one for me last week."

The detailed questionnaire about an employee's work status was one way the Ascarian Federation of Allied Regions kept tabs on people like Emma and Judy. People born with ties to radical Amoran families. Families with magical lineages and a history of resistance and hostility towards the Commarasi, Ascaria's authoritarian government. Emma lived a relatively quiet existence, but the same couldn't be said for the generations before her and extra paperwork was penance for their sins.

"I might as well join a rebel group if they're going to keep treating me like I'm a part of one," she said through gritted teeth.

Judy laughed through her nose and shook her head. "That's exactly what they're hoping you'll do."

Emma unclenched her jaw and let it go.

"I found something in the basement I need you to look at. I think they're diaries from before." She gestured vaguely towards the museum. "All this."

Judy arched a perfectly penciled eyebrow. "I have to get back to Liam, but we should be done soon. I'll text you, and you can meet me in my office."

Emma nodded in agreement.

Judy's cat-eye glasses slid down her nose. "Don't go organizing any rallies in the meantime," she said pointedly.

"How about a letter-writing campaign?" Emma countered.

With her hand on the knob of the office door, Judy flashed Emma a stern look, then disappeared inside.

CHAPTER 2

LIAM

Liam stood in the foyer waiting for his eyes to adjust to the darkness. He struggled to get his bearings in the new space. His body was still feeling the effects of Emma's dark hazel eyes connecting with his and leaving him momentarily breathless. The deep green and dark brown rivaled the colors of moss on a forest floor. Her smile was friendly and comforting one moment, but alluring and seductive the next.

Where was Emma three months ago?

Liam wiped his sweaty hands on his jeans and fussed with his shirt collar. He ran his hands through his wind-blown hair a few times as though it would reset him to his default settings.

He tried to focus on the space. His space. His new office. And his new home for at least the next year.

To his right was a row of thick coat hooks holding heavy weatherproof jackets and insulated work pants to use when he worked outside. To his left was a steep flight of stairs made of brick and stone that would take him to the second-floor landing and the door to his apartment.

Walking through another heavy wooden door, Liam found his office. He turned in circles in the cluttered space, but he wasn't really there. Holding Emma's hand sent lightning through him, heating his entire body and liquifying his brain. The spark lingered in his veins, and he struggled to focus on anything else.

The sound of the front door slamming shut, and the rhythmic tapping of high heels, was a welcomed distraction. Again, he ran his hands through his hair and over his beard a few times, trying to pull himself together.

Judy walked into the space. "It's definitely not a corner office overlooking the River City skyline."

Liam smiled weakly and for the first time really looked at his new office. She wasn't wrong. The small room with its thick stone walls, dirt-stained floor, and functional furniture was a far cry from the office he walked away from five years ago.

"It'll take me a few weeks to get it organized the way I like, but it's perfect."

Judy crooked her finger and motioned for him to follow her. "Let me show you the apartment upstairs."

The corner-office version of Liam would have lost his mind if he knew one day he'd trade in his luxury suburban townhouse for a one-bedroom apartment over a garage. He had enough squirreled away in savings and investments that even on his nonprofit salary, he could easily afford a house twice the size.

But Liam was done with that part of his life. Done with acquiring things that were beyond his reasonable need. Done with symbols of status and wealth. The work required to keep up with that life almost killed him, and he wouldn't be going back.

Although the building looked cold and foreboding from the outside, the upstairs living space had a warmth and comfort about it. The curtains were drawn and the windows opened, letting in the sunshine and the sea breeze that carried the faint scent of pine as it brushed through the trees. Creamy white paint popped against the dark hardwood floors. He stepped closer to the wood-burning fireplace to admire the masonry work of the hearth. He ran a finger along the exposed stone that made up the entire wall. It seemed to hum under his touch, but Judy's voice stole his focus before he could give it more thought.

"All the stone was shipped from the Valen mountains. It made up more of the building, but over the years, much of it had to be replaced."

Liam backed away from the wall, hitting a bronze bucket of fireplace tools with his heel. He cringed at his clumsiness, but Judy didn't seem to notice.

"The heat is electric, and the fireplace really helps cut down on utility costs in the winter." Judy took a seat at the small kitchen table.

Liam nodded, thankful for the tip. Housing was included in his contract, but utilities were on him. He moved on to the kitchen. He half-expected fifty-year-old appliances and fixtures but everything appeared brand new.

"Belle is going to tear up these floors." Liam flashed her an apologetic smile.

Judy shrugged. "These floors can take a beating."

Liam wandered into the bathroom and made a mental note about the size of the linen closet.

"You know, Belle isn't the first dog to live here," Judy called from the kitchen.

"Oh yeah?" He peered into the large stand-up shower.

"Emma did a great series called *The Dogs of Yates Manor* for our newsletter last year."

Liam's stomach fluttered, and his eyes closed at the sound of her name, the heat of her touch still danced in his hand. He imagined brushing her long, hazelnut-brown hair off her neck and grazing his lips over her skin while digging his fingers into the soft flesh of her hips.

Judy encouraged them to collaborate. Is this how he'd feel every time Emma was nearby? He tried to remember the last time he was inexorably drawn to a person in this way, and he came up empty.

After some time, Judy yelled from the kitchen. "Are you okay in there?"

He combed his fingers through his hair to regain his composure and stepped out of the bathroom. "Sorry, I got distracted."

Liam pulled out a chair and sat across from Judy at the old wooden table.

"Just as perfect as your new office, I hope." Judy pulled a set of keys out of her pocket, put them down gently, and slid the chair away from the table.

"It will be. Just needs my dog."

"You should take your time getting to know the place without me hovering over you. Make a list of anything you need and bring it to the staff meeting later."

Liam offered her his thanks and with a smile and a nod, she left, leaving him alone with more optimism than he'd felt in years.

The second floor of the museum housed a mix of exhibition rooms and administrative offices. Liam had a vague idea of where he needed to go for the afternoon staff meeting but refused to admit he was lost.

"You look lost."

Until now.

Liam laughed and turned to face the voice that had greeted him. "Yes. I am."

He recognized the older woman from the beginning of Judy's tour. He gave her a hopeful smile and tried to remember her name without looking at her volunteer name tag. "Mabel, right?"

"The one and only." She opened her arms with dramatic flair. "Looking for the staff meeting?"

"Yes. I'm glad I gave myself some extra time."

"I'm headed there too. I'll let you escort me." Mabel hooked her arm through Liam's elbow and started walking in the opposite direction of where Liam was headed. "It's easy to get lost in this place. Especially on your first day."

Liam expected to slow his pace to account for the difference in their strides, but Mabel's petite, elderly frame was deceiving. She moved quickly, and Liam almost struggled to keep up.

"I did a little reading about the estate before my interview a few months ago. I should have studied the map."

Mabel chuckled. "It wouldn't have made a difference. The map only shows the public what we let them see. Much like people. They have a persona they share with the public, but it's only a small piece of who they are."

Mabel's casual observation sounded personal. Did Mabel know something about him or his past? He didn't hide his prior career in finance, but he was intentionally vague when asked any questions beyond the skills he'd need for his current position. A small nugget of worry pressed on Liam's chest.

Did she know about his family? *Their magic*?

Liam's quickening breaths were interrupted by a light squeeze. Mabel's slow exhales coaxed Liam's into matching hers. A comforting warmth spread through his body, easing that nugget of worry. By the time they reached a door at the far end of the floor, Liam's anxiety no longer had a hold on him. His questions remained, but they no longer concerned him. He wasn't sure why he suddenly felt safe and at ease.

Liam stood outside the door, letting Mabel walk in ahead of him.

"I found the new caretaker wandering the halls." Mabel flashed him a sly smile and a wink. "Didn't want to lose him like we did the last guy."

"I heard he's still roaming the third floor." An attractive man approached Liam with his hand out. His brown skin and his eyes both had a hint of copper that reminded Liam of late autumn maples.

The man could have been older, but his flawless skin and neat haircut made him appear no older than twenty-five. Liam needed to know this guy's skin-care regimen.

"I'm Hector," the man said. "The programming director."

Liam returned Hector's firm grip and introduced himself. "Maybe I should tie a bell around my neck so you guys can keep track of me."

A svelte woman introduced herself as Blair, the financial director. He'd only spoken with her over the phone and email, and this was his first time meeting her in person.

Thick black eyeliner highlighted her wide-set dark eyes, and a deep rose lipstick complemented the red undertones of her brown skin. Her short thick hair was gray at the roots but darkened to nearly black at the ends.

"I'm sure you'll figure it out. But if we're tying bells to people, make sure Emma gets one." Blair lifted one finger from her coffee cup and pointed across the table.

Liam's eyes met Emma's playful gaze, making his heart skip a beat. He forgot how to breathe, and every word disappeared.

"Because I go into the basement and disappear for hours at a time?" Emma guessed.

"Exactly." Blair laughed. "One day, someone is going to have to go looking for you down there and you'll be easier to find."

"It's probably not a bad idea." Emma conceded. "I swear that place gets bigger every time I go down there."

She put her water bottle and her notebook on the table, then hit Liam with another smile. "Hey, Newbie, how's your first day going?"

Miraculously, all his basic functions came back online.

"I haven't been fired yet." Liam shrugged. "So far so good."

"Yet being the key phrase." She winked and left for the refreshment table.

Liam wasn't sure how long he stood there before Mabel reached up and patted his arm. He pulled out the chair next to her and sat down.

When Emma returned to her seat, Mabel pointed a finger and said, "She's a troublemaker, that one."

Emma slid a plate of cookies across the table to Mabel. "She says that like she didn't teach me everything she knows."

Liam marveled at the friendly atmosphere. He'd been steeped in a toxic work environment for so long, he forgot there could be anything else. In his experience, a healthy work culture simply didn't exist. The competition and pressure of his last job made everyone the worst version of themselves, including Liam. For most of his coworkers, the lifestyle and salary was incentive enough to suffer through. Liam did for a long time. Even when it started ruining his life.

Judy began the meeting shortly after taking her own seat. She owned the room, but without the arrogance and aggression he was accustomed to. The six other people around the table turned their bodies toward her, their attention hers and only momentarily distracted by the snacks in front of them.

"I'm sure you've all noticed the new face at the table." She nodded at Liam and everyone's eyes turned on him. "Liam Doran is our new property manager. He's responsible for the maintenance team and overseeing the landscaping renovation starting next week. He'll be living on site with his dog Bluebelle."

A collective cheer erupted.

Emma clapped her hands excitedly. "It's been so long since we've had a museum puppy!"

"Liam, why don't you tell us about yourself before we dive into the rest of the agenda?" Judy relaxed back in her chair signaling that he had the floor.

"Oh. Okay." He shifted in his seat and cleared his throat. He didn't anticipate introducing himself, though the practice was probably normal at most jobs. "I'm sure you'll quickly find that Bluebelle is the most interesting thing about me, but here it goes."

He smiled awkwardly. Emma snagged his gaze and held it, her wide smile soothing his nerves.

"Thank you for the warm welcome. Everyone I've met has been really great, and I'm looking forward to getting to know you. I've been a landscaper for almost five years, doing smaller design projects, and I'm really excited to do something bigger. I'm from Asters Valley. I'm really good with spreadsheets. That's it, I guess."

Judy thanked him and took back the reins. She instructed each of the staffers on the museum's small team to go through their projects and their goals for the coming month.

With Emma so close, Liam could observe the little quirks and details that he rarely noticed in others. Emma took almost as many notes as Mabel, the acting staff clerk. When her pen wasn't flying across her page, Emma fidgeted with it and used it to emphasize her ideas.

Without the light jacket she wore outside, a collection of colorful tattoos on the inside of her wrist and forearm were visible, though not clearly enough that he could make out exactly what they were. She ate the chocolate side of her black and white cookie first, followed by the vanilla.

When the conversation circled back to programming, Liam was deeply distracted by three raised beauty marks on Emma's collarbone.

"I'd like to start developing classes that would be a good fit for the nature classroom," Hector said, turning to Liam. "Could we set up a meeting for the end of the week to go over the construction schedule and design plans?"

Liam cleared his throat and sat up. His face warmed with the embarrassment of being caught not paying attention.

"Definitely. I should have an update from our contractors by Wednesday."

Hector wrote something in his notebook, then spun his chair to face Emma.

"Is Regan still interested in teaching a few backyard astronomy classes?" He asked. "Depending on the timing, we can hold it in the classroom instead of the back patio."

"Ohh, she'd love that," Emma replied. "She said May would work best with her teaching schedule."

"Cool. Can you tell her I'll be in touch next week after meeting with Liam?"

Emma nodded and scribbled a note. "I'll tell her tonight."

Is Regan her girlfriend? Liam's stomach clenched with curiosity and disappointment.

Judy sat forward, her arms crossed on the table. "I think offering an astronomy class is long overdue. But Hector, I need to remind you to be mindful of how you word that program description. Regan has been teaching astronomy long enough that I'm sure she can craft something that won't get flagged, and I'd like to review it before it goes live."

"Of course," Hector said with a sober nod.

Judy ended the meeting after Liam gave a rundown of the tentative construction schedule. "Enjoy the rest of your evening, everyone."

Liam looked at his watch and tilted his head in confusion when he saw it was only four.

"We leave early on staff meeting days." Emma's voice carried over the shuffling of notebooks and friendly small talk.

He nodded and collected his things. "So what's there to do around here with all the extra time after work?"

Emma shrugged. "Depends on what you're into."

"What are you into?"

Emma brought the top of her pen to her mouth. Focusing on the way she tapped it on her deep pink lips, Liam missed his other coworkers leaving them alone at the conference table. Judy and Hector talked quietly just outside the door, but otherwise, the room was empty.

"Do you drink?" She finally asked.

"A bit. Not like I used to."

She held out her hand across the table. "Can I have your phone?"

Without hesitating, he unlocked his phone and handed it to her.

"Island Cidery is a little place downtown." Her thumbs tapped across the screen. "The owners are fifth generation distillers, or something like that. Most of their ingredients are sourced locally, and what they can't get in Belhaven, they get from Willow Ridge."

Emma reached across the table and handed back his phone just as hers buzzed on the table.

"It'll give you a true taste of the area." She pushed the chair back and stood up. "And now you have my number if you need anything more specific."

Liam stood up but continued to stare at the sent message in his phone. Even as coworkers, he didn't expect to get her phone number that quickly.

"Just don't send me any nudes." She smirked. "We don't know each other that well yet."

He locked the phone and slid it into his pocket. Usually a locked book of secrets, Liam was ready to tell Emma anything she wanted to know. She only had to ask, and he'd share his entire life story.

"Yet being the key phrase."

Emma's face turned mischievous. He grew hot as her eyes raked his body. She had him in a chokehold without saying a word.

"See you tomorrow, Newbie."

He took a deep breath when she left the room, grasping for what little control he had of his body.

And it was only Monday.

CHAPTER 3

DIARY OF SARA CORTESE

Belhaven Island, late winter circa 1620

Seven days and nights of rain have fallen to the earth. The bloated creeks that carve through the isle threatened to wash our village into the sea, but this time, we were spared from destruction. We emerged from the storms grateful for the nourishment that will feed our young crops and fill our wells. I've added gifts of gratitude to our Goddesses to the family alter.

As foretold by the skygazers, the rain that brought us life also brought us death. When the village elders called for me, I knew the rains claimed Maryanne Banner's life. I'd long known that Maryanne named me her successor as our village's keeper of lore. A heavy heart escorted me on the muddy journey from my home to the temple.

Though sixty years old, Maryanne was far from frail. Despite her vigor, she believed her journey to Terultimi was near. Shortly before she died, Maryanne told me that when the elders pass me her quill to record our people's stories, I must continue to keep my own.

"Keep them separate and keep them hidden."

In a voice as sharp as lightning, she claimed it would be my truth that would come to be of great importance. That would be the last time in this life that we would speak. On the seventh night, her corporal form was all that was left in this realm.

When I arrived at the Banner home, a small herd of unicorns was standing vigil at the forest edge. No doubt they felt the loss of their caretaker. As a keeper of mystic animals, Maryanne tended to many of the creatures that journey between the realms. If the unicorns were there, I suspect other beings were as well.

Maryanne's partner Eliza puts on a brave face as she prepares for the funeral rituals that will guide Maryanne safely through Teremedi to join her family and the Goddesses in paradise. I visited with Eliza only long enough to give her a basket filled with the plants she will need for our sacred rituals and a few balms and tonics to aid her through her grief.

The people of my island village are intimately familiar with death, and we embrace it as part of our pact with the natural world. In my heart, the cause of Maryanne's death was not part of our natural world.

CHAPTER 4
DIARY OF SARA CORTESE

Belhaven Island, early spring circa 1620

The deep browns of winter have given way to the vibrant color of spring. The earth took blessings from the clouds and turned them into wide green leaves and delicate pink buds.

From autumn's heavy blanket, the smallest of souls emerge from their winter sleep. I hear their scurries through the forest as I search for the tender hearts of the redbud tree. My stores of this precious ingredient are low, and the tonic for which they are required is desperately needed.

At the village full moon feast, I was offering gifts to the moon Goddess when I was approached by Piper Dawson. Accompanying her was Bethany Clement, a doula from Willow Ridge, a small community on the land beyond Belhaven's southern shore.

I was struck speechless by Bethany's beauty, mesmerized by the way firelight danced in her large emerald eyes. The magic that surrounded her whispered to mine, curling together like the ringlets of her hair. Sweet dimples appeared on her light, freckled skin every time she smiled, which she did often. I'm ashamed of how my attention to Piper wavered when in Bethany's presence, especially due to the serious nature of Bethany's arrival in Belhaven.

Piper's father, John, collapsed in his stables shortly before Maryanne's death. I saw him then, offering a balm to ease his pain. Though he sat by the fire, his skin was remarkably cold. His pains have worsened since and violent nightmares keep him from proper rest. His aches keep him from his craft, and Piper has stepped up as the village blacksmith.

At the guidance of the Willow Ridge skygazers, the elder healers stationed Bethany here and John Dawson became her first charge.

Doulas like Bethany require the assistance of an herbal alchemist, like me. The gift of the Goddesses' healing magic is a great honor, but it comes at a great price. Doulas must share their essence with the sick. Working in partnership with medicinal healers allows them to rest and care for their own bodies so that they can continue to care for others.

I'm not the only alchemist in Belhaven, but Bethany wished to work with one that Piper's family held in complete trust. I'm humbled and honored that they've chosen me. I would do anything to help the Dawson family, but this feels more than aiding a beloved member of our village.

It feels like destiny.

Chapter 5
Emma

The delicate parchment of the 400-year-old diary tugged lightly at the binding as Emma carefully turned the page. She wondered if anyone had opened the book since Sara Cortese penned the entry on the final page.

The small collection of Sara's personal diaries were packed with the official records she took as Belhaven's keeper of lore, a title Emma didn't know existed until she found them. The books were packed well, suggesting that someone intended to keep them safe while being moved. To where and from where remained a mystery.

Emma spent three days sifting through the museum's digital and paper records looking for any clues for how the museum or the original owners of the property came into possession of the trunk. Though frustrating, it wasn't surprising that her search yielded little that she didn't already know.

The Yates family, like many in Belhaven, had a complicated history with magic. During Sara's time, the Yates' were considered some of Belhaven's bravest warriors. Among others, they were chosen by Amora goddesses to guard the rift to Teremedi—the realm between the natural world and the afterlife—and prevent malevolent creatures from crossing over. Their battle skills were required during the Commarasi's violent push for power, leaving the rift vulnerable.

No one knew why the Yates family eventually partnered with the same people they spent hundreds of years fighting, and if they did, they took that knowledge to the grave. Many of Belhaven's oldest Amora families still consider them traitors and refuse to speak their names in good faith, Emma's Grandma Rose included.

But Emma's exploration of the family's manor painted a more complex picture. The Yates may have razed the remains of the sacred temple and surrounding village to build their estate, but as Commarasi leaders ordered the destruction of Amoran literature, texts, and official records, someone must have used their own influence to protect artifacts connected to their family history. The more Emma poked around the forgotten items, the looser those connections became. She suspected someone did what little they could to prevent their culture from going extinct.

Emma stood up and leaned on the hand-carved dining table she used as a desk. The large surface was cluttered with pieces from several projects. She rounded and arched her spine to release some of the tightness that settled into her back and shoulders. She reached across the table for her stack of sticky notes and continued to mindlessly rock her hips while she jotted down the names Sara mentioned in her entry.

To prevent people from learning their family history, the Commarasi burned most of Ascaria's census records from before 1900. They kept their own copies, of course, but the public couldn't access those. Even with little to go on, Emma had a few research tricks up her sleeve.

A knock on the door pulled her attention from the old tomes. Her breath hitched when she saw Liam leaning against the doorframe. How dare he have the audacity to do something that sexy at their place of work?

"Hey, are you busy?" He took a few steps into the room and removed his dusty baseball cap.

His smile was both charming and intoxicating, and it made her drunk with desire in a way that surpassed anything she'd ever felt for a person. His rich syrup-colored hair intensified his expressive eyes of calcite blue. His shaggy, untamed locks were the perfect length for twisting between her fingers. She couldn't tell the texture of his neatly groomed beard but knew it would tickle her most sensitive skin.

At first, she thought her attraction was purely physical. Just the whole look of him ticked every one of Emma's boxes as though he were created by a goddess and placed on earth just for her. But despite their infrequent interactions, that physical attraction became an unyielding pull that twisted with her magic like vines gripping a nearby tree.

She swore off coworkers as romantic or sexual partners; she went through several in her twenties, and it took her too long to learn it always ended badly. Now at thirty-eight, it was the sort of workplace drama she actively avoided. Her coworkers at the museum became family, and a broken relationship held too much potential for tearing her family apart.

Regardless, any involvement with Emma put a target on her suitor's back.

She sat in the office chair behind her. "I'm reading a 400-year-old diary. Its urgency ran out a long time ago. What's up?"

Liam walked toward her desk and sat in the tattered but cozy armchair she kept nearby. He leaned forward, putting his elbows on his thighs. "Can you do something with me today?"

Intrigued by his vague choice of words, Emma crossed her arms on her desk and leaned forward. "What did you have in mind?"

"I just came from a meeting with Judy, and she suggested filming a quick explanation video about the renovation. The thing is, we'd have to film today since it's going to rain tomorrow, and the project starts Monday."

"Hmm," she mused. She leaned back in her chair and crossed one leg over the other. "This sounds more like a project for me unless you know how to edit video."

Liam's sun-kissed cheeks reddened a touch, and a ghost of a smile formed on his lips as he mirrored her posture. His tall, athletic build overpowered the old chair.

"You're right. It's not exactly a fair ask. But if there's a project here or a personal project at home that I could help you with, I'd be happy to return the favor."

Emma bit her lip, enjoying this flirty back and forth with her coworker far too much. "Say please."

Liam's resolve crumbled into laughter, taking Emma's with it.

"Please, can you help me with this project that our boss wants us to work on?"

"Yes. Of course I'll help you." Emma opened a nearby drawer and pulled out a small video camera.

Emma's sexual attraction to men seldom lasted after they opened their mouths. This little project was exactly what she needed to prove that under those seductive eyes and inviting mouth was just another disappointment. She told herself that this ridiculous sexual attraction to Liam would wane, and she could once again go about her day without thinking about all the places she wanted that mouth.

Walking side-by-side through the quiet museum made it easier for Emma to see the finer details of his face: the dappled selenite white in his beard, and the little folds between his brows when he smiled. He smelled like freshly turned earth and the forest after a heavy rain.

"So, 400-year-old diaries, huh?" He asked, breaking the silence.

Emma forgot she mentioned the diaries to Liam and his question took her by surprise. She and Judy agreed that Emma should work with them quietly and avoid talking about them with staff outside the collections team. Judy's background check into prospective employees dove deep into their potential Commarasi connections. Judy only hired people who she determined weren't outright hostile to Amora, but even the staunchest of allies have been known to turn with enough pressure from authorities.

"Yeah, it was a really cool find." She bit her nail to avoid spilling more details.

"What are you going to do with them?"

"I'm not sure. I'm still going through them. The historical commission has a lot of rules about how we create exhibits and the information we can share. Anything that goes against the regional or federation official record is illegal. I've never worked with anything this old before."

It was all true except for not having any ideas. Emma had an entire page, but most weren't viable under the country's censorship laws. She begrudgingly accepted those boundaries as a necessary part of her work, but now that she had a first-hand account of life before the Commarasi, it was tempting to push up against them.

They used a side door that opened out to one of the original rose gardens that only exploded with color after meticulous care and pampering. Emma knew from reading

Liam's proposal that he was going to tear out whatever was left of the roses and replace them with plants better suited for a beating by the salty winds.

"There wouldn't happen to be a list of plants in there, by chance?" Liam asked as though reading her mind.

"Not a list, exactly, but the one I'm reviewing now is partially a nature diary. I saw a few plant sketches, but I don't remember the names offhand," Emma lied.

She remembered all of them. Many of them grew in her backyard, planted and nurtured by her grandmother. The others could be found on the edges of the museum property. Sara cataloged more than two dozen plants and about as many animals. She detailed uses for each plant and recipes for elixirs and balms.

And if that was all, Emma wouldn't hesitate to show them to Liam; Sara's diaries were also her spell books and spell books were the kind of illegal that ended your life.

Emma and Sara, as it turned out, had the same kind of magic. The kind of magic that enhanced the medicinal and mystical properties of plants. While anyone could make a cup of yarrow tea to ease an upset stomach, their magic amplified yarrow's healing abilities to cure the most painful of digestive ailments within hours. Sara was one of several island pharmacists, but Emma only had enough training to cure a mild stomach flu.

Liam stopped walking in the middle of the garden and began bouncing on his toes. His eyes sparkled like a child who was promised a fluffy animal for their birthday.

"Knowing exactly what plants were on this property before it became all this would be amazing. The undeveloped sections gave me some really good clues, but confirmation would be next level."

The impact of his beaming smile caught her by surprise. It sent a quiver of excitement racing through her. It was far too tempting to break all the rules to keep that smile from fading.

"I have to be really careful about handling the books, but I can make a list for you," she offered.

"Yes, please." Liam winked.

Emma's quiver became a throb. She struggled to keep an even breath.

Apparently satisfied, Liam began turning in slow circles.

"I thought the video could highlight the projects that are going to make the biggest difference on the property." He gestured vaguely around the garden. "All this stuff is getting ripped out so we could start here."

"Yeah. Sure," Emma croaked. If she couldn't get her body under control, she'd be forced to submerge herself in the icy sea water below. She busied herself with turning on her video camera and checked the light.

"Then we could move to where the nature classroom will be." Liam shifted his gaze again, this time towards the front of the museum. "And then we could head back here to the parking lot where the new pavers and rain gardens will go."

His eyes returned to her, a look of genuine interest on his face. "What do you think?"

"That sounds great." She smiled.

He looked pleased with her praise, then held out his hand. "Any chance you want to be in front of the camera instead?"

"Oh no, sir," she said with a laugh. "This is The Liam Doran Show. You're managing this whole renovation. My job is in the basement. Literally and figuratively."

Liam sighed, and she almost gave in to his pleading eyes. "You can't blame me for trying."

She pointed to a shady tree nearby. "Start walking back toward that tree behind you."

Liam stepped backward.

She followed, monitoring the light on the small screen. "Listen, I review our social media demographics pretty regularly, and if I thought putting a gorgeous woman on screen would be good for engagement, I'd absolutely do it."

Emma held up her hand indicating he was in a good spot.

Liam took off his hat and ran his calloused fingers through his hair a few times. He placed the hat a little higher, allowing more light to shine on his lightly weathered skin. Then he flashed her a coy smile and arched a brow.

"So, what are you saying?"

"I'm saying you and your whole rugged, outdoorsy, strong-man aesthetic would be more appealing to our social media following."

He lowered his head with a sheepish smile, but his eyes simmered. "So, I'm just clickbait then?"

"Pretty much." She winked and pressed record before he could respond. "And you're on."

Considering Liam's protests, Emma anticipated he'd be boring or awkward in front of the camera, but he came alive once prompted. He was charming and approachable, and endearingly goofy. He explained the science behind each project without sounding arrogant or condescending. Emma chimed in with questions that he graciously answered with the contagious excitement of someone who truly loved their work. She wanted to listen to him talk for hours about native plants, rainwater management, and soil retention.

"Personally, I think the coolest part of the nature classroom will be the living roof that will span over the seating area. In the summer, these vines will provide shade for us and a food source for lizards and birds."

Liam paused to catch his breath when the shrill chime of his phone cut through the quiet. "It's one of the subcontractors. Can we break for a few?"

Emma nodded and took the opportunity to sit down on a patch of brittle grass overlooking the water. Feeling a mild ache in her lower back, she reached her hands to her toes. The people of Belhaven remained especially close to their Amoran roots, however thin they might be. That meant treating their little slice of the island as a habitat they shared with all earth's creatures. The kind of care Liam was taking came instinctually for Belhaven's longest residents. Liam was an outsider, and highlighting how he made the island's ecology a focus of his design would go a long way with the locals.

"I can't wait for this little spot to have benches," Emma said when Liam joined her on the ground. She ran her fingers over the dry grass, pulling some as she went.

"You don't like this straw poking you in the ass while gazing out to the open sea?"

"Not without getting to know me first." She shot him a playful smile and threw a tuft of grass at him. It came apart in the breeze and floated onto his outstretched legs.

"Noted." Liam responded by throwing his own handful of grass.

"What exactly will the living roof be made out of?" She asked between giggles as grass sailed between them. This grown man tapped into an adolescent silliness Emma rarely experienced as an adult. It filled her soul in a way few things could.

"Probably Virginia creeper. It's not flashy but the autumn berries are good for birds. And it doesn't destroy the stuff it climbs."

Emma nodded thoughtfully. "Virginia creeper is pretty abundant in this area. There's enough direct sunlight that trumpet vine could do well. It's sure to attract hummingbirds, which are my personal favorite."

"Trumpet vine it is then."

Liam's boyish smile made her blush and in that moment, a spark of something passed between them. It buzzed through her and left goosebumps in its wake. Liam ran a hand over his opposite arm, and she wondered if he felt it too.

"You know a lot about plants for someone who analyzes social media demographics all day." He leaned back on his hands and briefly lifted his face to the sun. He squeezed his eyes shut, deepening the wrinkled corners.

"I learned a lot from my grandmother. She taught me the importance of balancing human existence with all earth's beings. I live in her old house downtown and many of the plants on the property have been there for two or three generations. They're my responsibility now."

Emma silently scolded herself for oversharing. She needed to change the subject before she started rambling again.

"While we're here, can I meet your dog?"

Liam beamed like a proud parent. "You really wanna?"

"I absolutely do!"

Liam laughed.

"Say please." His playful smile did little to temper his suggestive tone.

"Ugh." Emma feigned annoyance. "Please can I meet your dog?"

"Jeez, Emma. You don't have to beg. Of course you can meet my dog."

She rapidly tore out several handfuls of grass and threw them at Liam just as quickly. "Thank you, Liam!"

When Emma finished her barrage of grass and pine needles, Liam brushed himself off and got up with ease. He offered his hand and Emma hesitated a beat, knowing that once their bodies connected, there would be no going back.

Liam

Emma's hands were so unlike his, but somehow perfectly matched. When Liam's palm made contact with hers, warmth beamed from deep within his bones, molding to Emma's skin like invisible glue. The sensation intrigued him.

How could something so unfamiliar feel so right?

He barely registered pulling Emma to her feet and his hand remained tightly clasped around hers. The pressure of her grip hadn't loosened either. Liam knew he should let go before it got awkward and uncomfortable, but breaking their bond was akin to cutting off his own limb.

A cold gust of wind came off the frigid water, chilling the warmth that bound them. Emma's hand trembled slightly, triggering Liam to release his hold.

"Your dog," Emma prompted, taking a step forward.

"Right. My dog."

Liam walked in step with Emma along the perimeter of the property to the maintenance building.

"Her name is Bluebelle, but I call her Belle. Sometimes BeeBee." The name of his sweet mutt never failed to make him smile. "I went to pick up my lunch from the sushi place next to a pet store and came home with an adoption application."

Emma smiled. "Don't you hate it when that happens?"

Liam recounted how the sandy retriever took up the entire shopping center sidewalk with a stubborn steadiness that forced him to a halt. It wasn't the first time a potential pet tried to wiggle their way into his heart, but having recently quit his job, he finally had the schedule to consider it.

"She absolutely refused to move until I sat down beside her. I can't explain it, but I just knew she belonged with me. Three days later, she was taking up half my bed."

Liam wasn't ready to open up with the whole truth, however, and he gave Emma a sugarcoated version of the story. He didn't mention that picking up lunch was the first time he'd left his house in weeks. The takeout wasn't just for himself but also for his niece and brother who used lunch as a ploy to force him outside. He didn't tell her that he barely took care of himself, and it was his magic that kept his neglected houseplants alive. He didn't tell her that Belle forced him outside every day for a walk no matter the weather. He definitely left out that Belle probably saved his life.

"Sounds like you were meant to find each other," Emma said.

"It definitely feels that way."

"I love dogs, but I don't have one right now." Emma's voice was tinged with sadness. "What are your thoughts on cats? Your answer will determine how I feel about you."

"Wow. No pressure or anything." He ran his hand over his beard. "I'm a dog person."

"But?" Emma urged.

"I like cats. I had a couple growing up, and they were definitely not evil."

"Hmm." Emma tucked her hair behind her ear. "I'll allow it. For now. My cat Luna isn't evil either, but I have some exes that would disagree."

"That probably says more about your exes than it does your cat."

The path opened to a small clearing with a gravel driveway and parking pad. The dark stone of the building's exterior melted into the earthy greens and browns of the surrounding forest. Its distance from the overly manicured gardens of the estate allowed for a more natural space.

White pine and redbud trees grew to the heavens with little interference. Cottontail rabbits and chipmunks scurried between tufts of cinnamon fern and moss-covered logs. At the water's edge, ospreys added sticks to their oversized nests on top of the tallest trees along the shore. The sprawling wooded acreage with its wetlands and rocky beaches offered Liam a mental separation from work and home even though they were one and the same.

Belle's excited bark echoed through the front door. Her cries intensified as they stepped up the drive, the gravel crunching underneath their feet.

Liam put a hand on the knob and punched in the code. The lock whirred and beeped. A golden blur slid through the opening and barked with unfettered joy.

"Hey, BeeBee!" Liam bent over and rubbed Belle behind her soft floppy ears. Her tail swung side-to-side making a *fwap* sound when it hit his canvas pants. "I'm happy to see you too! I brought a new friend."

Belle ran to Emma and rolled onto her back, exposing her white belly.

"Hello, sweet girl! I should have come so much sooner to give you so many belly rubs." Emma's voice climbed several octaves with excitement.

Liam took a few steps back to retrieve a few dog toys but lingered while Emma used her short nails to lightly scratch Belle in her favorite spots. His energetic dog had been lulled into a temporary calm by Emma's soothing touch. He let out a quiet breath of relief. Belle was often wary of new people, and strangers seldom earned her trust as quickly as Emma had. Liam didn't know if it meant something, but he wanted it to. He wasn't raised to believe in signs or messages from ancient deities. Allowing himself to see something in Belle and Emma's instant connection felt emotionally dangerous.

Liam dropped a few toys on the ground and Belle twisted onto all fours. He launched a neon green tennis ball deep into the woods. Belle bolted after it, her dark beige fur hiding her path among the trees.

Emma stood up straight, cringing as her knees cracked on the way up. Liam was still impressed with how easily she moved her body. The transition from a desk job to one of manual labor wasn't an easy one, and his work had taken a toll. He regularly ached like he was much older than thirty-seven.

Belle jogged out of the woods and dropped the ball at Emma's feet. She picked it up and scrunched her nose at Belle. "Wet tennis balls are so gross, but I'll pick this up for you because you're just so freaking cute."

Emma threw it into the woods and Liam sent another one after it.

Emma sat down at a nearby picnic table and rubbed her hands on her jeans. "Have you always had a green thumb, Liam Doran?"

Did he imagine the sensual way she said his name? He kept his eyes on the woods where he heard Belle sifting through the leaves.

"Maybe."

Belle emerged and dropped the ball at Liam's feet. He picked it up and launched it again. "No one taught me anything about gardening. My parents just maintained whatever plants grew around our house. Getting my hands in the dirt just feels really natural."

It wasn't exactly a lie but, again, it wasn't the whole truth either. Starting friendships with lies of omission was a well-worn practice drilled into him from an early age. It mattered less at his previous job, which was in no way connected to his magical ancestry. Liam was at the end of a long line of Amora who wielded earth magic deeply connected to the physical land. Plants nurtured by their hands thrived in the poorest of conditions. But for reasons no one ever explained, his ancestors began following the Commarasi, left their farms behind, and few dared speak of their magic again.

"Cutting grass is a great way to build up a customer base. Design is the fun part. It's a living puzzle, and I love the challenge."

Emma curled a strand of her wavy hair between her fingers. "This must be a dream job for you then."

Liam bent over to pull a few stray leaves and twigs from Belle's coat, taking the moment to weigh the risk of divulging too much detail to Emma. Asters Valley was a small town in a part of Valen that wasn't kind to people still considered Amora, regardless of their ability to perform magic. The local laws against magic use were some of the more strictly enforced in Ascaria and pitted neighbors against each other by offering hefty rewards for cooperating with law enforcement. His parents and three of his four siblings still lived there, but he visited as infrequently as possible.

Belhaven Island, though, had a different reputation. The lax enforcement of federation laws made this job opportunity especially appealing. As a landscaper, he never purposely used magic—he didn't know how—but it was only a matter of time before someone connected his ancestry to his day job and filed a report.

"Living in a cabin in the woods and not having to pay bills would be the dream." He sent three tennis balls sailing into the woods.

"It's an ideal job. I get to turn this blank slate into something resembling what it used to be. I spend minimal time in front of a computer, and I only have one client to keep happy instead of ten. Unless I do something absolutely abhorrent, I'll have a consistent paycheck for at least the next year."

He moved towards her and sat down on the bench, sliding in close.

Too close?

She turned sideways and rested her cheek on her fist. Her lean into the table accentuated the curves of her torso. Her long hair slid off her shoulder exposing her neck. Liam felt pulled to her like she was the earth, and he was the moon, unable to resist being in her orbit.

It may be too close, but it wasn't close enough.

"It's almost everything I need right now," he said.

The corners of her mouth curled into a curious smile. She leaned in slightly. "So, what are you still needing, Liam?"

Fuck.

Nothing he could say out loud.

Unless she wanted to hear him say he needed the sensation of her touch again. He craved whatever it was that made him feel like his skin was liquid being poured into the mold of her hand. He needed to hear her say his name in whispered breaths. He needed to know if she also felt this enchanting gravitational pull.

Belle returned and made her appearance known by aggressively pawing at Liam's hand until he was forced to acknowledge her. He narrowed his eyes at Belle, silently scolding her for interrupting whatever had been happening between him and Emma.

"We should get moving." Emma stood up and stretched. "We still have the parking lot to film."

"I guess we are still on the clock." Liam picked up Belle's toys and replaced them in the storage bin.

"C'mon, Belle. You're perfect for social media." At the sound of her name, the dog left Liam's side and trotted over to Emma.

"You sure?"

"Absolutely." She turned to walk away, Belle following her. "A rugged, outdoorsy, strongman getting love from his dog is very female gaze."

"What does that even mean?" Liam called after her.

It was late afternoon by the time they called it quits on filming. The sun was beginning its slow descent towards the horizon.

"Enough eye candy for your social media audience?" Liam winked.

"Well, you had that group of hot moms looking pretty interested in the benefits of pavers over traditional asphalt for stormwater management."

Emma tilted her head in the direction of a few women hanging around by their minivans and SUVs. "I'm pretty sure the strawberry-blond lost sight of one of her kids there for a minute."

Liam glanced over at the group, now trying too hard to fake a conversation. He gifted them a smile and a little wave, eliciting embarrassed giggles that sent them running for their cars. Emma laughed too and it was the only sound he ever wanted to hear.

"I'm sure I'll be fielding a lot of messages about your availability."

"Tell them they could do better." It slipped out of Liam's mouth before he had a chance to filter his thoughts. He spent the bulk of his post-college adulthood being a less than stellar boyfriend.

He worked constantly, spending long days at his office during the week and being emotionally unavailable on the weekends. His dedication to his job instead of his partners made him a c-suite favorite, and he was quickly rewarded with promotions and bonuses. Liam's lucrative career also fueled a hedonistic lifestyle, leaving a trail of failed relationships and broken hearts in its wake. He never quite forgave himself for that season of his life.

Emma's face softened, a bit of sadness flashing in her eyes. Liam tried to save the interaction with a broad smile and a change of subject. Maybe their shared interest in nature would distract her from Liam's lecherous dating history.

He pointed at a tiny black and white bird sifting through one of the feeders. "Do you know what kind of bird that is? I don't think I've ever noticed them before."

Emma shielded her eyes from the sun as she squinted at the feeder. "Where? I don't think I see what you see."

"It moved. It might be hard to see from where you're standing." Liam moved behind her. He reached his arm over her shoulder and pointed in the direction of the palm-sized bird. He tried to maintain his distance as warmth filled the space between them. The heat radiated from deep within, making his bones hum.

Emma's breathing quickened, and he became aware of the intimacy of their closeness. "Is this okay?" He asked.

"Yes." Her voice was soft and breathy.

"Do you see it? On the edge of the feeder?"

"It's a chickadee." She looked back at Liam with relaxed eyes, a spark of eagerness in them even as she spoke in hushed tones.

"I love them because they look out for their flock. Their songs are more like a language than other bird calls. When danger is near, they use a very specific warning call. Other animals picked up on the pattern so they're like an alarm system for the forest."

They watched silently as the chickadee was joined by two more. The world around them blurred, leaving only Liam, Emma, and the birds in the distance providing an anchor to keep the moment from spiraling out of control.

"Do they think we're dangerous?" Liam whispered.

Emma tilted her head in thought and after a long breath answered, "I think right now they feel safe and exactly where they're meant to be.

CHAPTER 6
DIARY OF SARA CORTESE

Belhaven Island, mid spring circa 1620

The warmth of spring has brought bees and nectar fairies to the early blooms and a buzz to the village square. No longer deterred by the cold seas, the bards resumed their visits to Belhaven, bringing with them news from Amoran villages across Arcanos. I often enjoy when the bards pass through our island. My deep love of storytelling is why Maryanne chose me to be her successor as the keeper of lore. This spring, however, I've begun to dread their visits to the village pubs.

They speak of Amora who have forsaken our people and are antagonistic towards other creatures of this realm. They make their home in floundering villages where they quietly turn people against Amora Goddesses. These humans cast blame on the Goddesses for the suffering of these villages. They call the Goddesses vengeful and unsympathetic.

The elders die without naming successors and villagers fight amongst themselves to take power. The use of magic is controlled by village leaders for the benefit of a few instead of all. Children inherit their magic from the soul of the body that created them and as such, these humans believe birthing and feminine people have too much power. They are stripped of their ability to lead businesses and own property under these false beliefs and willful ignorance.

Parents no longer teach their children how to use their magic and the rituals are forgotten. Without the free use of magic, these villages become susceptible to malevolent creatures from Teremedi. In only a few generations, the village will fall, and the Amora vanish.

In the evening glow of the moon, I sit by the fire with Stephen. Though we have fallen out of the kind of passionate love of which the great poets write, he remains a person in my life I care for dearly. I treasure his companionship during these times of worried contemplation.

We talk of our children who are just coming into their own magic. Without our counsel, will they be tempted to stray from everything we've taught them? Stephen believes the island will offer us some isolation from these humans and we will continue to thrive under the guidance of the Goddesses.

Stephen's pragmatism often sets my pessimistic mind at ease, but John Dawson's shadow lingers over our conversations.

CHAPTER 7
DIARY OF SARA CORTESE

Belhaven Island, mid spring circa 1620

John Dawson's illness and suffering are the worst the village healers and the Amora elders have ever seen. The days on which he is in too much pain to leave his bedchambers grow in number. Vivid nightmares keep him from a restful sleep so his mood has been most unpleasant. He will lash out at his wife Rebekah and their children, then weep his apologies.

Rebekah has taken the youngest children to stay with her brother and his partners to spare them from watching their father deteriorate. Bethany has been working day and night to provide him with as much comfort as she can while his family makes preparations for his journey to Terultimi.

Bethany doesn't speak much of her own exhaustion. I know she is weary from this work. Where she was once clear and assertive, she is now unsure and timid. The scattered silver in her sandy brown curls have become streaks of egret white.

It was only with Piper's insistence that I was able to convince Bethany to join me for a meal by the creek near the Dawson home. I spread a blanket on the edge of the water where we shared a loaf of bread, cheese, and jars of sweet jams and sour pickles made from the shared abundance of the Hartley farm.

She couldn't meet my eyes when she confessed that caring for John sometimes exhausts her beyond her will to eat. Bethany must care for herself so she can care for others, and she felt ashamed of this self-neglect.

"Then I will see to it personally that you eat, even if I must feed you myself," I said.

I piled fruit and cheese and bread onto her plate until she cried, "Stop!" with the most beautiful laughter.

I watched her eat as she spoke candidly of her worries. She fears John Dawson's illness is an omen of terrible times ahead. That his illness will start a loss of faith among Belhaven's Amora. She'd heard some elders already believe that a nefarious spirit walks amongst us. It was against my official duty as village scribe to relay secret conversations amongst the elders, but I confirmed those rumors as the truth.

As we sat quietly, watching the water's gentle flow towards the sea, I asked Bethany why her face twisted in pain every time she moved her right arm. Though her thick arms were strong, more than twenty-five years of doing her work will take its toll, she explained.

Healers, sadly, cannot heal themselves. I offered to ease her discomfort with a balm I made of maypops and cattails.

The corners of her vivid green eyes welled with tears. As a healer, she is often well cared for by the village in which she lives, but she said, "Few have ever offered to care for me the way you do."

My stomach turned in blissful knots, rendering me unable to speak. She loosened the ribbon on the neck of her tunic to bare her shoulder and her arm. Dark brown freckles speckled her light skin. I traced shapes with my eyes as I pressed my fingers deep into the tender muscles of her shoulder, arm, and hand.

The magic that radiated from her body swirled with mine, pulling at me from deep within. Never have I experienced such an overwhelming force.

As I pressed my thumbs into her palm and let them slide over her skin, she spoke quietly of the anger and sadness in John Dawson's body. Just being in his presence drained her. I confessed that I felt it too.

Our eyes locked and our fingers twisted together. With her free hand, she cupped my cheek and touched her forehead to mine. Before she kissed me and allowed me to taste the sweet honey on her lips, she said, "When you're by my side, it reminds me of what happiness feels like."

Chapter 8

Emma

Stepping outside onto the museum's large patio, Emma sucked in a breath of the salty air blowing in from Belhaven Sound. The heat from the early April sun masked the lingering winter chill. April was a fickle month, and the meteorological perfection Emma was experiencing could turn on them just as easily as it swept in. That's why she kept the bird feeders around the building stuffed with sunflower seeds and nuts well into May.

In a small greenhouse tucked in a corner, Emma loaded a garden wagon with large containers of birdseed and whole peanuts. Starting at the first feeder on the patio, she made her way around the large building, pulling the wagon behind her, its weight becoming lighter with each stop.

A grating caw from a blue jay grabbed her attention in time to see Liam driving up in a utility cart. She looked away to hide the ridiculous smile she couldn't contain.

A few birds flew off when he pulled up alongside her. Looking away was impossible now, and she wouldn't have been able to even if she tried. His hands rested on the steering wheel, his short sleeves riding up his biceps. For the first time, she was given a clear view of the tattoo that stretched across his long arms. A black and gray tree with almost lifelike texture throughout its trunk and sprawling limbs covered his entire biceps. The trunk ended above his elbow, becoming roots that snaked down his forearm.

Goddess thank you for the warm weather, Emma thought.

She squinted, trying to make out the details of the piece, but Liam interrupted her ogling.

"Ya know, that's technically my job."

Emma shrugged and dumped a cup of birdseed into the feeder. "I don't mind. I've been doing it for years."

"The old guy didn't do it?" Liam turned towards her, throwing an arm over the back of the bench seat.

Emma busied herself by getting another large scoop. Anything to keep her from staring at the way Liam's shirt stretched across his chest.

"Nah. He did a good job keeping up the place, but it was like his To Do List hadn't changed since the 80s. I'll have to find another excuse to get out of the building once your renovation is done and there's less need for these feeders."

Liam fidgeted with his hat. "You got time. It'll be a while before the new plants can support wildlife."

Emma was about to agree when it struck her that many of the small shrubs and trees that Liam planted had already grown quite a bit, which was unusual for this time of year. That thought sparked another.

"If you've got a little time," she said. "I'd like to cash in my favor."

"Sure. What do you need me to do?"

Me, she wanted to scream. Maybe it was Liam's tempting forearms or too much sun and sea air, but Emma's self-control decided to let her hormones drive for a bit.

"I'm preparing an outdoor exhibit on native plants and there are some large and heavy flower pots in the basement I'd like to use."

"And you need my rugged, outdoorsy, strong-man aesthetic to help you?"

Emma pressed her lips together to contain her laughter, which became increasingly difficult as Liam silently taunted her with a look of amusement.

"Yes. That."

Liam's knowing smile cracked into a belly laugh that echoed against the museum's stone walls.

Emma climbed into the passenger seat as he loaded the wagon and its contents into the back of the utility cart. She was unprepared for her body's reaction when he slid next to her, his hip bumping hers. A sizzle of electricity tore through her, causing a hitch in her breath.

"Where to?" Liam asked.

"Umm," she stumbled, searching for her words. "The back patio."

Liam drove the small vehicle like a go-kart, whipping around the building at top speed. It gave her little time to think about the possible consequences of taking Liam someplace where few employees willingly ventured.

Emma held open the greenhouse door, and Liam followed her inside, wheeling the wagon behind him.

"You can just leave that there." Emma pointed to a spot in the corner and closed the ornate frosted-glass door.

"Is this the part of the story where you murder me and put my body parts at the bottom of the flower pots?"

"I'd never do that. That's way too much work." Emma winked. "No, this is a shortcut to the basement."

She opened a heavy wooden door at the back of the greenhouse and flicked a switch on the inside wall. A dim trail of lights revealed a narrow hallway.

"C'mon." With a crooked finger, Emma coaxed Liam into following her.

"We're in the old servants' corridors," she said over her shoulder as they walked through the dusty passageway. "As you can imagine, they're the quickest way to get around the building."

She heard Liam drag a finger across the wall followed by the brushing of his canvas pants.

"They don't seem very well traveled these days," he said.

"Mabel uses them occasionally. Sometimes she includes them on tours. I definitely use them the most."

"Why's that?"

In the five years she'd worked at the museum, no one had ever asked her, and it took her a moment to pull together an answer.

"It's quiet. There's a lot going on at the museum. It's usually busy since we function like a community center. So it tends to feel," she paused to find the right word.

"Overstimulating?" Liam answered.

Emma stopped at a door at the bottom of a steep flight of steps. "Yeah. And traveling through these passages cuts down on some of that."

Liam was a step or two behind her, but she felt the closeness of his presence as though he'd pinned her against the door. Emma's magic always came alive when she was in the basement, but now, with Liam so close, it purred.

They emerged from a doorway near the main elevator. Part storage, part holding area, mostly dumping ground, the basement held a vast collection of Belhaven's untold stories. It was mysterious even for Emma who spent the most time there. She maneuvered a squeaky dolly cart out of a corner and guided Liam across the spacious room to a spot with wooden shelves holding large sculptures, small furniture, and the heavy ceramic flower pots she wanted.

Seeing Liam's curious eyes wander to the items that surrounded them, Emma sat down in a faded armchair, giving him a little time to explore. The physical distance between them created a mix of longing and relief.

"So what is all this stuff? Where did it come from?"

Emma sighed a laugh. "Figuring that out is the bulk of what I do. The Yates family was powerful enough that they were able to hold onto anything connected to their family lines. But they also loved stuff. Expensive stuff, exclusive stuff, unique stuff. They filled this building with it. But when the family's influence and wealth started to dwindle, they squirreled much of it away into the deepest part of the basement."

Liam's eyes widened. "You mean it's bigger than this?" He gestured around the room.

"Oh, much bigger. There are rooms that haven't seen a living person in at least seventy-five years."

Liam arched a brow. "Living?"

"I said what I said," Emma teased. "Anyway, the rest of it comes from private donations, usually when an older Belhaven resident dies, and their family is cleaning out their house. Most of it doesn't have historical value, but it's quality craftsmanship and can be repurposed."

"Like your flower pots." Liam pulled one to the edge of the shelf and examined the intricate design work.

"Right. Those were donated by a family whose matriarch just entered hospice care. The best stuff comes from hidden collections that are found during renovations. If something has historical value, it usually comes to us after a contractor took down a wall to expand a bathroom or something."

Liam lifted the planter off the shelf, his muscles tensing under the weight. Emma jumped from the chair to push the dolly closer and lock the wheels. She stepped aside and leaned against the heavy shelving frame. Liam pulled another planter to the edge of the shelf. Though similar in shape, it had a different texture from the previous one, and Emma held her breath as Liam ran a finger over the elaborate design. Until that moment, Emma was unaware that she could be jealous of a flower pot.

"What are you planting in these?" Liam lowered the piece onto the dolly, squatting with perfect form.

Safety first. Emma released a breath.

"Swamp milkweed, wild bergamot, river oats. And another I'm forgetting." In her current environment, it was nothing short of a miracle she remembered three of the four.

"Hmm." Liam squatted again to reach for a planter on a low shelf.

"What?"

"Just thinking." He lowered the planter onto the dolly with a controlled exhale. "Do you have a specific reason for those choices, or can I offer an alternative?"

Emma narrowed her eyes, initially put off by his response. But is it really mansplaining if their skills are evenly matched? And he asked first? "What were you thinking?"

Liam stood straight and reached his hands behind his back, stretching his shoulders. The fabric of his shirt pulled tight across his pecs.

Nevermind, Goddess.

She needed the return of winter and Liam in layers. If he was trying to seduce her, it was working. Her body flushed with heat that flowed from her chest. She crossed one ankle over the other, fighting her enjoyment of the growing pressure between her legs.

"I like your choice of river oats for that spot, but not in a planter. I think they'd do well in the ground, but there's just a little too much sun to keep the potting soil moist without a ton of amendments that the other plants won't need. Little bluestem, though, can handle it."

Their eyes locked. Liam reached over her shoulder, lightly brushing her hair away from her neck. The energy pulsing from his body landed on her skin and soaked down into the bone. Emma's magic beat in time with her racing heart.

"Can you feel that?" she whispered.

She regretted the question the moment it left her lips. Liam knit his brow and broke his gaze. His energy changed.

"Feel what?" He pulled a medium-sized flower pot from the shelf behind her.

"Nothing. Nevermind." Emma looked away and found a strand of hair to curl around her finger. "Little bluestem?"

Liam cleared his throat. "Right. I have some leftover starters. And they'd do well in pots like this. If you're interested."

"That's a great idea. Thank you for the suggestion." Emma took the flower pot from him and distracted herself with a chip in the rim.

"Definitely a better fit. I'll get another dolly, and we can get these loaded up too."

Emma darted away, back into the corner by the elevator. This was no ordinary crush or infatuation. This was a book of matches and Emma was playing with fire.

CHAPTER 9

LIAM

Liam slipped his weather-beaten hands into a pair of wool-lined work gloves. The temperate weather of the past few weeks left him mentally unprepared for the return of the icy cold that seeped through his skin and grafted to his bones. A biting wind came off the water and sailed through the open museum property. The young oak and cedar trees that he and his team planted along the shore would one day fend off the sea winds with their thick trunks and reaching limbs, but today, their scraggly branches made little difference.

The trees would grow on a timetable of which he had little control. He expected them to thrive though. His ancestral talents would make sure of that. Any soil his hands worked became the ideal medium for the plants within it. He squinted at the clumps of switchgrass planted in the once-barren sand. In just two weeks, they'd grown a few inches taller and began filling the space in between.

Not bad for not even trying, he thought.

Liam lacked the generational knowledge required to ever see the full potential of his magic. It was probably for the best though. Being too good at his job was risky and could put him on their radar. *They* being the government officials that enforced the ban on magic. It would start with a review of Liam's family tree to determine how far removed he was from his familial magic. Regardless of the outcome, he would get a warning.

Next came surveillance.

Then regular monitoring.

If an investigation followed, punishment was inevitable. Using magic to influence your success was still punishable by death.

Unless being too good made people rich.

Liam spent a decade making others incredibly wealthy. Sometimes he wondered if he was just that good, or he was being aided by the same weak magic that prodded a row of asters to bloom a couple weeks early.

Working with money was the opposite of working with the soil.

Soil required patience.

Money required speed. Meet goals quickly, taking as many shortcuts as possible to maximize the return. Exceed expectations for a handsome reward. But now the bar is set and locked in place. There's no going back.

Liam pulled the beanie over his ears, already red from the biting wind. He walked around to the back of his truck, opened the tailgate, and let it fall with a loud thud. He had about an hour to work before an excavation crew arrived to dig up some old sewer lines.

Picking up a shovel set against the truck, he took a heaping scoop of wood chips and dumped them on the nearby garden bed. He repeated the process over and over, covering delicate yarrow, milkweed, and coneflower with a thick layer of bedding to keep their growing roots warm. It was physically hard but mentally mundane. It grounded him, rooting him to the present, requiring just enough focus so that his mind wouldn't unearth some deeply hidden worry.

He brushed the last bit of wood chips out of the truck bed and spread them evenly around a section of young milkweed. Like the others, it had already grown a bit, but not enough to raise suspicions from an inexperienced eye. The magic that made it possible served his ancestors well. They were once revered for their ability to grow crops in fallow soil, producing an abundance of food that they shared freely with neighboring villages.

With his parents unwilling to share anything else about their family history, he knew little more than that. On nights when sleep was out of reach, he'd stare into the darkness and think about all the good he could do if he had that kind of power. Maybe he could make amends for his role in the harm caused by his former clients.

With the task complete, his truck bumped along one of the perimeter access roads to the worksite near the museum. A small crew milled around, setting up equipment and getting a backhoe into place. A tall, broad-shouldered man in a reflective vest and a hardhat walked up to Liam.

"You must be Liam. I'm Clint." He removed his heavy work gloves and reached out a dark brown hand. "I'm the foreman for this project. We spoke on the phone."

"Glad to finally meet in person, Clint." Liam shook his hand and followed him toward the excavation site. "I was able to review the plans since we last spoke. I was told some tunnels run underneath this place."

Clint nodded. "Yup. That's why we did some imaging last month. Nothing popped up in this spot, but you never know what you're going to hit on this island. A couple of years ago, I started adding a day or two into the estimate just to cover any surprises."

"What happens if you don't need them?"

"Well, the client ain't mad that they saved a little money, and it makes my team look good. But I gotta tell ya, Liam, it's rare that it happens. Belhaven's full of buried secrets."

Clint's ominous admission sent a chill down Liam's spine. "Well, I'll let you get to work then. Do you mind if I send our social media manager down for some pictures and video?"

"Sure, that's fine. Not sure how interested they'll be in a bunch of shitty pipes though."

Emma would be very interested in those shitty pipes. Liam knew enough about rainwater capture to include it in his design plans, but Emma knew about Belhaven's water. Where it came from and where it went when it seeped into the earth. She knew about every plant along the freshwater creeks and saltwater bay. Their conversations were far too short and infrequent. With his office on the other side of the property and a job that kept him outside, he had few opportunities to bump into her. Those moments were a taste that only made him crave more time with her, and he was jonesing for another hit.

A symphony of diesel engines interrupted Liam's thoughts. The backhoe's clawed bucket pierced the soft ground, sending a rumble under his feet. Liam didn't have to spend the whole day watching the crew, but any other property manager would have stayed longer than he did. He wanted to see Emma and the want became overwhelming.

He gave Clint a wave and walked toward the back of the building, slipped into the greenhouse, and through the door that led into the dusty servants' corridors. They really were the fastest way through the building, but Liam could swear he still felt Emma's energy vibrating through the narrow space. The hallway amplified whatever force pulled him towards her. It reverberated off the walls and soaked into his skin. Several weeks later, he bathed in its echoes.

Liam popped out of a narrow door in the back of the museum's lobby. He slowed to a casual pace, purposely stopping Hector as he was leaving the museum cafe. Hector had asked him about running a couple of children's nature classes and a short conversation would make the real purpose of his visit much less obvious.

After some small talk, Liam said, "I think I can make a Tuesday and Friday nature class work until school lets out."

Hector's lips curled into his signature lopsided smile. "That's awesome, man. I'll send you the details."

Moving on, Liam exhaled a quiet breath of relief when he saw Emma's open door. Emma had a spacious corner office with the best view of the water. The other nonprofits he worked with saved these offices for the people that regularly met with deep-pocketed donors. But Emma probably had the most space because she shared it with dozens of items being prepared for exhibition. The other offices were small and tidy. Emma's was organized chaos.

She sat behind her computer, her face tense with concentration as she moved a stylus across a touch pad lying flat on her desk. She leaned forward and the light from the monitor reflected off her glasses as she squinted at something on the screen. Whatever she did next must have worked because she smiled triumphantly and relaxed into her chair.

Liam knocked.

Emma's eyes met his and a wide smile appeared on her face. "Hi."

He replied with a quiet, "Hey."

Being near Emma always felt electric. Any time they got close, it was like his soul was attempting to step away from his body and fuse with hers. It never failed to leave him speechless.

She patted the seat of the stool next to her. A silent invitation for Liam to come closer.

He sat down, noticing an empty canvas on her screen. Whatever she'd been doing wasn't for his eyes.

"What were you working on?" He nudged.

Emma spun the oversized office chair until her entire body faced him. She leaned in, her face serious.

"I'm not supposed to show these to anyone yet," she said quietly. "Can I trust you?"

"Do you trust me?"

She searched his face for a moment. "Yes. But should I?"

I would die for you.

It was more a feeling than a thought. An instinctual feeling that rocked him to his core. He didn't have time to reflect on it. She asked him a question and the discomfort written on her face grew as she waited for his answer.

"You can trust me."

That seemed to be enough, and Emma spun back to face her screen. "I scanned one of those 400-year-old diaries I found. I'm cleaning up the images so they're easier to read and the originals don't have to be touched as much."

She clicked the touch pad so several pictures came into view. Each was an improved copy of the original, the lighting and color adjusted to make the words pop off the page.

"You're amazing," he said, his voice heavy with affection.

Emma chewed on her bottom lip and looked away. "Thanks."

He cleared his throat and sat up straight. "The foreman said you can take pictures of the work being done if you're interested."

"Cool. I can get out there in a bit. How's it going so far?"

"Good, as far as I can tell. Sewer pipe replacement isn't exactly in my skill set."

Emma lifted her reading glasses onto her head, pushing her hair away from her face. The tousled ringlets looked even more inviting for his fingers.

"Oh, and here I was thinking that you were perfect," she teased. "I guess you do have flaws."

He leaned forward. The delicate scents of citrus and magnolia danced off her sun-kissed skin. "I'm perfectly flawed."

Emma's chest rose and fell with a slow inhale and a nearly imperceptible sigh. If they were anywhere else, he'd pull her onto his lap and kiss her neck until those quiet sighs turned into desperate moans.

A heavy chill swept through the room, and Liam looked up expecting to find an open window, but they remained shut. The energy in the space changed. It grated his nerves like microphone feedback. A slight vibration ran through the desk, barely there, but strong enough that Liam lifted his hands in confusion.

Emma jumped up from her seat and looked around her office.

"Do you feel that?" Her face contorted. Her fingers dug into her chest. "It's like some kind of... I don't know how to describe it. Like my chest is tight."

"I feel something, but..." The vibrations increased to a low rumble. The exhibition pieces and antiques that covered Emma's office trembled until the rumbling strengthened to an earthquake. His face likely mirrored Emma's look of panic and confusion. Valen wasn't a region known for earthquakes. Snow storms, hurricanes, and the occasional water spout were all the weather conditions he prepared for. Geologic activity wasn't something anyone ever thought about.

Ceramic pottery shattered onto the stone floor. Liam grabbed Emma's hand, pulling her under the heavy wooden table. He ripped off his jacket and Emma slid into the space created by his outstretched arms. Pressing against his chest, her body heat warmed him like a furnace in the still mysteriously cold room. Liam tucked them both under his jacket the best he could.

Objects rained down beside them, some exploding on impact and pelting them with shards of debris. The old mansion was made of stone, but was it made to withstand an earthquake of apocalyptic magnitude? How much more could it handle before becoming a mountain of rubble? The nearby bookcase slammed on top of the thick tabletop above them. Emma screamed, and Liam squeezed her tighter, ready to take the brunt of the entire building if it would spare her from even a scratch.

Then the room went still.

The chill in the air disappeared.

It was utterly silent except for the frantic rhythms of their breaths. Liam lifted the jacket off their heads, but Emma's fingers remained tightly wound into the fabric of his shirt.

"I think it's over," he whispered.

Emma didn't release her grip from Liam's body right away. When she did, Liam almost gasped at the emptiness caused by the absence of her touch.

Liam laid his jacket on the floor and brushed aside bits of glass, stone, and clay as he crawled out from under the table. He took Emma's hand and helped her up. Her hair was messy and wild, and her chest and neck were red and glistening with heat and sweat. Impulsively, Liam ran his fingers across her hairline looking for injuries. He brushed his thumb across her cheek, his eyes focused on her softly parted lips. Every cell in his body ached for her kiss. The intensity of this yearning should have shocked him, scared him even, but it felt too natural and too right.

"Liam," Emma breathed.

His gaze snapped to hers, and he thought he recognized the same longing in her darkened eyes.

In his moment of hesitation, cries for help echoed through the hallways, severing their connection. They were slammed back to the present, mere moments after an earthquake had shaken a building made of rock and stone to its core.

"Go," Emma said forcefully. "I'm right behind you."

All of Liam's next movements happened in a blur. He found most of his coworkers still huddled under their desks, some surrounded by the personal items they kept on shelves nearby. None of the offices had the level of destruction as Emma's, but the same couldn't be said for the exhibition rooms, many of which lay in shambles.

With his coworkers safe and in the care of the museum's security team, Liam ran to the excavation site. Veins of separated earth fanned out across a field of hibernating grass. The ornamental trees with shallow roots lay toppled on their side, leaving craters of upturned soil.

When Liam arrived at the site, a group of workers were surrounding their foreman who was slumped against a pile of dirt taking slow sips from a water bottle.

"Clint, what happened? Is everyone else okay?"

"We're okay. We got away from the equipment in time."

Some of the machinery lay on its side, having toppled over when the sandy ground beneath it shifted.

"I fainted. I'm too old for this kind of excitement." He flashed Liam a weak smile and downed a sports drink a crew member handed him.

Liam looked out to the bay. Though the earth had stilled, rough waters crashed angrily against the rocky shore.

"I told you."

Liam turned back to Clint, who was wiping his brow with his sleeve. "What?"

"I told you this island is full of surprises."

Chapter 10

Emma

Emma stepped over the tree limb that remained in her driveway nearly two weeks after the earthquake sent it to the ground. Every morning, she vowed to take care of it after work, and every evening, she groaned because she didn't have the energy to deal with it. This evening was no different.

Aside from the limb and some overturned patio furniture, Emma's little house survived the earthquake unscathed. The museum took the brunt of the impact, and her days were spent alongside a handful of trusted archivists from all over Ascaria working on what amounted to a ridiculously large jigsaw puzzle. She was too busy to wonder why the damage was so localized.

Barely in the doorway, Emma dropped her things on a side table with an exhausted sigh. An equally loud meow greeted her.

"It's been a day, Luna." Emma bent down and lifted her black cat onto her shoulder. The low rumble of Luna's purr vibrated against Emma's neck, releasing some of the tension that remained in her shoulders. Emma walked into her bedroom and eased Luna onto the bed before collapsing beside her and opening her text messages.

EMMA: I just got home. Staying in or going out? I need to know if I'm putting on my home leggings or my going out leggings.

REGAN: There's a difference? Let's go out. I'm feeling social.

EMMA: Only in number of stains. I'll see you outside in 30.

Emma lobbed her phone onto the mattress. "Girls night out, Luna. I have to keep this bra on for a little while longer."

Already curled into a doughnut on Emma's pillow, Luna closed her eyes and drifted off to sleep. Clearly, Luna wasn't as invested in Emma's bra issues.

Emma and her best friend Regan met most evenings after work. This evening, it seemed they would be trading the porch for a downtown bar five blocks away. Feeling social was a requirement for any evening in town. Many of the local kids who left the island for college didn't return after graduation and started new lives in Valen or other regions in Ascaria. But enough made a permanent home in Belhaven that Regan and Emma always expected to run into someone from their past who insisted on trapping them in conversation.

Though Emma grew up in Hunting Woods on the Valen mainland south of Belhaven, she stayed with her grandmother during school breaks. Being related to Siena and Rose DiMarco made for strong island associations. Locals tended to forget she didn't come to live on the island permanently until her thirties.

Regan, however, was a Belhaven kid and, like Emma's, the roots of her family tree ran deep.

With the Healys and the DiMarcos close both spiritually and in proximity, Emma and Regan were friends as kids and closer as teens but drifted apart in college.

While Emma toiled away in River City at any low-level media or marketing job she could get, Regan returned to Belhaven with advanced degrees in astronomy and a job at a nearby university. How Regan was able to specialize in a science connected to her family magic, Emma still didn't know and never attempted to ask.

The Healys were one of Belhaven's oldest families and one of the few that still quietly observed Amoran holidays and rituals. Regan was one of the last in a line of skygazers that scattered across the Arcanos continent and went into hiding when the Commarasi made their push for power. Their magic enhanced their divination and wayfinding abilities, making them valuable to both Amora elders and Commarasi leaders, neither of whom had the skygazers' best interest at heart.

Emma's mother had no interest in Amora traditions or learning magic. The bits of her ancestry that Emma kept with her might have disappeared after her grandmother's death if not for the Healys sharing these traditions with her.

It was almost dark when Emma stepped out of her front door and onto her porch. The late-April air sent a chill through her, prompting her to pull her leather jacket closed and zip it to her chin. Her days of being uncomfortable for the sake of fashion were long over. She was too old and too tired to freeze her voluminous ass off in a more flattering outfit.

The blue door of the nearly identical shotgun house across the gravel street opened, revealing a woman in tight jeans and brown boots that clung to her calves. Like Emma,

Regan inherited her house from an elderly family member after her unsuccessful attempt to buy it outright as an unmarried woman.

Emma moved in three years after, and Regan welcomed Emma to the neighborhood with a container of her favorite soft-baked cookies. A decade had passed since they last spoke, but their bond remained. Being around Regan again felt like a missing piece had been put back into place. It was clear then that they were soulmates.

"Is that my sweater?" Emma squinted in an attempt to see the details in the dark.

The two women wore the same size, but their shapes differed a bit since Regan was a couple inches taller. The creamy cable-knit sweater fit Regan's body like she commissioned it to highlight every curve in the most perfectly flattering way.

Regan shrugged and met Emma in the middle of the gravel road. "Probably. Don't buy such nice clothes if you don't want me hanging onto them when you leave them at my place."

Emma thought it looked cute on her own petite frame, but she clearly didn't like it enough to notice that it'd gone missing.

"You keep it." Emma kissed Regan's warm bronze cheek. Regan's spiral curls were freshly dyed a deep sunset purple and pinned away from her square face.

"I can't deny the world the chance to see how amazing you look in it."

Regan linked her arm through Emma's, and they began walking in step toward Downtown Belhaven's Main Street.

"I was hoping you'd say that. Now I won't feel bad about not giving it back after I wash it." Regan's big smile scrunched her nose and deepened the lines of her cheekbones.

They continued down a quiet sidewalk lined with small homes that served as a living exhibit of the architectural changes over the past century. Many were still owned by the same family that built them, often passed down to unmarried daughters and nieces as a safety net should they decide not to marry. New residents without some kind of familial ties to the island seldom moved in. It's why Liam's arrival sparked a little excitement. And as Emma predicted, their social media audience were suckers for a sexy man and his dog.

The sky was dark by the time Regan and Emma arrived in Belhaven's central business district. The hum of open shops and restaurants filled the air. They stopped at a crosswalk and Emma scanned the bulletin board in front of town hall.

"Did you see this one?" Emma pointed to a fresh-looking notice that hadn't yet bleached in the sun.

"Anyone with information connected to unsanctioned equinox celebrations should contact their regional enforcement office," she read aloud.

Regan rolled her golden-brown eyes. "As though any seasonal feasts would've been sanctioned. The same notices have been plastered all over campus. They'll swap them out in June after the solstice."

Belhaven Island was one of the last Amora strongholds when the Commarasi violently came to power at the turn of the twentieth century. It remained a place that was more welcoming than most, but that also made it a target for enforcement campaigns by the Commarasi-led government. They picked up around traditional Amoran holidays.

"Things are getting heated on campus," Regan added after a long silence.

Emma didn't answer right away. A professor at Willow Ridge University was recently fired for teaching more Amoran history than the law allowed. How much more is being debated. Emma walked that line every day, and it was an easy one to cross.

Filling the silence, Regan said, "A group of students is talking about organizing a rally in support of rehiring Grace."

It wasn't lost on Emma that a woman named Grace was being given none.

"You should come."

Emma threw her head back with an exhausted laugh. Every couple of months, Regan tried to coax her into doing more to end Commarasi censorship of Amoran history and bring back the traditional feast days. But as much as Emma wanted the ban lifted, she wanted a quiet life much more.

"That's the last place I should be."

Regan exhaled loudly, and Emma knew her friend was stewing inside. This was the one topic that Regan didn't push Emma on, but Regan was incapable of hiding her feelings about it.

"Just being a DiMarco puts me under a microscope. Judy got three surveys for me in less than a year. I'll end up in questioning if I'm in town the same day as the rally. And I'll only say this once, but I think it's dangerous for you too." Emma found Regan's hand and gave it a tight squeeze. "You know I'm right."

"Fine." Regan groaned but her body softened.

The women unlinked their arms when they reached the door of the bar. A stocky bouncer stood by the entrance, eyeing people skeptically as he scanned IDs. Emma stepped up to the door and pulled hers from her wallet.

"It's been awhile, DiMarco." His husky voice fit well with his intimidating stature. "Been getting into trouble?"

"I live a boring life, Chris. Sorry to disappoint." Emma flashed him a confident and flirty smile. She held his unblinking gaze until he finally averted his stone-gray eyes to scan her ID.

The scanner beeped and printed out a bracelet with a green tag. "You're clear to enter and drink what you like."

Chris handed her the bracelet with a wink, a gentle expression that always looked at odds with his hardened features.

Emma stepped aside and fumbled with the plastic band. Occasionally, her license would get flagged for alcohol consumption limits for no discernible reason. Someone a hundred years ago decided that alcohol and magic were connected, and arbitrary limits were put into place, putting a damper on happy hours everywhere.

"What about you, Healy? Last time you were here, you were on a two-drink limit. What was that for?"

Regan handed over her license. "You know I'll never tell."

She hadn't told Emma either, only leaving it at, "Don't worry about it."

Which made Emma worry about it, but keeping secrets was one way that Belhaven's remaining Amora kept each other safe. Plausible deniability was a way of life.

The scanner printed out a green bracelet and Chris's mean-guy demeanor dropped long enough to give Regan a wide smile and a high-five.

Once inside, Regan headed straight to the bar. "I got round one."

Emma scanned the room for an empty table. There were plenty, but Emma chose the one in the farthest corner of the bar with a couple of overstuffed chairs facing each other. She sat down and shifted until she was sitting cross-legged and leaning into the corner of the chair's winged-back. This bar was Emma's favorite haunt. It catered to the older crowd that claimed the bar as their own; the drinks were expensive but well made, the seating comfortable on achy joints, and music reminiscent of their adolescence played at a reasonable volume.

Still possessing her college-era serving skills, Regan weaved through the small crowd with two brightly colored drinks and two glasses of water on a black tray. It was the first of several that would make its way from the bar to their table.

"Are you excited to teach that sky magic class at the museum?" Emma sipped her fifth drink, a cocktail named Belhaven Rock Candy, made with copious amounts of mead. She tried and failed to keep her voice steady, and she began to giggle.

"Shhhhh," Regan hushed. "It's a backyard astronomy class. You're gonna get me arrested."

"Backyard astronomy." Emma winked in an exaggerated way. Then she sipped more of her drink, which now tasted like actual candy.

"I could teach this class in my sleep." Regan set her wineglass down and made a point of sitting up and looking right at Emma who was now lounging back with one leg thrown over an overstuffed arm.

"But what I am excited about is finally meeting Liam."

Emma was too drunk to stop the involuntary smile that spread across her face. It had taken her days to recover from being pressed against his body under a desk as objects shattered around them. The cardigan she wore smelled like him until she reluctantly washed it. The entire ordeal was terrifying, and she'd happily go through it again just to feel the heat of his body melting into hers. Thinking about the way his fingers lingered on her face still made her stomach drop to her knees and her chest tighten with the anticipation of a kiss that never came. She ached desperately for that kiss.

Regan narrowed her almond-shaped eyes and pursed her full lips. "You're thinking about fucking him right now, aren't you?"

"I can't help it!" Emma covered her face with embarrassment.

Emma and Regan's connection as soulmates had a similar feeling. Mistaking their magical connection for romantic love, they dated, but only briefly. When they realized that beyond the bedroom, a traditional romantic relationship didn't work for them, they mutually called it quits. Emma and Regan were intimately tied in a way that was neither romantic nor platonic, but something else entirely.

Their bond wasn't nearly as strong and nowhere near as consuming as whatever was driving Emma's infatuation. The energy around Liam slipped into her skin and wrapped around the fibers of her muscles and the marrow of her bones. No person ever had this kind of hold on her.

The buzz of five drinks allowed a simple thought to plant its seed.

Is Liam another soulmate?

She didn't know much about the interplay between love, sex, and magic. Those were the first texts torched by the Commarasi. Grandma Rose taught Emma what she knew, but close as they were, sex was not a topic they willingly discussed.

Soulmates were an exception. Rose DiMarco loved love and intimacy and connection, and she could talk for hours about people bound not just by their shared affection, but through being perfectly matched spirits.

The magic that connected soulmates enhanced whatever bond they had; romantic, sexual, platonic, familial. In rare cases, even hatred. It was common to have several soulmates, each person filling an important role in the other's life.

"Em, just ask this guy out already."

Emma downed the last of her drink and considered Regan's advice. Everything with Liam felt overpowering, and she didn't like it, regardless of how right it felt.

"Yeah, we'll see," she finally responded.

Regan scoffed, then mimicked Emma's words back at her. "I'm not telling you to take him to prom, get married, and have his babies."

"Good, because he has broad shoulders, and I'd end up with broad-shouldered babies." Emma lifted her empty glass to her mouth and sucked in a few sugary ice cubes.

Regan lowered her head into her hands in defeat.

Emma pushed herself up from the chair, attempting to be graceful while so unsteady on her feet. "Let's get home before I get too tired to make us the Booze Eraser."

She reached out her hand to help Regan up and didn't let go as they moved through the now-crowded bar. Sufficiently drunk, the pair giggled and whisper-talked the five blocks back to Emma's house.

With a look of judgment that only a black cat could accomplish, Luna greeted them at the front door and led them into the kitchen. Regan fell back into a chair, and Luna jumped onto her lap.

Emma shuffled around the room, pulling jars of dried plants from her cabinets. Mountain mint for nausea, wild bergamot for headaches, anise for a restful sleep. From the refrigerator, she pulled a pitcher of water. Any water would do, but water that bathed in the light of the full moon always provided better results.

"What do you think, Luna Tuna?" Regan cooed. "Should Emma ask out the sexy landscaper man?"

Emma sighed loudly while pouring the water into her electric kettle. The room was small enough that she heard Luna reply with a loud meow and an affectionate purr.

"See! Luna agrees. And considering she is a gift from the Goddesses, it would be blasphemy to ignore Luna's counsel."

Emma turned around and leaned against the counter. Regan was scratching Luna in all her favorite places, no doubt as a reward for being on her side. Regan wasn't wrong though. Luna arrived at Emma's back door on the same night that Emma moved in. She was a cat in all senses of the word, but Luna's and Emma's magic were connected, giving them something close to a telepathic bond.

Lost in thought, Emma jumped when the kettle beeped for attention. She poured the water over the fragrant mix of leaves and buds into her grandmother's iron teapot. She whispered the familiar incantation. One of the first she was taught. The one that would channel her magic and supercharge the goodness of plants into a warm beverage that would ease the pain of drinking-while-almost-forty.

She brought the teapot and her favorite mugs to the table. Emma fell into the seat opposite Regan, the heaviness of a long day settling on her like Luna had settled on her best friend's lap.

"You'd know though," Emma said. She felt Regan's gaze on her, but she didn't look up from the strand of hair she was twirling through her fingers.

"If you read the stars, you'd know how Liam was meant to fit into my life."

Regan inhaled deeply; a familiar contemplative look appeared on her face. "I would never tell you to do anything that would hurt you. You know that."

Emma nodded. There was never a doubt, but even the reassurance wasn't enough to risk bringing Liam into her inner circle and ruining his life.

CHAPTER II
LIAM

Liam slowed his muddy pickup truck to a crawl. From the outside, the two-bedroom townhouse he once called home hadn't changed much. Everything about it remained picture perfect. Perfect lawn. Perfect shrubs. Perfect clean siding. As it always would.

For all the work Liam did to other people's yards, he never once touched his own. He wasn't allowed to per his contract with the townhome association. It was exactly what he needed during the ten years he used the place as a crash pad and storage facility; the inability to work his little piece of land grated at him until he handed the keys to his brother Tommy and drove two hours to Belhaven.

Liam pulled into the driveway next to Tommy's fifteen-year-old sedan. Both vehicles sent a stark message to the neighbors that someone of lower status was in their neighborhood. On paper, purchasing real estate in this wealthy town was a pragmatic one. But at its core, Liam just wanted to live somewhere that would impress people.

Belle whined and pawed at the door. Liam offered an apologetic ear scratch and eased himself out of the truck. The spotless walkway looked recently power washed. Another task Liam couldn't do on his own. The only bits of personality came from several small bird houses tucked in the corners of the porch. Liam laughed at a little sign by the door that said, "Warning: Attack squirrels." These little touches had his niece written all over them.

Liam let himself in and Belle ran ahead to explore the new smells of their old home. "Happy Birthday!"

"Uncle Liam!" Deryn's high-pitched voice carried from her bedroom.

Liam stopped in the doorway just in time to receive her arms around his neck. Though gangly, they squeezed him with a force that took his breath away. As a preschooler, her aggressive affection pulled him out of his lowest lows. She ignored all social cues and trampled over the walls constructed by his depression.

Even now, at eleven years old, she still hugged him like she was preparing for it to be the last. Maybe it was a habit. Maybe it was a refill or a reminder. Either way, Liam didn't care. He loved this little person as if she were his own daughter.

Belle pushed her way into the room and became the center of Deryn's attention.

Tommy Doran rounded a corner from the kitchen looking a bit frazzled. Though his light brown hair was cut much shorter than Liam's, Tommy ran his hand through it a few times. It was one of the few physical traits the brothers had in common. While Liam had their mother's sharp lines and darker coloring, Tommy had their dad's rounder lighter features.

"How's it going, man?" Tommy slapped Liam on the arm and offered him a beer.

"Not bad." Liam took it and followed Tommy into the living room. The space looked more comfortable than Liam left it a few months earlier. The room was filled with soft, well-loved furniture and the walls were adorned with Deryn's artwork.

Liam sunk into the corner of the couch. "Happy birthday, baby brother. Glad Mom and Dad didn't return you like I suggested."

"I'm sure it crossed their mind several times." Tommy clinked Liam's beer with his own and took a long pull.

At thirty-three, Tommy was the youngest of the five siblings but was the oldest soul among them. He took advantage of his exhausted parents, getting away with the same kind of adolescent trouble that got Liam banished to his room for weeks at a time. Tommy's teenage shenanigans turned into legitimate struggles that only settled when his girlfriend Cadence became pregnant with Deryn in their early twenties.

The young parents did okay, all things considered. Until Cadence went out to run some errands and never returned. Her disappearance flipped Tommy's life upside down, but for most of it, Liam was too wrapped up in work to notice, or care.

Liam smiled at the haphazard birthday decorations strewn around the kitchen and living room. He spent thirteen birthdays in this townhouse, but it wasn't until Deryn brought Liam a balloon one year that it saw any birthday decorations.

"I'm guessing the better three aren't coming for cake?"

Liam loved his other siblings—Joe, Cate, and Jennifer—but he didn't have much of an adult relationship with them or their families. Working seventy hours a week and partying in your spare time isn't conducive to building relationships of any kind. Despite his neglect as a brother and an uncle, Tommy and Deryn forced their way into his life when he needed it most.

"Nah." Tommy leaned back in his armchair. "But I didn't ask them either. I think Mom and Dad are coming just to see if Deryn is living in squalor."

The doorbell rang and Belle barked. "Grandma and Grandpa are here!" Deryn yelled from her room.

"Great timing." Tommy put down his beer and jogged to the front door, leaving Liam in a familiar but unfamiliar place.

Liam wasn't sure if Joe Doran's golf story was as funny as he claimed. A long day of playing dodgeball with controversial topics mentally exhausted him and he let his mind wander while he poked at the leftover cake icing on his plate.

"Great story, Grandpa." Deryn's sweet smile brought out the dimple in her chin, but no one could miss the tween sass in her tone.

Now that made Liam chuckle.

"I'll be outside." She tossed her plate in the garbage, picked up a book from the counter, and disappeared with Belle out the front door.

Diane Doran reached a manicured hand across the table and rested it on Tommy's. "This house looks wonderful, Tommy. So much cozier than when Liam lived here."

Liam sighed and straightened his back. "Because I barely lived here, Ma. I took the 6:30AM train into the city and the 9PM train out."

"I'm surprised it's so clean," Joe muttered behind the napkin he used to wipe his mouth.

It was Tommy's turn to sigh. His old place wasn't dirty, but it was as messy and cluttered as one would expect from a single parent who worked long hours and had a small child. "Well, when you don't have to pay rent, it's easier to afford hiring someone to help with cleaning."

Incredulous, Joe pointed at Tommy but spoke to Liam. "He's not paying rent while you're making next to nothing working at that museum?"

Liam pressed the heels of his hands into his eyes, willing his brain to keep from exploding through his sockets. "No, because the house is paid off. If anything, he should be paying Deryn rent. I transferred ownership to her with Tommy as the financially responsible party until she turns twenty-five."

"I wish you hadn't told her that, by the way," Tommy added. "She regularly threatens me with eviction."

Liam chuckled and caught their mother fighting a smile.

Their father slumped back in his seat. "Why would you do that?"

It didn't matter that Liam did it because it was the closest he could get to showing Tommy the same kind of support he offered Liam. Joe remained incensed that Liam left the job that gave him that sort of privilege.

But Liam didn't have a chance to answer before Tommy sat forward and spoke for them both.

"Because Dad, your buddies running the country made it really hard for unmarried women to own property unless they inherit it."

"In that case, you could have just bought Deryn a house instead of taking a job as a gardener."

Liam sat back while Tommy argued with their father on his behalf. It wasn't about the house or the money, really. It was the job. The job was too close to his ancestral magic and that was a risk most people avoided. They had the same fights when Liam started his landscaping business.

"Your family worked really hard to move away from that, and you're diving right back into it," his dad had said then and continued to say now. Joe became especially hostile after he retired and started playing golf at the same club as some of Valen's most powerful politicians.

Liam stood up when he couldn't handle the fighting anymore. He gave a look to Tommy who nodded knowingly.

"Liam, honey." His mom was always quiet during these fights, and he'd given up hope that she would ever back him. "We just don't want you to have the same fate as my aunt Georgia."

"Right, Ma. Happy birthday, bro. I love you."

The bickering continued as he walked out the front door and shut it behind him.

Belle's ears perked up when Liam stood next to her, but her eyes were trained on Deryn. She sat cross-legged on the small patch of grass that passed for a front yard. Her long, dark hair was piled over one shoulder. A squirrel sat on her knee reaching for the sunflower seed Deryn offered between her fingers. The squirrel ate it quickly, adding the discarded shells to a growing pile on Deryn's lap.

The squirrel skittered away when Liam sat down next to her. "Sorry I scared your friend."

"You didn't. She had things to do."

"Oh yeah? I didn't realize you were fluent in squirrel."

She rolled her eyes. Tween perfection.

"I hate that you're so far away." She pouted. "Does your new job make you happy?"

"You, sweet niece of mine, make me happy. But I am happy at my new job. It was the right choice for me."

A pair of robins landed a few feet from them. Deryn placed a few seeds on her open hand. "You should ask that Emma girl out."

The unsolicited dating advice hit Liam like a brick to the face. When did she get old enough to have opinions on his love life? "What? Why?"

Deryn watched the robins gently peck at the seeds in her palm. "Because you like her. You mentioned her like a million times. And every time you said her name, you had this doofy smile on your face."

"You have a doofy smile."

An exasperated sigh followed another eye roll. "You need to spend forever with anyone who makes you look that ridiculous."

"I'll take that into consideration. What do I owe you for this therapy session?"

"Ten dollars should cover it."

Liam stood up so he could reach into his back pocket for his wallet. He handed his niece a twenty. "Add a credit to my account for next time."

A couple of finches joined the robins at her hand. Liam kissed the top of her head and marveled at how quickly Deryn earned the trust of these little creatures. "I love you, kiddo."

"I love you too. Text me when you get home."

"I always do."

Liam let Belle into the car first, then slid into the driver's seat.

"What do you think?" Liam scratched Belle's chest, sending bits of fur wafting into the air. "Should I ask Emma out?"

Belle barked and Liam was taken aback by the unexpected response. "Huh. Okay." He turned the key in the truck's ignition. He had two hours alone to marinate on Deryn—and Belle's—advice.

CHAPTER 12
EMMA

The first time Emma thought she heard a dog barking, she ignored it. Her smutty book was finally getting sufficiently smutty. She lay on her belly, her feet hanging off the edge of her blanket. She absentmindedly wiggled her toes in the coarse sand as she read.

There was no mistaking it the second time. A rush of excitement took over and she tilted up the brim of her hat to look up and down the shore. Emma huffed when the barking dog failed to materialize and went back to her book.

It wasn't unusual for her to come to the museum on a Sunday. The wooded corners held medicinal plants that haven't done well in her own garden. It wasn't exactly a secret that she often strolled through the undisturbed areas and spent some time reading on the beach before heading home. The beach at the end of her street was under water during high tide and covered in seaweed the rest of the day. The beach at the museum was a lot nicer.

It had absolutely nothing to do with possibly running into Liam outside the confines of work. That was just a bonus.

The next interruption of her hyperfocus almost sent her into a rage. But the flames of her anger were extinguished by Belle's excited licks and nudges with her cool wet nose.

Emma laughed through the dog's affectionate attack until Liam called her off with a breathless apology.

"Oh, thank fuck! It's you." Liam's body relaxed, and he put his hands on his thighs to catch his breath. "She just took off running for this stranger laying on the beach. She never does that, so I panicked."

Emma slid over, making space for Liam. "Well, sit down before you have a heart attack."

Still panting, he awkwardly eased himself down onto his stomach and rested his forehead on top of his folded hands. "Beach running is a special kind of cardio hell."

His shaggy hair still had a hint of dampness, causing the ends to curl just slightly. The chemical perfume of generic man-brand body wash overpowered his usual earthy scent of sea salt and cedar. He wore a clean athletic shirt, loose running pants, and sneakers instead of his heavy work boots. It felt strangely intimate seeing Liam in what amounted to his private time outside of work.

"Agreed. There are other cardio activities that I prefer." The sexy read notwithstanding, Emma found it almost impossible to have a conversation with Liam without some flirting. It was more than impulsive; it was almost instinctual.

Liam lifted his head and arched a brow. "Oh yeah? Like what?"

"Swimming, kayaking, hiking." She winked.

Liam laughed through his nose and returned his forehead to his hands. "I didn't expect to see you here," he said, his voice muffled by his arms.

Emma closed her book and set it aside. "I like hiking in the woods. Then I usually read for a bit. What were you up to today?"

A muffled groan and a half-hearted laugh escaped Liam's crossed arms.

"Something good, then?"

Liam rolled onto his side and propped up his head with his hand. "Do you ever feel like you were meant for something bigger?"

Emma didn't expect the conversation to get deep so quickly. Only a Belhaven outsider would ask her that. The locals already assumed she was part of something bigger. It came with her family history. After the initial shock, though, she felt immense gratitude that he would ask her such a vulnerable question. She shifted until she was mirroring Liam. The late afternoon sun caught the freckles on his cheeks and deepened the shadows in the wrinkles around his eyes. The flecks of white in his beard reflected a touch of silver. Everything about him seemed softer.

"Every day."

His eyes widened like he was surprised by her answer.

"But I don't want to be."

"Why not?"

Emma looked out to the water, giving her thoughts time to organize themselves. She almost laughed at the ridiculousness of having this conversation twice in forty-eight hours.

"I'm on the list." Emma watched the slow realization form on Liam's face. "As far as I know, no one I'm related to has tried to overthrow the government in the last hundred years, but it doesn't matter. I still have the surveys and the monitoring, and the random loyalty checks as though I'm a real threat to their power. I had a hard time finding stable work after college, and I think it's because prospective employers didn't want the added hassle."

The words started to flow like a river through a busted dam. "I sincerely love my job, but it's complicated. The Emma of five years ago was full of spite and fire. But attempting to teach people about our past within a very specific set of historically inaccurate parameters is infuriating. I continue to push up against those parameters as best as I can, but I'm tired."

Emma shifted again until she was back on her stomach and the horizon stretched in front of her. The breeze picked up, and she held her floppy sun hat down until she was convinced it was safe to let go.

"Doing this work also feeds into the belief that I'm somehow a threat, and I accept that. But I don't do serious relationships anymore because the person I'm with is targeted. And if they're also from a monitored family, the enforcement gets worse for both of us. Just for being connected to me."

Emma watched Liam turn onto his stomach. His eyes followed Belle as she sniffed up and down the beach, occasionally running toward a flock of seagulls until they scattered into the air.

"So I take it you're not seeing anyone then?" Liam averted her gaze, now focusing on the woven pattern in her blanket.

Emma bit back a smile and tried to match his casual tone. "Not at the moment."

From the corner of her eye, Emma caught a slight nod and a hint of a smile.

"I've never told anyone this," he hesitated a beat. "My mom never met her aunt Georgia."

Liam's voice was so soft, it was almost hidden by the gentle crashing of the waves against the shore. Emma gave him her full attention, but the privacy of keeping her gaze on the water.

"When Georgia was in her twenties, she lived in this little house on a huge plot of land up north in the mountains. The growing season was short, but she never had a problem because she could grow anything anywhere. And she always had an overabundance of it. She made money selling fresh fruits and vegetables in the summer and canned stuff in the winter.

"The factory or a lumber mill, or something like that, caught fire and most of the townspeople lost their jobs. And she just started giving it all away to anyone who couldn't afford it. She just fed the entire town. Then the following spring she taught people how to plant gardens. Most people could do the basics, ya know? But this was a manufacturing town in the mountains, so no one really had a subsistence garden anymore. And it didn't make up for the income loss, but people didn't starve. Kids weren't malnourished."

Emma heard what Liam wasn't saying. To the uneducated eye, everything he put in the ground looked like it was growing as expected. But these were native plants that Emma spent her whole life around. She knew everything was a bit farther along than it should be and thriving despite it. He had Georgia's magic. Liam didn't have the training to do what Georgia did, but he had the potential.

Emma understood his question, but her answer remained the same. "What happened to Georgia?"

"She was executed." Liam clenched his jaw. "Some of the townspeople tried to hide her. They were arrested and never seen again."

"And the town?"

"Abandoned within a generation." He shook his head with a frustrated laugh. "My parents think I'll end up like her."

"Because of your work here."

Liam nodded. "Yep."

It wasn't likely unless Liam raised some red flags. In Emma's experience with the federation's enforcement offices, it would be pretty easy for a guy like Liam to fly under the radar. Being a man always helped. He hadn't said anything about being a monitored family, and Georgia's magic use would have definitely added her siblings to the list. It was hard, but not impossible, to be removed if you had friends in high places.

"Most days I just want people to forget I exist," Emma said.

Liam turned until his troubled eyes met hers. His conflicted emotions swirled in the energy around him.

"If you want to push some buttons, I'll introduce you to Regan when she's here on Friday," Emma offered. "She teaches astronomy at the university and pretty tapped into the trouble the kids are causing these days."

He smiled but it didn't reach his eyes. "I'd like to meet her, but I should probably hold off on making any waves."

The blanket wasn't very wide. They were only inches apart; it would be so easy to close the gap. Emma's fingers itched to stroke his cheek and feel the texture of his scruffy beard against her skin.

"Anyway, I'm sorry about the heavy conversation topic." Liam began to press himself up. "You came here to relax and here I come talking about dead family members."

Emma impulsively grabbed his shirt.

"No, you don't have to leave." Her voice bordered on frantic, and she took a breath while he settled back into an awkward half lean.

"What I mean is, don't be sorry. I don't mind hearing about your dead family members. Or your living family members, especially the ones that make you question what you're doing with your life."

Though still half-sitting half-leaning, Liam relaxed into it, bringing them closer together. The space between them now was only a sliver. Emma slowly released his shirt, hoping he was unaware that she still had him in her grip.

"Before I got into landscaping, I worked in finance. Stocks, hedge funds, all that high-level stuff. And I was good." Liam's voice deepened, like the memory was pulling him back to a darker place. "I made myself rich and a lot of other people even richer."

Emma didn't know much about Liam, but there was nothing about him that would have led her to believe he had ever been wealthy. The sand shifted underneath her as she turned her body towards him, her legs now brushing up against his. The light contact felt anything but.

"I figured you majored in botany and grew up some kind of flower child."

Liam laughed. "Definitely not. My parents actively pushed me away from botany or anything related to it and pushed my older brother and me into finance."

"Because of Georgia."

"Right." Bitterness tinged his voice.

"You must have liked it on some level to pursue it for as long as you did."

He shrugged. "I was extremely good at it, but I didn't like it. I liked the money and everything that came with it. If I wanted something, it was handed to me without question. I was a kid, and my entire world was a candy store."

Emma was intimately familiar with these kinds of entitled men. She dated plenty in her early twenties because back then, she found their arrogance and power attractive. It gave her the false impression that she was powerful by association.

She leaned in. "What did you want back then?"

Liam's eyes darkened and the corner of his mouth lifted into a half smile as though he relished reliving the days he could have anything.

"I wanted everything. Rare bottles of wine, invitations to exclusive parties, custom-tailored suits, the purest drugs, nameless sex with beautiful people." He wet his lips. His voice got low. "Power."

Emma's breath hitched in her chest, and she fought to keep her composure. Maybe she was still attracted to toxic entitlement. Or maybe it was just that Liam made her feel safe and the arrogance wasn't a real threat.

The air had changed around them. Charged, like a lightning storm ready to strike. The tension pulled too tight and ready to snap.

She needed to throw some ice on the conversation. "So what happened? How did you get here, Liam?"

"I crashed. I spent a decade killing myself from the inside out. I damaged almost every relationship to the point of no return. I woke up one morning, and I just couldn't get out of bed. I texted my team and said I wouldn't be in. And I never went back."

Maybe too much ice.

"At some point, I felt good enough to realize that being in my house wasn't what I needed. I started cutting lawns and doing some light landscaping. I was really good with money, but working with plants just felt so natural. The physical work was hard, but the job itself was effortless. Competition increased, and I had to hustle more. I felt myself slipping back in. This job seemed like..." he trailed off. He looked to the horizon with a thoughtful look. "The right fit for my life right now."

Emma took some time to absorb everything Liam told her. The puzzle pieces were falling into place and the reason for his initial question was clearer. "Has this job turned out to be the right fit?"

Liam

Liam considered her question. Sometimes he missed the hedonism of his old life, but occasional visits were enough to scratch the itch. No amount of money or power could convince him to go back to being the worst version of himself. Depression and anxiety would always be there, but that was the nature of mental illness. At this moment, he was the healthiest he'd ever been.

"I think so. Though," he leaned in, "I do look great in a perfectly tailored suit."

Emma raised her eyebrows in consideration, then brought her finger to her lips, pulling Liam's attention to her mouth. Her eyes moved slowly up his body like a hungry lioness assessing her prey.

"Hmm, yes." Emma's voice turned low and breathy. "I can see how that's an aesthetic that some people may find attractive."

Liam welcomed the return of their flirty banter as a balm for the rawness left by exposing so much of himself. With it, though, came sexual energy that pulsed between them, thick with anticipation. The rational voice that would have reminded Liam about the complications of messing around with coworkers was clocked out for the weekend. He leaned in, his mouth hovering close to her neck. On her skin, the breeze left a hint of the sea mixed with the familiar scent of citrus and magnolia.

"And what about you?" He whispered. "Is that an aesthetic you find attractive?"

Emma turned her head, her lips dangerously close to his. Liam's restraint was hanging on by a thread. How much longer could he resist tasting her mouth?

"It's okay." She shrugged and turned away. When she looked over her shoulder at him, her lips curled into a coy grin.

Liam knew their game wasn't over. He shook his head in mock offense. "Ouch."

Emma swept her legs underneath her until she and Liam faced each other. Her floppy sun hat lifted a bit in the afternoon wind. He gingerly removed it from her head, releasing a cascade of soft, loose curls made by the salty sea air. The mossy green of her hazel eyes brightened in the glow of the waning sun, but there was a hint of seductive darkness.

Emma ran a finger down Liam's sleeved biceps and traced the ink on his exposed forearm, leaving a trail of icy fire over his skin. "My type is more rugged and outdoorsy."

His heart hammered against his ribs. Her words alone were his undoing. He took Emma's chin in his fingers and guided her mouth to his, stopping to ask, "Am I your type?"

Emma's wet lips brushed against his. "Yes," she sighed.

"Can I kiss you?" Liam whispered.

Emma quietly moaned, "yes."

He pulled back. "Say please," he teased.

She lowered her head and met his gaze through her lashes. A sinful smile told him she didn't intend to. "Make me."

Liam was already grasping onto what little restraint he had left. Emma's playful defiance required self-control, and he was in short supply. He wanted to ravage her, and he was ready to break. Ready to give her all the pleasure she desired. Ready to make her drunk with orgasms and bliss.

Liam brushed his thumb over her mouth and slid his hand into her hair, exposing her neck. He skimmed her collarbone with feather-light touches of his lips. Emma's breath quickened. His fingers twisted into her locks. She whimpered with every restrained push of his tongue.

Her lips sought his.

He tried again. "Say please."

"Please," she begged.

"Good girl." He kissed her with an insatiable hunger for which her mouth was the only cure. His hands traced the form of her body, memorizing every sweet, soft curve. Emma's fingers found their way to his hair, the gentle tugs becoming more needy with the growing intensity of their kiss.

Emma pulled away, momentarily severing their connection and laid down on the blanket. In the brief disconnect, he remembered they were out in the open on a public beach. But they were alone. Even Belle was giving them space as she dozed in the sun.

Liam bent down to nibble on her neck, and he was met with an approving giggle. His thumb drifted along her stomach, teasing the edge of her leggings. Emma lifted her hips into his hands and moaned into his mouth.

"Do you want me to keep going?"

"Yes," she moaned, her lips barely leaving his.

Liam slid his hand under her waistband. Emma's breathing quickened and the grip on his hair tightened.

He lingered there, digging his fingers into her hips, and savoring every kiss like it would be his last.

He pulled back. Emma found the sweet spot on his neck, and he groaned with pleasure, almost coming undone.

"Emma." His low voice rumbled the clear command, forcing their eyes to meet. Emma looked at him with feverish anticipation. "Do you want my fingers inside you?"

"Yes, please."

Emma swore quietly when his hand slid under the band of her underwear. His fingers explored every inch of her as he watched the way her body responded to his touch. He caught every hitched breath, every moan, and every soft cry. He circled her slippery center until she pleaded for more. Then he slowed. Just enough for Emma to take a deep, panting breath before starting again.

Her body tensed. She gripped the blanket. When euphoria hit, he kissed her to subdue the sounds of her pleasure. Emma's lips danced lazily with his. Her body went limp, and her breathing slowed. Liam kissed her deeply and slowly, drawing out every meeting of their lips and tongue.

Liam could have spent the rest of the evening pleasing Emma. As the moment cooled, despite his dick screaming otherwise, he knew he needed to slow things down.

She looked at him with sleepy eyes. Flecks of sand stuck to her glistening skin. He was absolutely enamored with her, and it must have shown on his face.

Emma brought a hand to his cheek. "What?"

"There's no way I could ever forget that you exist."

Chapter 13

Diary of Sara Cortese

Willow Ridge, Arcanos, late spring circa 1620

In the heat of the late-spring sun, Bethany and I sailed from Belhaven to Willow Ridge.

The operator of the small craft that took us across the water warned us that the voyage is longer without the assistance of his sea goat. He set it free when it became unusually hostile and unpredictable, nearly capsizing one of his larger crafts. I've heard stories of other ferrymen experiencing the same. Where once the sea around Belhaven was a safe home for these unearthly creatures, something has caused them enough fear to flee.

While the creatures belonging to this realm, Tereprima, fare well, those that visit from Teremedi have been behaving in curious ways. Some animal keepers believe it's connected to the Commarasi sowing discontent for the Amora goddesses. To quell more violent uprisings, gatekeepers are being pulled away from their posts guarding Teremedi's rifts, allowing more malevolent beings. Bethany and I didn't come to Willow Ridge seeking this information, but it quickly consumed my attention.

My tried-and-true spells offer John Dawson little relief for his pain and sleeplessness and only slow his worsening symptoms. Bethany depletes her lifeforce to precarious levels with no success. She sought counsel from the elder healers while I scoured the texts in the temple library.

When the sun was high, we left the temple at Willow Ridge to meet our ferry. We would be returning to Belhaven with little more than we already knew. I saw the frustration in Bethany's sullen features, and I pulled her into my body for a deep embrace. I gifted her a tender kiss and with a content sigh, her body relaxed heavily against mine. Our magic fused, and wrapped around us like the caterpillar's cocoon.

I brought her to the shade of a tall oak and guided her to rest her head on my thigh while we waited. I watched her fight her heavy lids until she finally succumbed to her exhaustion. Running my nails over her scalp, I noticed the brittleness of her hair. It catches easily around my fingers. The streaks of white have almost taken over its former golden-brown color. The cool blue of her light skin took on a gray hue. Her peacefulness allowed me to see the toll this work is having on her body, and should this continue, I fear what may come.

Chapter 14
Diary of Sara Cortese

Belhaven Island, late spring circa 1620

Bethany and I were met with an interrogation shortly after our return to Belhaven. I had not realized how many in our village had become rattled by the news of the Commarasi. We were whisked away by the village elders before we could share our knowledge with our community.

The Council of Nine requested our account, and we shared the news with them freely. When I reached for my ledger, however, I was told no official record of our meeting would be necessary. Not all conversations with the elders are recorded, but surely one of such high importance and consequence should be. Before we were dismissed, the Council advised us to avoid causing a stir within the village. Panic on our little island would be disastrous, they said.

Bethany left to care for John Dawson, leaving me with my restless thoughts. That night, I sat with Stephen at our table, a cup of warm stock between my hands. Its comfort reminding me of Bethany. Stephen sat quietly while I recounted the events of our journey and the concerning response of the elders.

"Your duty to this village," he said, "is to preserve our history and traditions so that our descendants will be able to look to the past for guidance."

He needn't say more. I understood.

CHAPTER 15

EMMA

"I'd let any one of them handle me like one of those trees," Blair uttered with her hand lightly gripping her chest.

Emma erupted into laughter and covered her mouth to stifle the sound. At work, Blair was the utmost professional. As the financial director, she spent the most time with the wealthy donors that kept the museum operating, and she cultivated a demeanor of seriousness and neutrality.

On the rare occasion Blair said something inappropriate at the office, it was equal parts shocking and hilarious.

Conveniently, Emma's office had the best view of Liam and his maintenance crew cutting and clearing trees damaged by the earthquake. She had plenty more visitors than usual the past few days, all wanting to get a glimpse of the crew's strength and athleticism. It set off something primal in all of them and no one could get enough.

"Mmm hmm," Hector hummed. "Especially the new guy. I want him to break me apart."

"Liam?" Emma asked, not taking her eyes off the man in question as he sorted cut logs into piles. His ratty t-shirt was drenched in sweat and stuck to his skin, outlining the peaks and valleys of his shoulder muscles.

"I'd let him tear me apart, too, but someone else is occupying his attention."

Emma shrugged with a coy smile.

Hector hip bumped her. "I was talking about Jake. The new new guy."

Emma let her vision wander to one of Liam's recent hires. Jake Mackenzie was the new mechanic and a bit of a mystery. Judy cleared him, but he didn't have much of an interest in getting to know anyone else on staff. Emma could see why Hector would be into him. He was an enigma wrapped in a muscular build with dark wavy hair against warm beige skin.

"I wouldn't kick him outta bed," she conceded.

"What are we looking at?" Judy's curious voice echoed through the room, startling the threesome away from the window. She peered out to the scene below and clicked her tongue. "Y'all are animals. Stop ogling your coworkers like you're at the zoo."

Blair and Hector giggled softly while slowly backing out of Emma's office.

Judy took one last glance out the window, then turned her attention to Emma. "I got your paperwork back. Do you want to go over it now, or do you want to schedule something for tomorrow?"

Emma groaned and fell into her chair. "Let's get it over with."

Judy handed Emma a manila envelope before taking a seat across from her. "Congratulations. You aren't a threat to the establishment."

With an exaggerated eye roll, Emma pulled out the paperwork and shuffled through it, scanning each page quickly before moving onto the next.

"Your check came back clear, and you've been approved to continue working in your current position."

"For how long?"

Judy huffed a laugh. "A week? A month? Five years? You know they never give you a timeframe. And even if they did, it wouldn't mean anything."

Emma stopped when she got to the report that concerned her the most.

Known Professional Associates.

A list of every employee Emma spent time with professionally or personally. The administrative team worked as a skeleton crew, taking on more work for a bit more pay in order to keep the staff small. Publicly, Judy said it was to keep expenses down. It was cheaper to pay one person a little more to do two jobs. The fiscally conservative board of directors loved that.

Privately, Judy said that it was to give her more control over who she brought on board. All department heads were listed on Emma's form. They'd all see extra scrutiny.

Except Liam.

Emma scanned the page for a date. Liam got a pass because the timing of his hiring worked in his favor. Judy completed the list on Liam's second day of work. Judy knew Emma and Liam would work together on occasion, but the date gave her an excuse for not adding him.

Emma flung the papers on her desk. "Sometimes it feels like things are inching forward, but being guilty by association is such shit."

Judy straightened her glasses and trapped Emma in an empathetic gaze. "I know."

"How did you and Celeste deal with all this extra scrutiny?" Emma had a close relationship with her boss, but Judy often held a firm line between work and home. She didn't mind personal questions before or after her work day and Emma usually respected that boundary. Sometimes her impulsivity got the better of her.

Wistful wasn't a look she often displayed, but when her 'Work Judy' features softened, it was usually because her wife was the topic of conversation.

"Our life together started under much different circumstances. At the time, as far as the federation was concerned, I had a more agreeable career as an attorney."

She paused, her eyes drifting upward as though searching for the right words.

"And I had a less antagonistic body. It picked up a bit more after I transitioned. They thought because I was living in a more traditionally feminine body, my ability to access ancestral magic would strengthen. And they would know that's not how it works if they didn't spend a few hundred years rewriting our history. Anyway," she waved her hand, "when I took this job, Celeste and I were already bound legally and spiritually. Poor woman is stuck with me."

Emma had a thousand questions, but Judy was gracious enough to answer one while they were on the clock, and she was already moving on to the next subject. Judy reached into her blazer pocket and pulled out a familiar leather pouch.

"I have some feelers out about this necklace, but I think you should hold onto it."

Emma had forgotten the ornate necklace she found with Sara Cortese's diaries, but she felt a brush of relief now that she held it in her hand. She opened the pouch and let it slip into her palm, seeing it in the natural light for the first time in weeks. Tendrils of Emma's magic seeped from her skin, seeking out the energy that radiated from the glistening stone.

"Do you know anything about it?"

"Nothing definitive, other than it's made up of quartz that was found on the island." Judy sat forward and lowered her voice. "Whatever this is, it's powerful. It needs to be kept in a safe place. And don't tell anyone else about it."

Emma slid the necklace back into the pouch. "Maybe I shouldn't keep it, then."

Judy stood up and straightened her blazer. "No, you probably shouldn't. But you know it belongs with you."

Emma couldn't be sure how she made it home in one piece. She barely remembered the events between getting into her car and pulling into her driveway. Her brain crammed an hour's worth of contemplation into a fifteen-minute commute.

What was this necklace all about?

Why did it feel like it belonged to her?

Should she keep things up with Liam?

Would doing so put a target on his back if there isn't one already?

Does he even want to?

She had barely heard from him since Sunday. Though he could say the same thing about her.

She stepped over the fallen limb that remained in her driveway. As she trudged up the steps of her front porch, a piece of beach glass on the railing reflected the late afternoon sunlight. She was running her fingers over the water-worn edges when a crow landed on the railing and eyed her from a few feet away. Emma smiled and the crow returned her greeting with a curious head tilt.

"I don't think I have any blue glass in my collection," Emma said softly. "Thank you."

Emma didn't possess animal magic, but Grandma Rose once told her that some Amora were just more in tune with the earth's creatures. It could explain why the crows left her little trinkets, but Emma believed it had more to do with years of putting out peanuts and fresh water.

She pocketed the glass and went inside, moving through the motions of her after-work routine. Taking a bottle of hard apple cider from the refrigerator, she made her way back out the front door with Luna at her heels. After stopping to place the bottle cap on the railing, she plodded across the street to collapse in one of Regan's rocking chairs.

Regan emerged from the backyard, a beer in one hand and her phone in the other. She stared hard at the screen, her furrowed eyebrows making little lines in her usually smooth skin. Luna hopped into Regan's lap as soon as her ass made contact with the chair.

"What's going on?" Emma asked.

Regan began with an, "Umm," and took a bit to finish her answer. "I'm texting with Peyton. Their deli is being audited. It's closed for a week."

"Fuck," Emma groaned. She downed a few long pulls of her cider, wishing she had something stronger.

Every business anticipated it at least once every few years. But small restaurants like Doolittle's Deli weren't audited often. Delis weren't known to use magic to guarantee success or for being particularly sympathetic to the underground Amora resistance. Being audited twice in six months meant the federation thought they had a reason to believe otherwise.

"Does Peyton know what prompted it?"

Regan's face twisted slightly, and Emma knew the answer.

"Officially? No. Unofficially? Me." Regan frowned. "I'm the only thing that changed in Peyton's life since their last audit."

Peyton was taking a business accounting class at the university where Regan worked. Their class schedules were similar enough that riding together and splitting the cost of the ferry made sense. It didn't take long for a forty-five-minute commute to turn into coffee or drinks after class. Coffee and drinks turned into meals, which turned into whatever Peyton and Regan labeled their dynamic.

Emma started scraping the label off her bottle, unsure what to say. Neither of them had evidence that Peyton's association with Regan is what caused the added scrutiny, but it happened enough over the course of their lives that Emma would have bet her grandmother's house on it. "How's Peyton doing?"

Regan put her phone on the table between them. "Okay, all things considered. You know Peyton. Little fazes them. But I still wonder if they're holding back because they don't want to make me feel bad."

Emma stretched over two wooden armrests until she found Regan's hand. Her golden-brown eyes were already wet with tears, and Emma wanted to set the world on fire for making her best friend sad.

"Peyton is blunt as fuck. If they blamed you for any of this, they would tell you. Peyton is also the most pragmatic person I've ever met. I'm sure they weighed the risks of spending time with you before even suggesting you ride together. And they clearly determined that being in your magnificent presence was worth it."

A tear rolled down Regan's cheek, taking some mascara with it. She used her other hand to wipe the rest away, ensuring it would be the only one. "I am quite magnificent."

Emma squeezed her hand tightly before letting go and returning to a more comfortable position in her chair. While Regan was distracted by the purring cat making biscuits on her fleece jacket, Emma swiped through her own phone until she landed on the last text message from Liam. Her thumbs hovered over the keyboard at a loss for what to say. She hesitated until the screen went black to save power. Somewhere in the back of her mind, though she knew it was ridiculous, she took the phone's dark screen as a sign it was best to say nothing at all.

Chapter 16

Liam

With an exhausted grunt, Liam lifted the tailgate of his truck and slammed it shut. The split wood would be emptied from its bed on Monday. Five days of felling trees and turning them into mulch and firewood took its toll on his middle-aged body. His low back ached, and his shoulders screamed anytime he lifted his arms. Feeling left out, an old sports injury in his knee decided to visit for a spell. Everyone was hurting though. His five-member crew worked themselves ragged trying to impress the rotation of audiences.

It pained him to admit it, but the attention gave him a rush he hadn't felt since his twenties. He wasn't yet at the height of his career, but the upward trajectory started putting him in circles with wealthy and well-connected people. Suddenly everyone from old high school classmates to acquaintances from the gym wanted face time with him. Liam knew he was being used, but he didn't care. Their desire for him fed his ego no matter the reason.

The shy smiles from stay-at-home moms and hollers from feisty elderly women barely registered compared to the few moments he caught Emma peeking from her office window. The thrill of her gaze sent gasoline through his veins, feeding his body fuel to take down one more tree, one more stump, one more load of firewood.

But that fuel burned quickly. The mysterious earthquake left its mark on the land, doubling Liam's workload. He also had to rework his design, his project schedule, and his budget. Physically and mentally exhausted at the end of each day, he crashed on the couch after walking into his apartment. Long days weren't unheard of in the landscaping business, but Liam had a tendency to work too much, running himself, and his relationships, into the ground. He could forgive himself for an occasional busy week, but a busy week immediately after hooking up with Emma—his coworker—felt like a return to his old life.

Liam parked his truck behind the nature classroom. He replenished the firewood visitors could use in any of the new fire pits or take home for themselves. The museum had plenty to spare.

He inspected the pointed leaves of the trumpet vine creeping its way up the pergola's wooden posts.

"Don't grow too fast," he muttered. The young plants had only been in the ground a couple of weeks and they were already at his eye level.

He unlocked the door to the education building and scanned the room for anything amiss. He didn't expect there to be. Only two other classes had used it since its completion a few weeks earlier. Crossing the room, he unlocked the steel and glass doors that looked out to rows of wooden benches. The doors rumbled along the track as they rolled up to the ceiling. A few birds scattered into the trees.

With the room open, he could officially call it quits for the day.

But he didn't. He lingered. Awkwardly.

Someone from the museum's administrative staff had to stick around during the class. He got a tip that staffer would be Emma. He was tired and achy, but he didn't want to miss his chance to catch her.

Liam stepped out of the building when he heard tires crunching over the gravel access road. A boxy SUV pulled up next to Liam's truck and out stepped a stunning woman with bold purple ringlets pulled into a high ponytail and wearing a polo with the Willow Ridge University logo.

"Hey, I'm Regan. I'm teaching the class tonight."

"I was just unlocking the room for you. I'm Liam, the property manager." He stepped aside to let her through the door.

"Nice to finally meet you, Liam." She hoisted her tote bag onto the table at the front of the room and started unpacking.

Finally? As Liam pondered what she meant by *finally*, his eyes caught the tattoo on the inside of her wrist. A telescope and a mortar and pestle inside a border of intricate floral and celestial elements. Emma had the same tattoo in the same spot.

"I've heard a lot about you," Regan said knowingly.

Liam's face warmed, and he rubbed the back of his neck. "Yeah?"

"Well, Emma's my best friend," she said, while sifting through her materials. "So, we talk."

"Oh?" Of course they would. He felt stupid for being surprised.

"About everything," she added, looking up from her things.

Understanding dawned on him. His eyes widened, and his breath caught. He recovered, but not quickly enough to hide his embarrassment and his words were even slower to come. Liam shifted awkwardly in the uncomfortable silence while Regan continued setting up for her class.

"Is this where you threaten me with bodily harm if I hurt her?" He joked.

Regan set her papers aside with the unmistakable look of a professor at the end of the semester who was absolutely over it.

"No. Emma is a grown woman. I don't need to fight her battles for her. Don't underestimate her though. Anything she comes up with will be far worse than whatever I suggest."

That sounded very much like the Emma he was getting to know.

"Anyway, she'll be here in a few minutes," Regan said.

"Oh?" He cringed, realizing how often he'd uttered the phrase.

"This is why you're hanging around, right? To talk to her?"

Liam stumbled through an incoherent response as Regan's smile widened with evil glee at his discomfort. She finally put up a hand to stop his rambling.

"Lemme give you some advice. I'm not worried about you hurting Emma, because she's going to try like hell to keep you from getting that close. And if she lets you in and allows herself to be that vulnerable, I know you'll protect her heart by any means necessary."

"What if she doesn't let me in?"

"Don't give her the option."

Liam needed her to elaborate. This was valuable intel. Why would Regan violate Best Friend Code by telling him all this? Was Regan being a good friend or a bad friend?

"Why—" he began but never finished. Emma arrived in one of the utility carts, cutting off his chances of learning more from Regan.

"I come bearing gifts." Emma stepped into the building carrying two takeout cups. She put one of the containers on the table next to Regan's things. She looked down at her cup, then sheepishly at Liam.

"I didn't expect to see you here. I would have gotten you something."

"You can get me next time."

He stopped by specifically to see Emma, but now standing only a few feet apart, Liam couldn't find his voice.

"Thank you for the coffee." Regan stepped between them and kissed Emma on the cheek. Emma jumped. Had she also temporarily forgotten Regan was there?

Taking the cup with her, Regan turned back to the dry erase board and continued writing a list of constellations.

"Can I steal you for a minute?" He asked.

"Umm, Regan do you need anything?" Emma spoke to her friend but didn't take her eyes off Liam.

"Nope. Class doesn't start until seven so you can steal her for a whole forty-five."

Liam led Emma around the back of the building to his truck so they could have a little bit of privacy should any amateur astronomers come to class early.

"I figured you and Regan were friends, but I didn't realize you were so close," he said. "Makes sense why you volunteered to work."

"There are few who come before my regularly scheduled Friday night debauchery. Regan is one of them."

Liam stepped closer, the familiar energy pulsing between them. Being near her was a balm for the ache of their distance the past week. He yearned for the connection they shared on the beach. The honesty and openness that shredded him raw and mended by her kiss.

"Are your Friday nights anything like your Sunday afternoons?" He winked.

Emma slowly licked her lips. She bit back a smile. "Sometimes."

He was within arm's reach, but didn't reach out. The electricity of her touch was a drug for every cell in his fingertips and he had something to say before he got high. "I'm sorry. For not reaching out more this week."

She narrowed her eyes. Somehow in the same day, he managed to have two women look at him like he said something stupid.

"There's nothing to be sorry about. I didn't reach out either."

"No, but still. I wanted to. I was just..."

"Tired?"

He breathed a laugh. "Very much so."

"It's okay. Really." Emma took him by the shirt and coaxed him closer until she had his body pinning hers against the door of the truck.

Liam didn't think he deserved to be let off that easily. Maybe it was unresolved guilt for so many ghosted lovers. He had plans to make it up to her. Perfectly wholesome plans that were in danger of being tossed aside now that her body trembled against his.

He leaned in until his lips ghosted the crook of her neck, leaving goosebumps in their wake. "Let me make it up to you."

Emma's grip on his shirt tightened. "What did you have in mind?"

He didn't answer right away, savoring every soft whimper that he teased loose with his mouth on her skin. "Let me cook you dinner tonight. After your class."

Her throat shook with a low laugh. "Okay. Dinner is good."

Liam lifted his head from her neck to find a subtle pout on Emma's deep pink lips. "What's so funny?"

"Nothing. Dinner is wonderful. It's just not what I thought you were going to say."

He kissed her lightly, pulling away every time she tried to deepen their kiss. Every meeting of their lips thundered through him like a storm rolling over the sea. It was nearly impossible to hold back, but Emma's tightening grip on his shirt suggested she was enjoying this game. She breathed a low sigh when he returned to her neck. One hand released his shirt and found the back of his head. Her nails ran along his scalp, catching his hair between her fingers.

"Were you expecting a repeat?" Liam whispered.

A silent nod was her only reply.

Liam was delusional if he thought their conversation would go any other way. Lust unlike anything he'd endured enveloped him anytime she was near. It was an overwhelming, almost spiritual desire to fill her body with pleasure and bliss.

With the faintest pressure, Liam pressed his thigh between her legs. "Use your words, Emma."

She sucked in a breath. Her nails dug deeper into his skin. "Yes."

"Do you want a repeat right now?"

Emma's breaths grew heavy, her voice a whispered plea. "Yes, please."

He smiled against her skin. Maybe she liked the exhibition and the risk of getting caught. Maybe she was too aroused to care. Liam could relate to both.

He kept the pace slow and intentional, his lips fighting against the desperation of hers. His hands slid down the curves of her waist to her hips. One slipped under her shirt. The pads of his fingertips were extra sensitive to every freckle, scar, and stretch mark, making a tactile map of her body.

The other hand followed the skin of her soft belly down to the warm mound between her legs. Emma shuddered, and her eyes rolled up to the darkening sky. His constrained movements didn't hinder her pleasure. She pressed her hips into his hand, grinding against his circling fingers. Liam no longer heard the ambient sounds of nature around them. He tuned out the crashing waves below and the nearby calls of sea birds. He only heard Emma's heavy breaths and quiet moans. He pressed his forehead against hers.

"Don't stop," she ordered.

"I wouldn't dare."

Her mouth hung open, and her breathy moans grew louder. Liam hushed her with a deep kiss, and she released herself over the edge. Emma's body stiffened then fell apart, turning to liquid in his hands. She kissed him frantically while he teased out the last bit of ecstasy.

Following her pace, he slowed when her breathing slowed, drawing out every kiss. He smoothed her hair away from her glistening face. "I'd still like to make you dinner tonight."

"Yeah. Okay." She choked out, her voice dry and hoarse. She cleared her throat, then ran her hand down the front of Liam's pants. The thick fabric was no match for the stiffness beneath. He sighed a moan with the gentle pressure of her touch. "I'll tell Regan you said bye."

Liam managed a quiet laugh. "That's probably for the best."

CHAPTER 17
EMMA

Emma's heart was still thumping against her ribcage when she walked to the front of the building. She stumbled into the classroom drunk on a cocktail of feel-good hormones, neurotransmitters, and magic bliss. Physical contact with Liam was as close to a transcendent experience she could ever hope to encounter.

Regan greeted Emma with a needling smile. "Good talk?"

Emma cleared her throat, attempting to gain her composure. "There was some of that, yes."

Emma picked up her coffee from the table. She'd been gone long enough that it cooled to the perfect temperature. "He said he wants to cook me dinner tonight."

"Well that's adorable. You're going, right?"

Emma nodded. "I think so."

"Uh oh. Insecure Emma has entered the chat."

Emma sighed. The happiness from her orgasm gave way to her more irritating emotional residents, anxiety and depression. "I just don't want Liam to become the next Peyton."

Regan sat down and squeezed her in a tight hug. "Maybe you need to let Liam decide if he wants to be the next Peyton."

Emma groaned, but she knew Regan was right.

"But until then, let him cook you dinner and give you more orgasms."

Emma laughed. When Regan put it that way, she'd be a raging asshole not to spend time with him. "If his hands are as good at cooking as they are at everything else, then I'm done for."

"Atta girl." Regan patted Emma's thigh before getting up. The first students were starting to arrive.

With her hand on the knob of Liam's front door, Emma hesitated a breath before stepping into the foyer. She wanted anything and everything that would come after stepping through that door. And the intensity of that want terrified her. Her nerves almost got the better of her, but Liam wasn't someone she could ghost and avoid for a few weeks.

The foyer was filled with rock music that leaked from the open door at the top of the stairs. A savory scent beckoned her.

Emma hadn't been in the apartment since Liam moved in, and she took in his personal touches. The built-in bookcase displayed a mix of books and DVDs. His phone was plugged into some kind of multi-media player in the corner of the room, but a vinyl record was the source of the music. She was most curious about the acoustic guitar that hung on the wall. They talked about music often, but he failed to mention being musically inclined himself. She failed to mention she was a pretty good singer, but this wasn't about her.

A woven blanket hung over the back of a worn couch dusted with dog fur. The armchair next to it looked almost new.

She greeted Belle with plenty of belly rubs, then followed the dog into the kitchen where Liam was stirring a small pot of tomato soup. "That smells good."

"Thanks, but I can't take credit for it. Doolittle's Deli made it. I'm just reheating it."

Emma flinched hearing the name of Peyton's temporarily closed business. "Well your wooden spoon technique is impressive."

"It's all in the wrist." He winked.

Her face grew hot, and she averted her gaze. On the counter she saw a loaf of bread, cut in thick slices, and a few short towers of cheese stacked on a plate. "I'm already here, you know. You don't have to woo me with bread and cheese."

Liam put the wooden spoon on a plate in the middle of the stove. "No, but I do distinctly remember you telling me a couple of weeks ago that you're motivated by carbs."

He leaned in and kissed her softly, twisting her stomach into knots. It was sexy in its tenderness. It complemented the fiery passion that fueled their exhibitionist encounters. He slowly pulled away, daring her to pull him back in. She let him go, though, because like he said, she was motivated by carbs, and she was legitimately hungry.

Liam tossed a slice of cheese to Belle who was sitting quietly at his side. He assembled the cheese sandwiches while a frying pan warmed on a burner.

"Can I help at all?"

"Drinks and plates?" He pointed to a cabinet on his other side, and Emma ran her hand across his back as she moved across the kitchen.

"I know grilled cheese and soup probably wasn't what you were expecting when I invited you over for dinner," Liam said, buttering a slice of bread.

Emma placed two bowls and two plates next to him. "These are my three favorite food groups: soup, cheese, and bread."

She moved to the refrigerator, peeking inside for an alcoholic beverage.

"I never really have the opportunity to cook for anyone." Liam put both sandwiches in the pan. They sizzled and the smell of warm butter filled the tiny room.

Emma opened two bottles of hard cider and placed one on the counter next to Liam. Their conversation at the beach flashed into her mind.

"I guess it's tough to make someone dinner if you're always at the office." How many meals did he have at his desk, she wondered.

"Bingo." Liam flipped the sandwiches showing off a perfectly golden crust. "And then I was too sick to feed myself let alone someone else."

Surely Liam has dated since, she thought. Landscaping was a seasonal job. Even if he worked from sun-up to sun-down, he still would have had a slow winter. "Not even the past few years? No one worthy enough to be courted with bread and cheese?"

A wicked smile appeared. "I've made breakfast for a few people."

Liam slid the sandwiches onto the plates, the gooey cheese leaving a long trail of melted goodness from the pan. Then he ladled the soup into bowls and moved them to the kitchen island. Emma followed with both plates and her drink bottle tucked in the crook of her elbow.

Liam slid onto the chair. "Those exceptions aside, if I'm cooking for someone else, it's usually my niece, Deryn. And it's usually some variation of pre-made soup and grilled cheese."

Emma pulled apart her sandwich, watching the strings of cheese drip toward the plate. "I'm honored to be amongst the special people for whom you bestow your reheating skills."

During one of their many conversations at work, Liam mentioned having a whole brood of nieces and nephews but only Deryn's name came up with enough frequency that she remembered it. "You two seem really bonded."

"We are. For a million reasons, but I think mostly because I get her. We're a lot alike. Thankfully, my brother isn't parenting her like our parents parented me."

"So it's just your brother and Deryn?"

Liam nodded, releasing a sad sigh. "When Deryn was about two, Cadence went out to run some errands and never came back."

Emma's heart shattered. She had so many questions, but none of them seemed appropriate.

Did she practice magic?

Did Cadence run away or was she taken?

If she was taken, were the kidnappers civilians or the government?

"That's awful. I'm so sorry."

Liam shrugged. "It's been almost eight years now. We've all kind of moved on."

A silence fell between them as they ate. Though heavy, it was comfortable. Natural. Emma dipped her grilled cheese into her soup, watching Liam rub his shoulder in between bites.

"Is your shoulder bothering you?"

Liam huffed out a laugh.

"My everything is bothering me." He leaned over his bowl to take the last bite of his grilled cheese. He sat up slowly as though an ache had settled into his lower back. "I usually spend the afternoons in the office doing paperwork. The past few weeks have been a lot of heavy lifting and little rest. My body's reminding me I'm not twenty-five anymore."

"You made it look easy."

Liam gasped dramatically, putting an offended hand on his chest. "You were watching?"

"Don't look so hot while working if you don't want the attention," Emma teased.

Liam leaned in and kissed her, and she tasted the sweetness of the cider lingering on his lips.

"I do envy the outside part of your job," Emma said when he pulled away. "If I'm not in front of a computer, I'm poking around underground."

"Why didn't you apply for this job?" Liam asked. "You know just as much about plants as I do."

Emma swished the last bit of her grilled cheese in the last bit of her soup.

"I thought about it," she said, not meeting Liam's curious gaze. "But as much as I love working with the natural world, I love storytelling more. I get to do that through our exhibits and the projects I create. I hate the rules I have to follow, but the actual work of storytelling is one that I really enjoy. Plus, I'd rather walk through flames than do all that accounting paperwork you deal with."

Emma shuddered for effect, and Liam's laugh echoed through the room. She took their empty dishes and brought them to the sink.

"Sorry we couldn't get a dishwasher in here." She turned on the water and squeezed some dish soap onto a sponge. "I suggested it several times while they were doing the reno and it just never happened."

"Just leave them. I'll do them tomorrow." Liam tossed his empty bottle into a nearby recycling bin. He took the sponge out of her hand and put it back on the edge of the sink. "I can think of a million other things I'd rather you do by hand."

The lighthearted tone was gone, replaced by one low and seductive.

Emma bit back a smile. "How about I start with your achy shoulders?"

Liam's smoldering blue eyes lightened with relief. "Please. Yes. They really hurt."

Emma told him to sit on the floor in front of the armchair while she fished through her bag for a small glass jar. "Do you have any skin allergies?"

Liam sat down and narrowed his eyes. "No?"

She twisted the lid and handed Liam the open jar. "It's an ointment for the usual aches and pains."

"It smells good. Maypops?" Liam handed it back.

"And cattails. It's an old family recipe." One that she also found in Sara's diary, but she wasn't ready to tell Liam that. The balm was one of the few bits of magic that Emma regularly used. She only did so because the ingredients were found on the island or grew easily in her backyard. It didn't require any specifically timed rituals, and the small batches made them easy to conceal when sharing with those she trusted.

She eased herself down onto the chair, swinging one leg over Liam so he sat between her knees. Running her hands down his back, she stopped when she got to the hem of his t-shirt. She leaned in. Her lips hovered by his ear. "Can I take this off?" She whispered.

"Yes," he breathed.

Emma pulled Liam's t-shirt over his head and let it fall next to him. She drank in his artfully decorated skin, letting her eyes wander over half-a-dozen loosely connected, large and intricate pieces that marked his upper body.

She warmed her hands and pressed her fingers into the muscles of his back and arms, making a mental note of everywhere Liam groaned or hissed through his teeth. Once she had his tender spots mapped, she dipped her finger into the jar and dotted a bit of the ointment on each spot.

"So, about earlier," she said, feeling emboldened by the lack of eye contact. "I get the sense that you like the thrill of fucking around at work."

He breathed a laugh and hung his head down as she worked out a knot in his shoulder blade. Emma's fingertips buzzed with magic, sending an extra burst of strength to the ointment's healing properties.

"I'd say the same for you." He turned his head just enough for her to catch his devilish smile.

He wasn't wrong. Emma generally lived a risk-averse life, which meant her impulsive tendencies manifested in other ways. "I'd like to keep fucking around outside of work too. And maybe in between, we can catch a movie or go out for coffee."

Liam exhaled slowly when she pressed down on a spot on his triceps. "I thought you didn't do relationships."

Over the past few years, Emma had this conversation several times. They were always straightforward, leaving no room for misunderstanding or negotiation. Most of those liaisons fizzled because they lacked the emotional intimacy Emma refused to acknowledge she needed.

"I don't do serious relationships. I don't get involved with people who want love and marriage and kids. I keep things low-key and off-the-books because being with me is a red flag."

"So friends with premium benefits."

"I guess you could say that." Emma usually avoided labels. It was easier to walk away when things ran their course.

Everything about this particular conversation, however, felt different. The words were the same, but they didn't feel authentic. They felt like a lie. Her anxiety climbed with every second of pregnant silence.

Would she change her stance if he didn't agree to her terms? She didn't want to find out.

"Works for me," he said finally. "For the record, I can't have kids." He made a scissor gesture with his fingers, implying that he had had a vasectomy.

"I use an IUD." Emma was happy living a childfree life, and she didn't want her children to inherit a legacy of surveillance.

"Do you have this arrangement with others?"

"I occasionally have fun with a few people that I trust enough to let into my inner circle."

"Literally or figuratively?"

She heard the smile in Liam's voice. Emma laughed. "Both."

No longer feeling any knots under his skin, Emma traced the lines of his muscles and the ink that ran over them. She wasn't ready for the vulnerability of eye contact just yet. Liam leaned back against the chair, his broad shoulders spreading Emma's knees wider.

"I get tested regularly. They were negative," she offered.

She slowly raked her fingers through his hair. Liam tilted his head and leaned into her hands. "Same."

"How do your shoulders feel?

Liam began to shift and turn until he was on his knees between her legs. "Amazing. Thank you."

His hands slid up her thighs, and she cursed the fabric of her pants for keeping their skin apart. Liam's hands slipped under her shirt to explore the curves of her hips and stomach. Emma let him pull her shirt over her head. Her breath caught after a quiet gasp when his lips met the dip between her breasts. She barely noticed her bra coming undone and falling loose around her arms.

Liam touched her body with restrained fervor.

Rough and sweet.

Desperate and patient.

Unable to hold herself up anymore, Emma leaned back into the chair. The buttons of her pants were being undone much too slowly for her liking and that made it so much more enjoyable.

With her pants and underwear gone, she was ready to beg him to do anything that would end his sensual torture. Greedy for pleasure, Emma lifted her hips as Liam dragged a finger between her folds.

Liam teased a few soft moans from her lips by kissing inside her thighs. "I've wanted to taste you since the moment we met."

The darkness in his tone had her coming undone. Her clit ached with the vibrations of his breath. "So stop talking and do it already," she dared.

She felt a smile against her sensitive folds. In between breaths, Liam glided his tongue over her. Emma responded with a high-pitched gasp, the relief of his touch filling her with gratitude before turning into a desperate need for more. Liam read her body like a book, giving her everything she wanted without having to ask. The pleasure flowing through her swirled with the hum of her magic becoming more than just erotic bliss. She wanted to live forever with Liam in this blanket of euphoria.

The fire inside her grew. Her moans became louder.

"Shhhh," Liam hushed.

His cool breath against the heat of Emma's wet and swollen lips made her scream again.

"Hush, Emma." He slipped a finger inside her, and her hips rolled with her silent cry.

The sweeping of his tongue and the slide of his finger would be her end. One hand gripped the arm of the chair, while the other got tangled in Liam's hair. Emma pulled it with every soundless scream and with every pull, Liam took her harder and faster.

"Does this make you want to scream, Emma?"

She opened her eyes in time to see the smirk he wore before pressing his tongue against her clit. She wanted to deny him the satisfaction of an answer, but a flood of ecstasy was building inside her, and she was powerless to hold it back much longer.

"Yes." Her voice a whisper.

He kissed the inside of her thighs then locked his gaze with hers. "Scream for me, Emma."

Her orgasm washed over her like ocean waves slamming into the shore during a storm. She threw her head back and rolled her hips. Her mouth went dry from her cries of pleasure in between gasps of air.

With his touch, Liam had brought her body to a place only few had helped her travel. She sat up straight and cupped his cheeks. Liam kissed her hungrily, sweeping his tongue over hers, her taste still on his lips. Their bodies pressed together, hot skin against hot skin. And when Emma pulled away, the chill sent a spark through her peaked nipples.

A mess of groping hands and twisted limbs, they tumbled to the floor. "Why are your pants still on?" Emma asked breathlessly.

Tightening the muscles in his chest and stomach, Liam sat up enough to slip his athletic pants and boxers below his hips. Emma pulled them the rest of the way, tossing them with the rest of their discarded clothes.

Liam arched his back with a loud groan when she wrapped her fingers around his girth.

"Shhh." Emma pressed her thumb into the stiff base and ran her tongue up his length to his dripping tip.

She took him slow and deep and tended to his body the way he tended to hers. It didn't take much. Everything with Liam was new, but it felt so familiar.

"Fuck, Emma," Liam swore, his chest heaving. He threaded his fingers through her hair, and she loved the insistent tugs on her scalp.

"Is that what you want, Liam?"

His breath quickened. He moaned, "Yes."

She sat up and straddled his hips, his hard cock against her wet labia. "Condom?"

Liam's eyes snapped to hers. "Pants pocket," he said breathlessly.

Emma made quick work of retrieving their protection. "You were confident."

Liam fingers feathered over her thighs while Emma rolled the condom down his length. "And you're motivated by carbs."

Emma's mouth dropped in playful shock. "I knew it!"

Liam grabbed her arm and Emma squealed as she fell onto him. Their passionate kisses mixed with laughter. He cupped her cheeks and ran his hands through her knotted hair. She eased herself down his cock, his fit pure perfection. Her giggles turned to contented moans.

Emma started off slowly to savor the pleasure of Liam throbbing inside her. She took him deeper, magical bliss enveloping her. She wondered if Liam felt it too. She didn't have the aerobic stamina to sustain this enchanting place, and her rhythm started to falter. Liam pressed his thumb to her clit, taking her to the edge and not stopping until she willingly threw herself over.

Liam wasn't far behind. Emma used her last bit of energy to take him rough and fast, relishing the ripples of pleasure that doing so sent through her body. He swore again. He came hard, digging his fingers into the flesh of her hips. When his body went slack, Emma collapsed onto his chest. Liam wrapped his arms around her and squeezed tightly.

Liam started to move. "C'mon, before we get too comfortable."

Too late, Emma thought. She was too tired to speak.

Liam helped her up, wrapped a blanket around them, and eased her back down onto the couch. He put his arm around her, and she snuggled against his chest, her body soothed by the sound of his heartbeat.

Chapter 18
Diary of Sara Cortese

Belhaven Island, early summer circa 1620

John Dawson is dead.

Some days ago, my dear friend succumbed to the mysterious ailment that caused him months of suffering and began his journey to the next world. His absence will leave a gaping hole in the heart of our village.

Our funeral ceremonies are meant to be joyous occasions as we celebrate the deceased's life on earth and the beginning of their new life with the Goddesses. John Dawson's was no less festive, but unease has settled amongst the village. He is the second this year to pass in such a sad and excruciating way; my mentor Maryanne Banner is believed to be the first.

I was distraught when Maryanne died, but John's passing aches differently. We were so helpless to ease his pain, and nothing we did brought him long-term comfort. Of course we die. We're not immortal. But the Amora Goddesses share their magic with us to aid in a peaceful life. To limit our physical pain. Our magic, sadly, couldn't help John.

For the briefest time, we thought whatever ailed him had finally run its course. His pain vanished and his nightmare ceased. He slept peacefully for two days leading up to his death. His body, however, had been ravaged beyond repair. We couldn't keep him from death and this we accept, but we couldn't keep him from pain either and that is truly devastating.

My anger is matched only by relief that Bethany is finally able to rest. It wasn't but two moons ago when I arrived at John's home to find Bethany collapsed at his bedside. She woke with no memory of how she came to be sprawled on John's floor. With some expected protest, I brought Bethany here for proper rest. Even with Piper Dawson's insistent blessing, Bethany confided that she felt guilt for leaving him and shame for the relief his death would surely bring.

For me it has, but Bethany, I'm not yet sure. She remains weak from using so much of her physical and spiritual body to provide John what little comfort she could. Stephen, sweet man that he is, offered Bethany his bed in our chambers so that I could better tend to her while she recovers. The cottage he's building himself isn't yet finished, but he seems to find peace in the primitive space.

Bethany doesn't sleep much, despite her exhaustion. She tells me that working with the sick changes the rhythm of her body, and she has difficulty sleeping under the moon. We spend portions of the night connecting with soft talk and sensual touch.

She says we're soulmates. She's right of course. To heal the body, one must connect with the soul. But I didn't need Bethany's magic to tell me that our spirits are entwined. I just know it, like the way my lungs know how to breathe, and my heart knows how to beat.

I worry, though, because questions about John's ailment continue to needle her, consuming her thoughts and disturbing her dreams. And Bethany isn't the only one with concerns.

I sit with the Council of Nine as they hear testimony from our people. I diligently record the villagers' worries and fears. Enough have voiced their grievances that the elders have debated an inquiry into the illnesses but are unable to come to consensus.

They are distracted, it seems, by word sent by the elders of nearby villages warning that more demons and beasts from Teremedi have been seen roaming the forests, trying to settle in this realm. Many protectors of the rift have been called away to quell violence between Amora and the growing Commarasi. We are not a people of conflict and war. Our fighters' only task is to protect us against malevolent creatures of Teremedi. Now they beg to add more to their ranks, but I don't believe any good will come from it.

CHAPTER 19

EMMA

With gentle hands, Emma turned another fragile page in the third book of Sara Cortese's collections of diaries. Her books were a wealth of knowledge about the mundane details of village life shortly before the Commarasi began their slow and quiet effort to gain power.

Sara's entries detailed the seasonal rituals that had been mostly forgotten and the way magic was woven into their lives to create a shared abundance. Emma's grandmother always told her that the most successful villages lived communally with each other and in sync with nature. Sara's diaries seemed to prove that.

The level of detail all but ensured that it was one of the few surviving records of this time period. The Commarasi didn't go straight to burning the books. They banned printing them first.

The kitchen timer on her desk sprang to life. "Holy fuck!" Emma gasped with a startled jump.

Her heart still racing, she got her things together for a meeting with Judy about the diaries. The old estate had always made her jumpy. The energy that flowed through its walls harbored a bitter sadness of the souls that never moved on. It only worsened after the earthquake.

Emma arrived at Judy's office just as the door squealed open, and Liam's boisterous laugh escaped. Three weeks of casual dates, deep talks, and amazing sex had strengthened Emma's feelings beyond their friends with benefits agreement, but she continued to exist in stubborn denial.

"Hey, Emma." Liam's friendly tone clashed with the lust in his eyes.

The secrecy of their relationship threw gasoline on an already hot romance. Dirty talk that looked like casual conversation and naughty texts during meetings. Lunchtime quickies in Liam's apartment. A passionate kiss and an ass grab in an empty office.

"I'm grabbing lunch from the deli later," he said, the agreed upon code for, *sex on my kitchen table?*

"Can I get you anything?" *Are you in?*

Emma tried and failed to hide a smile. Her inability to be cool about it, and his flawless delivery was part of the fun.

"Sure. Grilled cheese and soup would be great."

"Oh, that sounds good!" Judy called from her office. "Make it two, Liam!"

Emma took a step away from the door to cover her face, her body twitching and turning red with silent laughter, while Liam's face remained perfectly straight.

"No problem, Judy! I got it."

Liam winked at Emma and walked away. Emma fanned herself and regained her composure before stepping into Judy's office.

Judy was staring at a spreadsheet on her desk and rubbing her temples when Emma sat down across from her. "Are you feeling okay?"

"Just a headache," Judy replied. "They've been constant for the past month. Only when I'm here though."

Emma gave her a sympathetic nod. "This place feels different. I can't really explain why. It's just off."

"Maybe it's allergies with all the new stuff Liam has been planting. I'll have Blair look into fundraising for a new air filtration system."

Emma didn't suspect allergies, but considering the museum could use a new air system, she kept those thoughts to herself.

Judy leaned back in her tall office chair, her fingers clasped over her stomach. "Where are you at with these diaries?"

"The earthquake set me back, but I'm making progress with scanning now. It's a slow process, but I should be done in the next couple of weeks."

"And then we'll have a digital copy?"

Emma nodded and pulled up a few photos on her laptop. "All saved on an external drive."

Judy leaned forward and silently scrolled through the images. "What do you know about Sara?"

It was a big question, and Emma didn't know where to start. "Not much. From what I can gather, she had an official job as the village scribe, which seems to be part village clerk and part village reporter."

"So these are official records?" Judy moved the laptop aside and sat back.

"No, I haven't come across any of those yet. These are her personal diaries. I'm getting the sense that she didn't trust the Council of Nine, and this is a more authentic record."

Judy pursed her lips. "I always said the Commarasi didn't invent the rewriting of history." She let out an exasperated sigh and rubbed her temple again. "So what can we do with them?"

"Not much without risking federation officials confiscating them. But I had a couple of thoughts. Sara wrote a lot about the landscape and included drawings and basic plant IDs. We can use them in an exhibit, and it can be tied back to all the work Liam has been doing."

Judy looked up at the ceiling the way she always did when she was mulling over a suggestion. "How do we do that without exposing the rest of the books?"

"A bit of historical dishonesty."

Judy arched her brow.

"Nothing is really dated. We can unbind the books, pull the pages out, and rebind them into a new book."

"It's really no worse than what we're forced to do on a regular basis," Judy reasoned. "I'll think about it. Keep working on a digital copy, and I'll reach out to some people I trust in the meantime."

With her social media analytics reviewed and her timesheet saved, Emma took off her headphones and returned to her suffocatingly silent office. She pulled her cardigan tight across her chest, not for extra warmth, but to feel the compression of the fibers against her skin. Her magic vibrated deep inside her chest. Every day felt just a bit off. Like if something was out of place, but she couldn't figure out what. Adding to her discomfort, she felt an unrelenting urge to visit the basement. It was more than just a strong desire to work on a specific task. It was a pull and the longer she tried to ignore it, the stronger it got.

"I need to get out of here," she muttered. Emma headed for the bathroom. A walk around the building usually helped to clear the energy rumbling inside her. She followed her usual path that snaked through the old building, moving on autopilot as her brain turned over a million thoughts with few connections.

A noticeable change in the light and the atmosphere caused her to stop and take in her surroundings. She had autopiloted herself to the basement.

"Seriously?" Emma groaned. She sighed and rubbed her temples.

Goosebumps crawled up her neck. She stopped and listened, straining her ears to make sense of the faint whispers that floated from the walls. Too much time spent down there often led to mind tricks, but this was different. Something drew her there and wanted her to stay.

The pull of an invisible hand guided her forward to the darkest end of the basement. The energy around her slowed. She moved as if her consciousness were a few beats ahead of her body, noticing her surroundings long before her limbs responded. Each step felt like walking through the thickest fog. Hazy and heavy.

She approached a battered wooden door that she'd only seen a handful of times. She typically avoided coming this far. Nothing was stored back here. All it held was a deep sense of foreboding that typically told her to run. Today, however, it beckoned to look beyond.

Emma hesitated before placing her hand on the cool, smooth wood. She ran her fingers against the grain and the whispers grew louder. Her ears strained to focus on the sound, but her brain struggled to make sense of it. Her chest pounded like she was standing too close to a concert speaker with a thumping bass. The sensation heightened her anxiety to a near breaking point. But her fear wasn't enough to override the pull that demanded she go through the door.

She placed her hand on the knob, and it was curiously warm to the touch. She'd been told it was locked, but she knew today it wouldn't be. She took a breath and prepared to give it a turn.

"Emma." A concerned voice said her name and a gentle hand rested on her shoulder. The invisible force abruptly cut its ties. Emma gasped and looked around. Her recollection of how she got there wavered like a dream, and she grasped at the fleeting memory.

"Emma, are you okay?"

She turned her head toward the sound of the voice, feeling a wave of relief when she saw Liam standing next to her. Her eyes focused on him, allowing his grounding presence to draw her back from wherever she had been.

"No. I mean yes. But also no." She took a heaving breath and tears formed in the corners of her eyes.

Liam stepped forward and wrapped her in his arms. His physical touch was like a weighted blanket and warm tea. Deep concern showed in his crinkled brow. She inhaled, pulling in the faint scent of saltwater and cedar tattooed into Liam's skin.

"I thought I heard something coming from behind the door and this place is so creepy. It fucks with your head."

She loosened her grip and Liam followed her lead. She tugged on his shirt to bring his lips to hers. His kiss cleared the fog, though the heaviness lingered. "What are you doing down here?"

"To murder you, obviously. Isn't that what happens in creepy-ass basements like this?" Liam waved his hand to gesture at the space.

Emma's unexpected laughter released some of the tension she was holding in her body.

"I texted you about lunch, but when I didn't hear from you forty-five minutes later, I thought maybe you got lost in a project, and I started walking to your office."

"What?" Emma yelled. She squinted at her watch. Somehow, she had lost an hour wandering the basement.

"When I walked past the elevator, I just had this overwhelming feeling that you were down here." He looked away, as though embarrassed by the admission. "I can't really explain it. I just knew."

Temporarily speechless, she simply took his hand and led him back the way they had come.

Liam stole a long kiss when the elevator doors closed. "This whole basement makes me feel... uncomfortable," he said when he pulled away. "What's kept behind the door? Is that where the old caretaker ended up?"

"Maybe," she shrugged. "I was told he retired, but I don't have any proof."

As they stepped out of the elevator, Emma stopped speaking to wave at a few of their coworkers. The space between them was a comfortable distance for friends but felt much too far for lovers. Liam kept his hands in the pockets of his work jacket and Emma's fingers itched to reach for them.

"Liam!" Mabel's voice echoed through the granite lobby.

Emma and Liam followed her beckoning hand to the reception desk where she was speaking with a beautiful young woman. Her thick strawberry-blonde hair flowed down her back in big barrel curls. Simple makeup brought out the pink undertones of her pale skin. A pair of designer jeans and fitted tee flattered her hourglass figure.

Emma recognized her but couldn't place from where. The feeling happened often living on a small island. While Mabel and Liam talked, Emma busied herself with her phone. Her chest tightened, and her heart banged against her ribs. A deep melancholy caused a heavy pit in her stomach.

Feeling like she was being watched, she looked up to meet the hard stare of the buxom woman. Her piercing blue eyes were mesmerizing even as they glared at Emma with disdain. Emma averted her gaze. Her anxiety grew and no one noticed.

When Emma looked up again, the woman's eyes were no longer on her. The other woman looked attentively at Mabel and Liam as they explained something to her. She smiled sweetly and tucked a thick strand of hair behind her ear.

Did I imagine it? Emma's anxiety climbed as she tried to process the interaction.

"I'll see you next week, Nora. I'm glad we were able to get your son registered for class." Liam glanced back at Emma, his knit brows suggesting he saw her discomfort. His hand inched towards her, but before he made contact, he raised it awkwardly to fuss with his hat.

"What's going on?" Liam asked once they were back on track towards the front exit.

"I'm not sure," she said. Whatever she'd been feeling disappeared as quickly as it came. She took a few deep breaths of the warm sea air. "Just a little shaken, I think."

"Let's get a real lunch. I gotta pick it up for Judy anyway." Liam winked.

Emma smiled weakly, but his subtle way of caring for her made her insides twist like a teenager. "Yeah, I think real lunch is a good idea."

They climbed into Liam's truck, but before Emma could buckle herself in, Liam pulled her forward to steal a long kiss. The sticky tension in her body melted, making her feel more at ease.

Liam pulled the truck onto the main road heading for downtown. "I got some crazy news before I went looking for you. Did I tell you about the guy—Clint—who fainted during the earthquake?"

"You didn't, but I heard something about it. The foreman right? Is he okay?"

"Well, they thought he was," he cringed. "But then he got really sick with something and died a few days ago. A team is coming back tomorrow to see if there was some kind of chemical leak, but no one else got sick so I'm thinking it's just a coincidence."

Emma's eyes went wide, and she swore under her breath. "What kind of illness?"

"I'm not sure. The new foreman said something about headaches, but he didn't know anything beyond that."

"Hmm." Emma mused.

The sparse details about Clint's death gnawed at her. She felt like she was given a piece to a jigsaw puzzle she didn't ask to complete.

Chapter 20
Diary of Sara Cortese

Belhaven Island, mid summer circa 1620

The long days of summer often bring a bit of calm over the village. We are busy tending to our crafts to prepare for the lean winters. We find comfort in the heat and the creatures that awaken from their cold slumber. This season, however, has not brought the same joy and fortune.

Animal tenders have found their livestock mutilated in ways not possible by any predator of this realm. The mystical guardians that protect us from malevolent species have started to vanish. Children are being led from their beds and found at the edges of the village. Stephen and I keep watch of our children at night, taking turns before the other drifts off.

With little rest, I sit with the Council of Nine to record their meetings with our people. They are scared and looking to the Council for answers and comfort, but the elders have none to offer.

My responsibilities to the Council in the light and keeping my children safe in darkness have left me drained with little to give to myself or others. On the occasional evenings that I visit with Bethany, I find her worsening since her time caring for John Dawson.

She refuses to confide in me, brushing off her symptoms as exhaustion. I haven't been able to utter the words aloud, but I fear that she has contracted whatever ailment took John's life. Worrisome dreams have turned into nightmares and minor aches are becoming debilitating pains. Her skin is so chilled, I feel as though I'm being caressed by ice. When her lips meet mine, the air is sucked from my lungs, taking my magic with it. Being in her presence used to bring me warmth and comfort, but now my heart breaks with the struggle of being in her company.

Chapter 21

Liam

From a tall storage cabinet in the nature classroom, Liam pulled out a large plastic bin filled to the top with an assortment of craft supplies: glitter and googly eyes, pipe cleaners and pom-poms, felt squares and colored paper. It seemed a bit heavier and fuller since Tuesday when he used it last, but Liam spent enough time around small children to know this cache would run out before the month was over.

Liam had mixed feelings when Hector asked him to lead a children's nature class a couple of times a week until the permanent teacher started. Though he didn't want any of his own, Liam liked kids.

In small doses.

And when he didn't have to be responsible for their wellbeing. Unless they were related to him.

In spite of himself, Liam found it hard to say no. He wondered if Hector had some kind of magic of persuasion or if it was just his magnetic grin and expressive brown eyes. When Liam posed the question to Emma, she said it was probably both.

He didn't expect the classes to heal his inner child. Little Liam had a passion for nature that his parents actively tried to suppress, pushing him toward hobbies that kept him away from anything resembling gardening. Now he had ten preschoolers looking to him as their guide to the natural world.

He was making small piles of materials at each table when he heard the exuberant cries of young children. He looked out the open side of the room, trying to spot the noisy beasts. Much like birds, their small bodies were hidden by an expanse of green foliage and colorful blooms, but their laughter floated through the space as they called out to one another. Within a few minutes, the wooden benches in front of the classroom were filled with children and their frazzled parents.

Liam stepped down from the classroom to meet a mother walking towards him. She fiddled with her blonde top knot and smoothed out her wrinkled t-shirt.

"Hi, Jessica. What's up?"

She smiled shyly and toyed with a charm on her necklace. "I got a text from Nora. She'll be here with Jaxon and Maddy, but she's running late."

Liam nodded. "Thanks for letting me know. They didn't make it on Tuesday so I'm glad they'll be here today."

"Yeah ..." she trailed off. Jessica continued after a breath of hesitation. "Nora has been on the struggle bus lately. I told her I'd watch the kids while they're in class so she could disappear for a bit."

"I'm really sorry to hear that," Liam said gently.

The news didn't surprise him. Jaxon and Maddy were program regulars since registering for the class at the last minute. Over the past few weeks, Liam noticed a drastic change in their mom's appearance and personality. He suspected some kind of illness, either physical or mental, or both, but it wasn't his place to ask.

"She's lucky to have you as a friend," he said.

"Thanks, Liam. You're sweet." Jessica turned her head to hide her reddening cheeks. She swept her bangs behind her ear and looked up at him through her long lashes. "And so great with kids. Do you have plans this weekend?"

Liam's mouth hung open as he processed the conversation's hard turn. He had to end it before it got even more awkward.

"Just spending it with my girlfriend." Liam excused himself and walked around her.

"Alright, kids!" he shouted. "Who's ready to make a mess?"

They screamed with excitement. The parents cringed. In Liam's mind, both were acceptable responses.

Liam harnessed their attention and made quick work of explaining the day's lesson. "We're doing some nature art today. Everyone's getting a bucket, and I'd like you to fill it up with things you find around the classroom."

A slight pressure weighed on his chest. He paused to clear his throat, then continued. "There are a few rules that are very important. Nothing alive. So, no bugs or frogs or other critters."

A few disappointed groans helped him smile through the discomfort. "Nothing growing. So don't pull any leaves or flowers off the plants. These plants are still new and young, and we need to give them time to grow. They can't grow if they're naked."

The class giggled. He waved at Nora, who had just walked into the space with her children. She gave them a quick kiss before walking away with a book in her hand.

"So just things on the ground, okay?"

He began handing out plastic buckets, noticing that the pressure in his chest started to ease. The momentary bout of anxiety had disappeared but the unease it brought lingered. Liam tried to hide it as he milled around the group, answering questions from his curious students. He had trouble describing simple concepts and zoned out when the kids talked about their projects. They were an observant bunch and likely noticed that he was uncharacteristically distracted.

The hour-long class usually flew, but he checked his watch every few minutes, anxious for the day to end so he could get back to his apartment.

"Okay, kids! Time to clean up!" It was a little bit early, and he hoped no one would complain.

Liam's announcement was met with a chorus of boos from children knee deep in glue and glitter. He zipped through the space, helping parents and students reorganize their supplies, only slowing down when he felt the pressure in his chest return.

A quiet voice broke through his growing unease. "It looks like they had fun today. I'm glad we made it."

Nora returned from reading her book and held her kids' projects while they cleaned. Liam stilled as he took in her appearance. Nora had deteriorated in the week since he'd seen her last. Her thinning strawberry blonde hair had lost more of its shine and fullness. Not even the sunlight could hide the gray pallor of her skin or the dark circles under her eyes. The change shocked his system, and he stumbled over his reply.

"Yeah. We are too."

Liam engaged her in some small talk as everyone else did their best to return the building to its original condition. He shifted back and forth on his feet, feeling restless with the growing anxiety. Nora's presence triggered something inside him that screamed a warning.

He wasn't safe.

His fight or flight instinct pulled at his legs to move.

Once he saw everyone else packing their things, he made a show of checking his watch. The afternoon class happened at the end of his work day, and he often lingered to socialize with other adults, but that couldn't happen today regardless of the alarm bells blaring between his ears.

"I've gotta get going, Nora," he said.

The remaining color drained from her blue eyes becoming almost gray. Her smile didn't waver, but her demeanor changed. For the briefest of moments, he felt guilty about cutting their conversation short.

"I'll see you and the kids on Tuesday though, right? You'll be here?" He tried his best to sound supportive.

"Yes. I hope so." A forced smile appeared on her face.

"Good." He smiled and yelled a goodbye to the rest of the group, resisting the urge to run back to his building.

The fear eased as he put more distance between himself and Nora. By the time he returned to his apartment, his adrenaline had stopped pumping, but the experience left him drained.

Sensing something was wrong, Belle followed him around until he fell back onto the couch, and she could lay beside him with her head in his lap. He scratched behind Belle's velvety ears and thought about the day he found Emma in the basement. Her hand was on that creepy wooden door and in a trance so deep, he said her name five times before she responded. Even though she insisted everything was fine, she had seemed distracted the rest of the day.

His phone rang before he got too deep into his own thoughts. An old picture of Deryn with a gapped-tooth grin stretched across the screen announcing a video call. In truth, he was too tired to attempt meeting Deryn's explosive energy, but he never denied her call unless he had to.

"Hey, blackbird," he answered, using one of his affectionate nicknames for her.

"Hi! Why do you look like that?" She squinted her light blue eyes at the screen. Deryn had her dad's eyes, which were lighter than Liam's but shaped the same. The rest of Deryn's appearance took after her mother, including the pouty lower lip and chin dimple that became distorted as she leaned closer to the phone for her inspection.

"Uhh, rude. Like what?"

"A hot mess," she answered. "Are you super depressed again?

Liam heard his brother reply off screen. "Deryn, he plants shit for a living. How do you expect him to look?"

"That's a gross misrepresentation of what I do, Tommy." Liam sat up a little straighter and propped his arm on a pillow. He could hear Tommy roll his eyes from ninety miles away.

"No, I'm not super depressed. I'm doing really well right now. In fact, do you want to help me pick something to wear for my date with Emma tonight?"

"You did ask her out!" Deryn squealed. "Is this your first date?"

Liam rubbed his stubbled cheek. "Uhh... no."

Tommy laughed in the background, likely picking up on the implicit reason for Liam's hesitation.

"But this is our first really big date." Liam groaned as he got up from the couch and walked into his bedroom to pull out a few options for the evening. He already had an outfit planned, but for a long time, he'd spent days in the same dirty pajamas. Deryn would dig through his closet and do it herself. It rarely matched but it was always clean.

Helping him pick out his clothes became their thing, and he cherished it.

His brother moved into view after Deryn offered her recommendation. "Where are you taking her?"

"I'm taking her to the Oceanic Wildlife Foundation fundraiser at the art gallery in Willow Ridge." Liam examined a light blue dress shirt for wrinkles before throwing it over the back of a chair.

"Weren't they one of your clients?" Tommy slid a chair next to his daughter.

"Yup. And every year, they throw a very expensive fundraiser in Willow Ridge."

"How expensive?" Deryn asked while she penciled something on a piece of paper.

Liam cringed. "Tickets start at a thousand a piece."

Deryn stopped drawing and her eyes went wide. "Dollars? Like One. Thousand. Dollars?"

"Fuck, bro." Tommy leaned back in his chair and ran a hand over his mouth. "Why?"

Liam and Emma spent most evenings on the couch wearing their most comfortable lounge clothes, drinking craft alcohol, and eating dinner out of takeout containers. Occasionally, they walked through downtown with their fingers entwined and laughing while indulging in moderately expensive cuisine and overpriced drinks in a dark restaurant.

He didn't have a good answer, not one that Tommy would understand anyway.

Because he could afford it.

Because sometimes it was fun to cosplay as his old self without the impending mental breakdown.

Because it was likely he'd run into someone he used to know and some small part of him wanted people to see that he was doing just fine. Liam hadn't been the first rising star to burn out. He was just the latest cautionary tale.

Because he was falling in love with her and didn't care how many lists that put him on. The government could bury him in paperwork and tap his phone lines for all he cared.

Liam finally answered with a shrug. "Why not?"

CHAPTER 22
EMMA

"Hey, Em." Regan's voice startled Emma enough to bounce her book from her hands. Sitting down in the rocking chair next to Emma, she added, "Well, you're jumpy today."

"No kidding." Emma flipped through the pages until she found her place and stuck her bookmark against the binding. "I've been on edge since the earthquake."

"Trauma will have that effect."

Emma picked up a small glass vial from the table between them. "This is for you."

"Goddess bless you." Regan sighed, taking the vial.

In these moments, Emma truly envied Sara's freedom to practice magic. Being found guilty of using magic to create a few ounces of medicinal tonic could end Emma's life. She did it anyway because medication for *afflictions of the mind*, as they called it, were hard to come by.

"I've been using it for a week and it's definitely helping me stay focused. Just one drop. If you take too much you might never unfocus."

"Noted." Regan put the vial in her pocket. "Shouldn't you be getting ready for your fancy date tonight?"

Luna hopped up onto Emma's lap and rubbed her head against Emma's fingers. She'd been dreading this date since Liam suggested it. The details remained a surprise, but she knew it would be far more public than they were used to, and she had to get all dolled up. "Yeah, I should."

"Could you tone down the excitement a bit?" Regan snarked.

"I'm excited. Just worried too."

"About what?"

Emma scratched Luna's cheek while searching for the right words. "It feels like we're crossing a line into relationship territory."

Regan rolled her eyes. "For fuck's sake, Emma. Just let someone fall in love with you."

"You love me."

"Yes, and sometimes you make it really fucking hard."

Emma couldn't deny that.

"But you know what I'm talking about," Regan pressed. "You're only keeping yourself from the happiness and love you deserve."

Emma could deny that, but doing so would only further irritate her best friend. So she avoided it instead. "You sure you're good to check in on Belle and Luna?"

"Yes. I have a date tonight too, but I will after I get home. Just enjoy yourself. Liam cleared his plans with me, and I think you're going to have an amazing time."

Emma sat up straight. "And you're just telling me this now? Whose side are you on?"

"Yours, which is why I'm keeping his surprise. Stop stalling and go get dressed."

Emma huffed as she pushed herself up from the rocking chair. "You're a terrible friend. I love you."

"Not as terrible as you." Regan got up and pulled Emma into a tight hug. The kind that warmed her soul like hot chocolate on an icy day. "I love you too."

In her en suite bathroom, Emma was applying another layer of mascara when she heard the familiar beeps from the lock on her front door. Liam was only the third person to have the code to her house, a privilege she never even thought of giving her own mother, let alone whatever she and Liam were labeling their romantic entanglement. An entanglement that wasn't supposed to be serious, but the slinky dress on the back of her door and their hotel reservations hinted otherwise.

Luna, who had been sitting quietly on the vanity, lifted her paw with a quiet meow.

"It's just Liam and Belle, but you can go check if you want," Emma said while she compared two different shades of lipstick.

Luna jumped off the vanity and darted out of the room just as the front door opened and Belle's nails tapped on the hardwood floors. Liam's heavy footfalls followed and grew louder until he was leaning against the door frame.

Emma froze at the sight of him in the mirror. It always took a moment to process him in nicer clothes. She spent so much time with Liam while he wore clothes with frayed seams, caked on dirt, and grass stains. A hat always flattened his hair and sometimes he went too long without cleaning up his beard. Her brain always had to recalibrate when he was dressed in anything else.

But if jeans and a nice sweater caused a glitch, the look he donned now caused an absolute malfunction. A little bit of product tamed his shaggy hair away from his face, allowing his muted baby blue dress shirt to draw out the hints of turquoise in his eyes. He paired it with a dark gray vest that created perfect lines from his broad chest and shoulders down to his waist. His perfectly pressed pants were tailored to fit his narrow hips and his long, thick legs. She suspected he had a matching jacket in the car, but to dress down the entire look, he undid the top button of his collar and rolled his shirtsleeves halfway up his forearms.

The face of his brushed silver watch caught the bathroom light and triggered a memory from the first day they met. She still didn't know what came over her that day. Her unrelenting infatuation with Liam started with lust at first sight but always felt more than that.

"Your cat hates me," he said with a hint of frustration.

Emma blinked a few times, breaking her trance, and returning to her lipstick. Liam obviously hadn't been similarly taken aback by the stained tank top and pilled leggings Emma wore while doing her hair and makeup. Nor did he realize he had engaged her in foreplay just by existing.

"She doesn't hate you." She blotted her lips with a tissue, noticing Liam watching the movements of her mouth in the mirror. "I wouldn't have kept you around this long if she hated you."

"I guess that's true."

Emma noticed his half-hearted shrug and unwillingness to take her bait. She replaced her makeup in its case and turned to face him. "What's on your mind?"

She waited patiently while he seemed to find the right words.

"Have you ever been around someone that just made you really uncomfortable? It's not the conversation, but just the person?"

A younger Emma would have rolled her eyes and shot back with a hefty dose of sarcasm. But she tried to temper her response because she was an adult pushing forty.

"So, basically my entire college experience with straight men?"

Well, she tried. It could have been worse.

"Yeah." He frowned. "Sorry."

She took his hand and squeezed it softly, narrowing her eyes in thought and reflecting on how she'd been feeling lately. "But this felt different? Not normal discomfort? Something deeply unsettling."

He nodded but remained quiet. "I dunno." He sighed. "Never mind. We can talk about it later if it's still bothering me."

His face said otherwise, but Emma knew not to push and let Liam open up at his own pace. Liam easily shared the good parts of his life and could speak of the hard times in a detached and casual way. The deeper emotions, though, required patience and a promise not to push or pry. Bit by bit, Liam let his guard down and let her in.

"Okay. We can do that." Emma pulled him in for a soft kiss that made her bare toes curl. She pulled away before the intensity could build. It wouldn't be the first time a soft kiss turned a date night out into a date night in.

She couldn't help but run her hands along the soft fabric of his vest. "Please wear this more often."

Liam raked his eyes over Emma's body. "Only if you wear this red lipstick with everything and nothing from now on."

Apparently, he did notice.

Chapter 23

Liam

Liam inched up behind a spotless white luxury car in the valet parking line. Emma's six-year-old SUV didn't stand out as much as he'd expected, likely given the fundraiser attracted environmental types that wanted to give off the impression that they weren't extremely rich.

When Emma stepped out of her bedroom, Liam considered forgoing the entire evening. The twilight purple dress draped over her body, conforming to all of her delicious curves in all the right places. She'd tamed her long natural waves into bouncy curls and pinned them away from her face. The neutral palette made the mossy green in her eyes pop.

The neckline dipped low, held in place by some strategically placed body tape. The way it crossed behind her neck perfectly exposed the intricate artwork she wore on her skin. Flowers, birds, animals, and celestial bodies were a mélange of intentional chaos.

She'd put so much time and effort into getting dressed, and Liam would have gladly burned two grand to tear off her clothes and spend the night at home.

The heels though. They'd have to stay even if they never touched the ground.

The valet motioned them forward and their opportunity to ditch the party disappeared. Liam stepped out of the car and handed the keys to the valet as another opened the door for Emma. The young man took her hand and tried to avert his gaze as Emma gracefully slid out of the car. Liam watched her hungrily, enjoying the way her skirt inched up her thigh before skimming back down her leg when she stood.

Liam offered her his arm, and she took it with a curious smile. "So where have you taken me?"

He followed the crowd into the main gallery where fashionably dressed guests mingled among modern art that Liam tried to appreciate, but didn't really understand.

"This is an excuse to eat very good food and drink very good wine while we watch very rich people pat themselves on the back for doing the bare minimum to support a good cause."

Emma's laugh floated above the music and the sound released the last bit of discomfort lingering in Liam's chest. He placed a finger under her chin and lifted her smiling mouth to his.

"Let's have some fun," he whispered, his lips meeting hers for a deep kiss that made the world fall away.

They spent the evening savoring the taste of extreme wealth: Wine so perfectly aged it would have been a crime not to relish every drop. Tables of food artfully arranged, and trays passed around by servers who glided through the rooms like ghosts.

At the peak of his career, Liam never had to shell out a dime to attend one of these ostentatious parties. His ticket was paid for by someone who desired his presence, either personally or professionally. Tickets to this annual gala came with the retainer. Sometimes, he brought someone he wanted to impress, other times he came solo. Either way, he never left alone.

And maybe that was why he wanted to bring Emma to this particular event. Because she wasn't impressed by this kind of shit and even though he knew it, he needed to prove it. Not to himself, but to the anxiety and depression that fed his deepest, unconscious insecurities.

After procuring another two glasses of merlot poured from bottles that could fund a month of oceanic research, Liam returned to Emma's side as she made conversation with a man who appeared to be old enough to be her father. It made the man's lecherous gaze all the more disturbing.

"What is it that you do?" The man asked.

"I'm the chief LMCO for a multiregional firm located in Glendale," Emma answered with conviction.

Liam tried to stifle his laughter with his glass of wine. It was the third meaningless job title Emma had come up with in the past hour.

"Well, I'll have to look you up. What was your name again?"

"Buffy Summers."

Liam almost choked on the piece of fruit he'd just put into his mouth.

"I hope you do. It was lovely chatting with you." Emma hooked her arm around Liam and led him away from the leering old man.

"You can't leave me alone like that anymore. I'd call men like that vultures, but vultures actually benefit humanity."

A familiar voice called Liam's name and cut off his answer. His stomach dropped. Liam expected to see people he knew, and he already bumped into those most likely to be in attendance. But there was one face he was hoping to avoid.

"Hey, Preston."

Preston Kavanaugh.

Liam hooked up with plenty of people from work. Sometimes the place felt more like a sex club than a financial services company. Of all his coworkers though, his fling with Preston was the only one that still made Liam feel like a piece of shit. Not because Preston was his boss, but because screwing the boss was a power trip worth being unfaithful for. Almost ten years later, it remained kindling for the voice that told Liam he didn't deserve anyone's love. It reminded him of all the relationships he destroyed, if not with infidelity, then with pure negligence and selfishness.

But Liam wasn't that guy anymore.

Right?

"Liam Doran." Preston gripped Liam's hand in a business-like shake that went on just a bit too long. "I knew you couldn't stay away from this. Back to making dreams come true?"

Whose dreams? Liam wondered. Definitely not his.

Preston was in his mid-forties but maintained the youthful appearance of someone half his age. His light olive skin was perfectly smooth, and his short dark hair was untouched by gray. It was all a mask for a man who was deeply afraid of becoming irrelevant with age.

"Nah, just trying to support a good cause." Liam's voice wavered with dwindling confidence.

"So, what's up, man? What have you been up to?" Preston rested a hand on Liam's bicep and gave it a squeeze. "Besides the gym. You look amazing."

Preston let his hand graze down Liam's arm before finally letting go.

"Thanks. Yeah, it's been a ride." Liam shifted his weight and ran a hand through his hair, forgetting it was stiff with product that now greased between his fingers.

Preston checked his phone with a disinterested frown. "I gotta answer this message, but if you two are up for some fun, I'm hosting an after-party."

After-party was a loose interpretation of the phrase. Preston never spent a significant amount of time at these kinds of events, usually arriving an hour late and leaving thirty minutes later. He mingled just enough to show his face and personally invite a chosen few to his beach house ten minutes away where a party was already underway.

Preston leaned in, notes of expensive whiskey on his breath. "You remember my after-parties, right Liam?"

No, Liam did not. Too many vices in one place didn't make for clear memories. "Yeah, those were some wild times."

"Well, I hope you and . . ."

"Wanda." Emma reached out to shake his hand.

"I hope you and Wanda will be there."

Liam struggled to form coherent thoughts as he stood face-to-face with the living reminder of the worst version of himself. He didn't know if Preston was inviting him back into his orbit as an act of social charity or salvation.

Liam found Emma's soft hazel eyes. They gazed at him without judgment. Just concern and the intuitive knowledge that Liam wanted to say no but struggled to say the word.

"Hmmm." Emma ran her hand along Liam's back, from one hip to the other, making his fine hairs stand on edge. "As much fun as that sounds, we're going to have to pass."

Preston scoffed and narrowed his gray eyes with slight offense. Even in heels, Emma stood almost a foot shorter than Preston, but her presence towered over both men.

With a hard stare and a devilish smile on her face, she said, "I'm not sharing Liam tonight."

People didn't say *No* to Preston Kavanaugh. Liam never saw a person willingly turn down a chance to be a part of Preston's inner circle.

Until now.

Standing a bit taller, Liam tightened his grip on Emma's hand and used the other to pat Preston on the shoulder. "Sorry, man. But I'm sure it'll be a blast. Be safe."

Emma led Liam through the crowd and past the candlelit tables, away from Preston, but Liam's past indiscretions followed.

Emma

Emma looked over her shoulder at Liam. Despite his calm appearance, the conversation with Preston affected him deeply. Emma felt it. She'd grown so used to the way his energy swirled around them that now she noticed only major shifts in its tenor. This shift was the emotional equivalent of being hit with a bat.

"I'm sorry," she said when they stopped in front of an extravagant display of cheese and fruit.

Liam handed her a small plate. "For what?"

"For whatever role that insufferable douche played in your past that made you so flustered just now."

Liam fidgeted with his sleeves, unrolling and rerolling the cuffs along his arm.

"Don't try to distract me by flaunting your forearms," Emma scolded.

Liam laughed and the energy around him shifted closer to its normal balance. "It's a long story that I'll explain another day. But he's just a toxic ex that I was hoping I wouldn't see here."

Emma eyed him with suspicion and added a few strawberries to her plate. She didn't buy it. Perhaps he'd tack it onto the list of things bothering him. If she let it go, maybe he'd talk to her about it later.

She nodded and quietly filled her plate with more berries and seasoned crackers. People buzzed around them, the voices becoming a hum of incessant white noise.

"Can we find a quiet spot somewhere? This is starting to feel too much."

Liam pressed his lips to her temple and the short hairs of his beard tickled her skin. Her eyes closed with a sigh, feeling some of the locked tension in her body melting away. With a light hand on her back, Liam led her to the outskirts of the main gallery.

They claimed an empty couch while people milled in their peripheries consuming art, food, and alcohol. Beautiful, vibrant pieces surrounded them, but Emma's senses had become too overwhelmed to truly appreciate the work. Verging on energetic depletion, her enjoyment of the night started to wane. The tingle of anxiety that lived in the pit of her stomach grew with each person that engaged her in conversation.

Emma pulled off her shoes and pressed her thumbs into her ankles. "It takes just one night in these heels to remind me why I embraced flats. Maybe I'll repurpose them as bedroom shoes."

Liam responded with an unholy smile. "I had the same idea."

Temporarily distracted, Emma's inside twisted with curious excitement. "Oh, did you? I'd like to hear more about your ideas."

Liam leaned in, but his gaze strayed from Emma's.

"Emma DiMarco?

Emma recognized the voice. That mildly aggressive tone taunted, harassed, and bullied her for years. The voice belonged to Kyle Nolan who had the same pale cherub face and slender build he had in high school. Little had changed in twenty years, it seemed. Nolan and everything about him, from his wispy blond hair to his irritating laugh, made up her worst childhood memories.

"Hi, Kyle." Though she didn't feel it, Emma remained relaxed against the back of the couch, making no effort to show any interest in his presence.

"I thought I saw you mingling with Preston Kavanaugh earlier, but I didn't believe it because that level of society has never been your league."

Emma had been a fiery kid with a temper to match. Kyle spent much of their childhood honing his ability to make Emma lose control of her emotions. Her run-ins with school authority figures were often a result of Kyle's constant prodding. He was either a grown man who had no idea how to talk to another human, or he was looking to pick up where they left off.

She reached forward and delicately retrieved her glass of wine from the table. "I like art. And ocean animals. Sounds pretty appropriate to me."

"Right." Kyle crossed his arms over his chest and pursed his lips. "So how do you know Preston? I didn't realize we have mutual friends."

"Really?" Liam piped up. The energy radiating from his body changed again. It pulsed with protectiveness that toed the line of possessive.

"Preston and I haven't worked together in a while, but I don't remember you, and he has a pretty tight circle."

Emma could have sat on Liam's smug face. His audacity had never been so sexy.

Kyle turned his attention to Liam and held out his hand. "I'm Kyle Nolan by the way. Emma failed to introduce us."

Liam glanced at Kyle's hand. He leaned back into the couch and crossed an ankle over his thigh. "Emma never fails to do anything she finds worthy of her time." Sitting up a little straighter, Liam reached an arm around her shoulder, a subtle yet effective move.

Emma kept her glass at her mouth to hide her smile.

Kyle stuck his hands in his pockets, an incredulous smile appearing on his face. "I'm just curious about how you got into such an exclusive party, DiMarco. Did you magic your way in somehow?"

Emma rolled her eyes with an exaggerated sigh, but she didn't take his threat lightly. If his accusation caught on, consequences ranged from being escorted out to being thrown in prison. Liam's connections with a handful of party guests were flimsy at best and no one gave her the impression they'd stick their neck out for him.

"I didn't realize you were working security tonight," Emma said calmly. "Please tattle on us. I'd love to see you look like an asshole when you waste everyone's time."

"I can save you the trouble, if you like." Liam reached into his pocket and pulled out his phone. "I still have the fundraising director in my contacts. Margot's always had a bit of a crush on me."

"Of course she does. I mean, look at you." Emma cooed.

Emma was nearing her limit for keeping her temper in check, but Liam's assistance with humiliating Kyle helped her stay cool just a little bit longer.

A deep flush spread from Kyle's chest into his face. His features contorted like a child who had just been embarrassed in front of his friends.

"Rumor has it that you're working at that museum on the island," he said through clenched teeth. "The one that everyone says harbors Amoran rebels. Maybe someone should check out the place."

"Okay," Emma groaned. "If you're done waving your dick around, you can go."

Kyle's eyes raged. "Watch out for this one, dude. Emma DiMarco and her whole family are nothing but trouble."

Liam sprung from the couch. Kyle flinched. Only a small table stood between them. Liam glared at him, his hands curling into fists. "She said you can go."

Kyle twitched with rage. He backed down with a malicious smirk crawling across his round face.

Liam continued to stand while Kyle walked away and disappeared into the atrium. "How the fuck do you know that guy?"

Chewing slowly on a strawberry, Emma willed her adrenaline to settle before answering.

"I had the unfortunate experience of growing up with Kyle Nolan in Hunting Woods. He's always been an asshole because he's a descendant of assholes and being an asshole is his birthright. And I come from a long line of people, but particularly women, who pushed back against his family as they were coming to power."

In truth, Emma didn't know much of the details. Her mother distanced herself from that part of their family lore, and Emma's time on Belhaven was a respite from the harassment. She seldom thought about her family's connection to Kyle's.

"He probably wouldn't have bothered with me as much if I sucked up to him like the other kids. He was wealthy and had cool things and what kid doesn't want to be friends with the kid who had cool things? He wasn't the center of my universe, and I made sure he knew I was unimpressed by him. So, regardless of family history, he hated me for that."

Emma slipped on her shoes and stood up, smoothing her dress and taking a breath to regain her composure. "We should go. I doubt he's changed much since high school and the drunker that asshole gets, the more likely he is to create a scene."

CHAPTER 24

EMMA

There was nothing like a belly full of expensive cheese, aching feet, and a solid buzz to make a person go from feeling like a sexy bombshell to a cranky toddler up past their bedtime.

The moment Emma stepped over the threshold of their swanky hotel room, she kicked off her shoes with a relieved groan. They flew farther than she planned, drawing her eyes to the sliding door at the opposite end of the room. A balcony looked over the bay, the dark water dappled with lights and the fragmented reflection of the full moon. Even when she was surrounded by awe-inspiring artwork, she thought the moonlight on the water remained the most beautiful sight. The salty breeze caressed her skin. Somewhere in the distance, a train blared its horn, the sound carried by the breeze like dandelion seeds. Standing in the light of the moon, Emma's magic glimmered under her skin. It moved through her veins like the waves that crashed on the rocky shore below.

Every wave cracked at the lingering irritation left by their encounter with Kyle Nolan, but she remained pissed. Likely sensing Emma's mood and not wanting to be on the receiving end of any hostility, Liam let her stew on the short drive over and continued to make himself scarce. The more she chewed on her anger, the more she wanted to fight it out.

Kyle Nolan and the system his family helped put into place may be the root of her indignation, but she wouldn't be fuming in this gorgeous hotel suite overlooking the water if Liam had stuck to their terms. Their casual, friends with benefits, low-key, secret-at-work terms. And she wouldn't be angry after eating so much amazing food and drinking so much amazing wine if *she* had stuck to their terms.

She heard soft footsteps come up behind her, and Emma braced herself for Liam's inevitable touch. She wanted to stay mad. His touch soothed her, and she loved it. She ached for it, but anger was easier. Once wrapped in his arms, Emma would be forced to feel all the other feelings and say all the hard things.

Liam kissed the crook of her neck, and her hardened emotions melted into liquid. "What do you need me to be right now?" He whispered. "I can be your listening ear. Or your punching bag. Or a distraction, maybe?"

She needed Liam to be her everything. That was part of the problem.

"We shouldn't have come," she said quietly, the words directed more at herself than to Liam. "I had so much fun, but we shouldn't have come."

Liam trailed soft kisses on her shoulder while squeezing her more tightly.

Emma leaned into him, feeling his solid body behind her. "Kyle's a piece of shit, but he's not completely wrong about the museum. Judy definitely isn't harboring rebels, but we're all vulnerable."

They never had a frank talk about magic. Doing so would push them over her arbitrary line into a legitimate relationship, and she absolutely couldn't have that.

She hesitated. Her thoughts heavy on her lips. "Except you maybe."

With a soft sigh, Liam rested his chin on her shoulder. "I am. I can't control it. Whatever I have. Aunt Georgia was the last one who could."

"Families have gone on the list for less. Do you know why yours isn't?"

"No. I suspect we were at one point, and my dad's family got us removed. The Dorans have deep ties with Commarasi politicians. My dad started indoctrinating us into that world when we were kids. That's why I'm such a raging disappointment as a professional gardener."

Emma chewed on Liam's admission. The lights reflecting off the water began to blur. She blinked back tears. "I wish you hadn't told me that."

Liam pressed his forehead against her shoulder. "I trust you."

"It's not about trust, Lee." Emma willed her voice to remain strong through the emotions that were bubbling up inside her. "It's about plausible deniability. The more I know, the more vulnerable you are. I trust Regan with my life, but even she doesn't know the full extent of my abilities. It's how we protect each other."

Liam

When Emma slipped from Liam's grip, he immediately experienced soul crushing emptiness without her touch. Emma's wet cheeks glistened in the moonlight. She looked frantic. Like she was trying to make a desperate decision in the middle of a crisis.

"We need to pull it back. This is too much. We had a discussion. And an agreement. And we've gotten too far away from that."

Liam didn't need or want Emma's protection. He just wanted her. He wasn't convinced the risks were that high. But to Emma, they were real and terrifying. In this moment, she'd never see reason.

And maybe it was better that way.

As soon as Liam pulled her deeper into his orbit, she got hurt. He brought her to the gala under selfish pretenses and inadvertently put his work family at risk. Emma didn't need to protect him from their world, but clearly Liam needed to protect her heart from him.

"You're right." His voice caught and the words came out softer than he expected. "I'm sorry about tonight. It was too far. Let's pull it back."

Liam didn't know what to make of the disappointment that flashed across Emma's face.

Emma wiped her check and wrapped her arms tightly across her chest. "I don't want to end everything."

"I know. Just getting back to our agreement. Casual dates. Great sex."

Emma laughed. "It is really great."

"Amazing even."

Emma's smile returned. Her body loosened and the harsh energy around her no longer pulsed. Liam held out a hand. "If you come inside and sit on the bed, I'll rub your feet until you scream."

Emma took it. "You should have led with that."

He pulled her back into their hotel room and stripped down to his underwear and undershirt. Emma's dress creeped up her thighs as she sank back into a pile of pillows against the headboard.

Liam took one foot in his hands and pressed his thumbs into her arch. Emma moaned a thank you, but otherwise, they sat together in silence, both decompressing from the evening in their own way. Liam slid his hands over her feet and ankles, listening for subtle cues that he should hang around in a spot a little longer. He was almost finished when Emma broke the silence.

"Do you miss this life?"

Liam sat with the question before answering.

"It's a fun place to visit, but I wouldn't want to live here. I don't need to do this again for a long time. If ever." He stopped rubbing her feet and slid off the bed to grab a bottle of water. "But it would be worth the money to see you look at me like you were doing all night."

"Oh really? And what look is that?" She waved her hand, encouraging Liam to proceed and then crossed her arms over chest in a way that was much more relaxed than earlier.

Liam didn't answer. He climbed onto the foot of the bed and crawled toward Emma, his hands sliding up the insides of her legs, guiding them open until he could kneel in between her knees.

"The look of pure, raw desire." He leaned in, and his wet lips met Emma's collarbone. She sighed a little laugh.

"Your eyes were begging me to fuck you."

"Will you?"

His lips grazed hers as he spoke. She tried to kiss him. He pulled back. "Not yet."

Liam lived to indulge her appetite for sexual anticipation. It was a delicate dance, building her desire then delaying her gratification. If he pushed her too far, made her wait too long, she'd take matters into her own hands.

He kissed her slowly, drawing out every meeting of their lips. She knotted her fingers into his hair and tried to pull him closer. Kiss him harder. Liam resisted and kept the pace slow. Emma groaned with frustration, and Liam's lips curled into a smile. She finally succumbed to his pace, and he relished the feeling of her mouth.

"Take that dress off."

He moved to give her some space and pulled his own shirt over his head, throwing it in the corner. His boxer briefs followed. He leaned back against the headboard on another pile of soft pillows. Emma kneeled on the bed, her dress flowing loose. She moved slowly, intentionally drawing out every motion to unhook the halter from around her neck.

Liam caught on to her little game. He smiled. "You're not listening."

"You didn't say take it off quickly."

Liam moved close enough to put one hand on her back, another tugged the straps out of her fingers so he could cup her now exposed breast. He massaged it roughly, pinching the tender nub of her nipple. Her legs buckled, but his firm grip on her back kept her upright. His lips moved to her neck.

"Take off all your clothes. Quickly." He dragged his teeth over her skin, inhaling the distinctive fragrance that would forever trigger thoughts of her.

"Why didn't you say so?" Her ragged voice still held her signature sass.

Letting her go, he watched her slide dress down her body until it fell into a pile on the floor, leaving her naked and ready for the taking. With her supple curves, soft belly, generous ass, and strong thighs, she looked like she'd been plucked from a painting. And like a rare piece of art, he could gaze at her body for a thousand years and never tire.

"Good girl," he growled.

In these moments, while drunk on lust and devoted only to her pleasure, Liam didn't care that Emma fought so hard to deny him the best parts of herself. He grabbed her hips and pulled her on top of him until she straddled his chest. Then pressing his hands into her ass, he guided her hips forward until her pussy hovered tantalizingly close to his mouth. It was almost impossible to hold back when he wanted so desperately to ravage her. Just one slow lick had her white knuckling the headboard. She trembled in his hands.

Emma knew her body was an altar, and Liam was there to worship. Pleasing her was akin to pleasing a goddess, and he would give this goddess anything she wanted. Liam may often hold the reins, but Emma always had control. Tonight she had both. She determined the pace, chasing bliss with purrs of, "Yes," and thrusts of her hips. Her nails grazed his scalp, guiding his movements. He complied with every firm demand. Every, "Harder," and "Don't stop."

It wasn't completely selfless. With every moment he spent between Emma's thighs, Liam's cock begged harder for release. As his own pleasure built, he dug his fingers into her flesh, devouring her at her direction.

"Yes, Liam," she moaned with sweet relief. Gripping his hair, she pressed his mouth to her swollen clit, and he drew cries of ecstasy from her lips. She melted into him, submitting to bliss.

Emma slid down his body, her skin hot and salty. When their eyes met, her pupils were so dilated, there was only a hint of the saturated greens and browns that reminded him of the forest floor.

"Now will you fuck me?" Even breathless, it was more of a dare than a request.

The mouth on this woman, he thought.

Liam flipped her until she was on her hands and knees, her body's position supported by a small tower of pillows. He teased her a bit with the tip of his cock before sliding inside her. The sensation of her body wrapped tight around him was nothing short of perfect. No longer holding back, Liam pounded into her, and Emma met him thrust for thrust, no doubt chasing another wave of euphoria. When it hit, her walls tightened and pulsed, demanding that Liam come now and come hard.

In the haze of sweet bliss, Liam could promise Emma the world. He could promise to wrap her heart in soft padding, never to be broken. But as he lay with her, and the evidence of mascara tears remained on the backs of her hands, he knew he'd never keep those promises.

Chapter 25
Diary of Sara Cortese

Belhaven Island, late summer circa 1620

I write with a heart heavy with fear and worry. My sweet Bethany has been banished to the depths of the temple and only the Goddesses know her true fate. She committed no crime, but the elders believe that she poses a danger to us all.

Since the death of John Dawson, Bethany has been unable to care for the village sick. For some time, she blamed the draining of her life force that made her susceptible to minor ailments. I knew, however, that these were lies she desperately wanted to believe.

More news of conflict on Arcanos has caused fear and suspicion to spread throughout the village. Small clusters have begun to form, some as small as a single family, and there is a hesitancy to care for one another as we once did. The elders cannot control what is happening beyond their borders but, they said, they can control more deaths from this mysterious disease by separating its latest victim from our people. The elders spoke of Bethany as though her inamorata wasn't sitting beside them, forging the official record of their meeting. Forgoing tradition, I argued on her behalf. They tolerated me for only so long before I was silenced.

Though she is plagued by the same nightmares and pain that hastened John's death, I think she has been less affected by the disease. Until her banishment. Caring for others brought Bethany joy and purpose. Even in the sadness of their deaths, Bethany was comforted knowing that she brought peace in their final moments. Now that she is separated from her patients and those she loves, I see the disease withering Bethany's body and mind.

The Council continues to debate her fate. No matter the decision, the end is death. The elders will either keep her separated until the disease takes her life, or she will be sentenced to a cleansing execution. It is the rarest of rituals for our people, only done for those who have committed the most heinous of crimes and have shown true and sincere remorse. Our laws require that these crimes must be punished with death, but the truly remorseful will have their souls cleansed so that they may spend eternity with the Goddesses and their loved ones. Bethany has committed no crime, and they only wish to try to clean their hands of the moral implications of murdering my beloved. I believe that fear of losing their status has made the elders act without logic, and the entire village will suffer.

Stephen believes that only I possess the magic and willful determination capable of healing Bethany without causing her harm. I visit her daily and bring a balm made of maypops and cattails to rub on her temples to ease the pain and help her sleep. At night, I lie awake, running my fingers over the quartz necklace she made for me. I know she is suffering, and it makes my heart ache. Something must be done.

CHAPTER 26
LIAM

Liam entered the small barn behind his garage looking for some gardening stakes and three hours later, still hadn't emerged. Once used for the Yates' collection of show horses, the barn now served as additional storage. The previous caretaker left this building much like he had his office: In complete disarray with a haphazard system that Liam could no longer tolerate. He lost the morning, but gained a truck bed full of trash and a storage system he could live with.

His original project now forgotten, he moved on to taking an inventory of everything he'd organized. Liam made a few notes and threw the clipboard onto a nearby cart.

A stack of fertilizer. Count the bags. Assess the quality. Make some notes. Repeat.

Lost in his project, he ignored the slowly increasing pressure in his chest until it became a struggle to breathe. Fear overwhelmed him. A blanket of sadness and despair wrapped around him. The plastic clipboard dropped to the floor, landing with a click that echoed like a crash. His brain screamed *run*, but his body remained paralyzed in its place.

"Hi, Liam." The muffled voice filled the space.

The same legs that kept him anchored to his place allowed him to turn to face Nora, the parent from the children's gardening class. Nora's presence had gone from causing him mild discomfort to an all-consuming dread.

She hadn't brought her children to his weekly nature classes in weeks, sending them with her father-in-law instead. "She's been really ill," the man had said and left it at that.

Looking at her now, "really ill," was an understatement.

Her physical appearance deteriorated, and she looked fifty years older. Limp white straw replaced her bouncy strawberry blonde hair. Her fair skin lost all of its glow, and her eyes were somehow bright with life and pools of darkness. Her hourglass figure shrank to a frail and slight frame.

Liam wanted to be concerned. He wanted to know what was wrong. But a raging river of adrenaline wouldn't let him feel any emotion other than fear.

"I'm sorry to bother you." Her raspy and hollow voice squeezed his chest like a vise.

"Hey, Nora." The increasing pressure in his temples made his voice sound low and muffled. "How'd you find me out here?"

Her eyes darted around the building, but she didn't answer.

He tried again, his panic rising. "Can I help you with something?"

"I always wanted a garden," she said wistfully. "I'd like to plant a garden this year."

Liam became aware of the dryness of his mouth and the warm air in the poorly cooled building. He needed to get somewhere with lots of people. He needed to get to the main building. Despite his size, he felt incapacitated by this frail and sick woman. Being around people would keep him safe. Emma would keep him safe.

"Okay. Let's go back to the museum, and I can show you the plants I started. We can talk more about your garden."

She nodded, but Liam didn't feel any relief. His rubbery legs moved forward.

He only had his back to her for a moment when a sharp pain radiated from his neck into his shoulders and back. Feeling for its source, his hand landed on a large bump on his neck.

The room grew fuzzy. He spun around. "What did you do?"

"I'm so sorry, Liam. I had no choice."

The throbbing pressure in Liam's skull was unlike anything he'd ever experienced. Even through closed eyes, the light above blinded him. He tried to shield his face, but his arm met unexpected resistance. Adrenaline shot through his body and the room came into focus.

He was sitting in an old chair, his wrists tightly bound to the armrests with rope and several layers of duct tape secured his ankles to the legs. A final strip was placed over his mouth. He struggled to move against his binds, hoping that with enough effort, he could get a hand free. He tried to look over his shoulder toward the faint sound of footsteps.

"I'm sorry, Liam."

Barely louder than a whisper, the harshness in Nora's voice grated against his ears. She slowly came into view. Her gray eyes were now obsidian pools.

"I didn't want to hurt you, but I have almost nothing left to offer, and it's chosen you to be next."

Nora floated closer to him as he struggled to free himself. Once so frail, Nora now had a towering, sinister presence. Cold radiated from her body, and her legs felt like ice pressed against his. She placed her frigid hands on Liam's bound wrists. He gasped at the intense cold. Her black stare bore into his eyes. Though his heart pounded blood through his veins, his body shut down.

Fight. Flight. Freeze.

"I just want the pain and the nightmares to end, Liam. I haven't felt peace in so long. I think a stronger person would have been able to fight against it. Whatever it is that shares my body."

She dug her nails into his skin. Liam let out a muffled cry. His lungs fought his constricted breath. Panic tore through him, but Nora's grip was so cold and so strong.

"This darkness, it chose you to be next. It won't let me rest until it has you. This is your burden to bear now, and I hope that you'll forgive me." Nora ripped the tape from his mouth and pressed her lips to his.

Liam's shock lasted only an instant before he felt the air being sucked from his body. Not just the air but his soul, his magic, the energy that made him human.

Flames engulfed his lungs. The fire ushered in a frost that swept through his veins until it reached the deepest parts of his living body.

As quickly as it started, it stopped, smothering him with heavy darkness.

CHAPTER 27
EMMA

The full-body pain hit Emma so quickly that it took her breath away. Pressing her hands into her stomach, she curled into a fetal position and gasped for air.

It started to subside just as she began running through her options, none of which involved the local hospital's emergency department.

"What the fuck?" She hissed.

Discomfort remained but her breaths came easier. It would be another fifteen minutes before Emma felt almost normal. Almost, because there was something she couldn't shake. Something was wrong.

She picked up her phone and drafted a new message to Liam.

EMMA: Busy? Can I come by?

Emma stared at the screen waiting for his answer. She barely let thirty seconds pass before shooting off a vague message in the employee chat about not feeling well and running out of her office.

Emma's SUV roared to life. Dirt kicked up behind her as she drove a bit too fast along the well-worn dirt road on the edges of the museum property. Her stomach grew heavy with dread as she neared Liam's building. With the windows down, Emma heard Belle's panicked barking over the engine and the tires crunching on the gravel driveway.

Forgetting her phone and keys, Emma jumped out of the car. Belle scratched frantically at the dog door. She needed the remote collar to open it, but Liam always took it off when he wasn't in the building.

"Liam!" Emma called.

She punched in the lock's code. Belle tore out of the building and sprinted to the old barn. Emma ran after her, ignoring the lead in her stomach, and the unsteady ground under her feet.

She stood in the barn doorway, allowing her eyes to adjust to the dusty light. In the middle of the room, on the cold, dusty cement floor, lay Liam's lifeless body.

"No." Her voice a choked whisper.

Belle licked Liam furiously, and Emma slid next to him just as he stirred. Despite her worry and panic, Emma remained calm. She called Liam's name and put a hand on his chest to feel his breathing.

"Emma? What's going on?" He reached up to push his dog's face away from his, but Belle wouldn't relent.

"I have no idea. We just found you like this." She patted her pockets and remembered that she left her phone in the car. "You need to go to the hospital."

"No!" Liam yelled, startling her. "I'm sorry, no. I'm okay. I don't need to go. I definitely don't need an ambulance showing up."

"What's the last thing you remember?"

Liam covered his eyes with the heels of his hands. "Just feeling really awful and anxious."

Emma ran her fingers across his scalp, feeling for a bump or blood from his fall. "You really should go to the hospital," she pressed.

Liam let out an exasperated sigh. Belle lay down by his side, her head on his lap. "I'm fine."

Emma pursed her lips. It was no use arguing. She knew Liam's mental health history made him wary of hospitals and doctors in general, and she didn't blame him. She had the same concerns.

Emma squeezed his hand and helped him sit up.

"Okay." She pulled over a chair. "Then you're coming to my place. I'll pack a bag for you."

Emma left when Liam nodded in agreement, his hands still pressed into his eyes. She ran up the stairs to his apartment, quickly stuffing some clothing into his duffle bag. Liam and Belle spent enough weekends at Emma's house that she'd become intimately familiar with everything the pair needed away from home. Much of it had already found spots in her pantry, on her dresser, and in her medicine cabinet. She focused only on the task at hand, running through her mental checklist. Her brain would make time for emotions later.

She found Liam still sitting with his head in his hands and Belle at his side. She leaned over him and gently touched his fingers. "Hey, all ready to go," she said quietly.

The next moments moved in slow motion.

Liam uncovered his eyes, and the color drained from his face.

His body trembled.

He screamed and launched himself backwards away from Emma.

Unprepared for his extreme reaction, Emma stumbled, falling hard onto the floor. A string of four-letter words left her mouth as she picked herself up and rubbed her sore limbs. Liam looked agitated and confused, his skin and eyes still drained of their color.

"Emma, I'm so sorry," he stammered. "Something about the way ... the way you leaned over me. I've never felt so scared."

He slowly stepped forward, reaching out his shaking hand. Emma hesitated. Then flinched when she interlaced her fingers with his. His hands were cool and slightly damp.

Liam pulled her closer until he curled his body around her. With her cheek against his chest, Emma felt his racing heart pounding against his ribcage. Tears collected in the corners of her eyes, but she refused to let them fall. She still had so much to do.

When they arrived at Emma's, Liam collapsed on the couch with Belle by his side.

"I'm going to make you some tea." Emma kissed the top of his head. "I'll be back in a bit."

Liam looked at her curiously but kept any questions to himself.

She headed for the back door, Luna following closely at her heels. Though still high, the sun had already started its descent behind the twisting limbs of the ancient white oaks that towered over her yard. Emma stuck a heavy key into a rusty lock protecting a mossy wooden shed in the back corner of her property. The door opened with a groan.

Luna took the lead and slipped into the dark space. A flick of a switch sent the hum of electricity through an antique chandelier hanging from the pitched ceiling.

A small wren nestled in a tilted flower pot eyed Emma with annoyance. "I'm sorry, sweet girl," Emma soothed. The wren shook her feathers and settled more deeply into her nest.

Luna jumped onto a workbench that ran along the back wall of the building and curled her legs under herself. Her light green eyes tracked Emma's movements through the space. Emma grabbed a few pieces of firewood and lit a small fire inside a pot-bellied stove in the corner of the room. To anyone else, it looked like an average garden shed. Gardening supplies hung from the walls, stood in tall piles on the floor, or sat neatly on shelves. The things Emma needed were carefully hidden from sight.

Kneeling on the floor in front of her workbench, Emma pulled up several loose floorboards and set them aside. From the hiding space, she removed a stone mortar and pestle, a deep cast iron pot, and several empty glass jars.

After replacing the floorboards, she moved to a thick wooden cabinet. She squatted next to it and felt underneath for a cold metal lever. Once found, it released with a smooth click. The top of the cabinet slid forward on its base just enough to allow Emma to turn the entire piece. Another lever released the lock that held a fake back in place. Emma swung it open and eyed dozens of carefully labeled glass jars. A few jars of popular herbs would go unnoticed, but a collection like Emma's was a beacon no one could ignore.

"What do you think, Luna?" Emma tapped her chin with her finger. "Old standard or do you think we should go stronger?"

The cat responded with a shrill meow and leapt from the workbench to the top of the cabinet. Emma watched her pace until she laid down and pawed at a leather-bound book underneath her.

"I don't love where this is going." Emma stood on her tiptoes to pull the book from the shelf. She leafed through the yellowed pages and stopped when Luna released another shrill cry.

Emma read the entry with a lump in her throat. "This is a protection spell. Don't you think that's a little over dramatic?"

Luna responded by standing and staring down at Emma with her judgmental feline eyes.

"Fine." Emma cradled the open book in one arm and began pulling jars from the cabinet. Having made her point, Luna laid down on top of the cabinet, her paws dangling over the side.

Emma never got around to explaining to Liam that Luna was no ordinary pet. On the night she moved in, the sleek onyx animal showed up at Emma's back door as a fluffy, malnourished kitten who didn't look old enough to be without her mother's milk. Waves of Emma's magic swirled with the creature cupped in her hands. Emma knew instantly that the Goddesses sent Luna to be her guide.

From a large glass bottle, Emma poured some purified rainwater into a kettle and set it on top of the stove, which was now throwing its warm glow into the space. She prepared the rest of the ingredients, many of which she grew herself, and others she foraged from various spots around the island. She had a few trusted sources with whom she traded, Mable being her favorite because she always threw in a batch of Emma's favorite chocolate chip cookies.

Mixing the water and her ingredients, Emma whispered the unfamiliar incantation until the concoction settled and its pungent scent transformed into something reminiscent of rosemary. She strained the earthy brown liquid into a thermos and sealed it with a worried sigh.

This was strong magic. Stronger magic than she'd ever dabbled in before. She never had a reason to because as far as she knew, a spell to protect against mythical creatures became obsolete when the rifts that connected the mortal world with the Middle Realm closed hundreds of years ago.

CHAPTER 28

LIAM

It was only when Liam heard the storm door slam shut that he realized Emma had been gone for almost an hour. He was in too much pain to wonder why it took her that long to make tea. He slouched low against the back of the couch despite the soft cushion feeling too abrasive for his pounding head.

He stared at the TV. A baseball game was on but the sound was off. The monotone voices of the local announcers were too much, but the visual kept him grounded in reality. Belle's chin rested on his thigh.

Emma walked into the living room and held out a steaming mug of a pungent liquid. Liam took it gingerly with a thank you.

"Before you drink that, I need to be clear about what I'm giving you." Sitting down on the coffee table in front of him, her face turned serious in a way that Liam had never seen.

He put the mug on the end table and shifted gingerly until he was sitting up straight. His head swelled with the movement, but he remained focused on her intense stare.

"A few weeks ago, we agreed to stop discussing magic."

That's not exactly how Liam remembered it, but he didn't interrupt.

"We have to discuss magic. I don't know much. I was taught foundations and very basic spells. Whatever healing properties a plant has, I can make it stronger."

"Like the ointment," Liam mumbled for his own sake. It was obvious, but he never bothered to give it much thought.

"Yes. That." She pointed at the mug beside him. "Is far beyond what I've ever done. It's a protection spell, and I know extremely little about it. My spell books were written over a hundred years ago by people who had generations of knowledge to fall back on."

"Protection from what?" Liam's head throbbed with the added mental effort of trying to understand if Emma was saying he was in danger.

"I don't have a fucking clue." The calmness in her voice started to give way. "Something magical? Something that hasn't been here since the rifts closed?"

Liam put his head in his hands, desperate for darkness. "What rift?"

He heard Emma suck in a long breath and let it out just as loudly. He recognized it as the breath she took anytime she was pissed off and trying not to lose her shit. "Sorry, Em, not all of us grew up illegally learning magic history," he snapped.

"I'll give you a history lesson later, but I'm trying to make sure you understand that I'm using very strong magic to protect you from something, and I have no idea what it is or what the outcome will be."

Confusion and frustration wrapped around him and Liam couldn't shake it. "Why? Why are you so sure you need to do this?"

"Luna," she said quietly. The bite had disappeared from her voice. "Luna guided me to it."

At the sound of her name, Emma's faithful cat jumped onto the coffee table next to her.

What he was hearing had become so ridiculous, Liam couldn't help but laugh. "Luna? Your cat? Unbelievable."

A low growl rumbled from Belle, who had remained by his side, but directed her warning at him.

"Animal guides exist, Liam," Emma said softly. "Whether you believe in them doesn't matter. Forgotten deities placed them in our lives when we needed them most."

Liam needed to move. Despite his pain, despite the increasing tightness in his chest, he needed to move. He stood up abruptly, and Emma flinched. He hated himself for causing her that kind of fear. But the guilt receded as quickly as it came.

"Emma, three weeks ago, you were adamant about not having this conversation. You threw ice on our whole relationship to avoid this conversation. We've been pretending everything's been fine for weeks, and we can't fucking talk about it. But your cat tells you what? I'm in danger? And suddenly everything's different?"

Emma's eyes glistened with tears. "Please don't fight with me right now."

He stared at her heartbroken face until Belle barked and broke his trance. His dog, the one that hadn't left his side since they met, stood protectively in front of Emma. Deryn was the only other person Belle had ever displayed this type of behavior for.

"If you can't trust me, at least trust Belle." Tears slipped down her cheeks.

Liam picked up the mug and brought it to his lips. He inhaled the woody aroma before taking a long sip. The liquid tasted like thick mushroom soup without enough onion. He swallowed and then continued to drink.

The warmth slid down his throat and into his stomach, spreading heat throughout his body. The pain in his skull eased with every gulp until it vanished with the last drop.

"How do you feel?"

A rush of energy filled the space left by the pain and for a moment, Liam felt like he could fight the whole world. "Better. A lot better."

He sat on the couch in front of Emma, still seated on the coffee table. Belle remained between them, but her body relaxed. "Em, I'm so sorry. I was in so much pain, and I felt out of control. I shouldn't have yelled at you like that."

Emma reached for his hands. "I understand. Let's get you to bed."

Taking her hand, he followed silently as she led him into her bedroom only letting go so she could cross the room and turn on a bedside lamp. He tried to slip off his shoes and remembered he was still wearing his dirty work clothes complete with his steel-toed boots. He groaned. Heavy drowsiness replaced the energy he had only moments ago.

Emma turned down the bed and walked over to Liam who felt irrationally annoyed with having to get undressed. She slowly undid his belt and the button-fly on his pants. When they fell to his knees, she placed a hand on his chest signaling for him to sit on the bed. Liam watched her with heavy eyelids while she untied his shoes and pulled them off, followed by his socks.

"I didn't sign up for this, you know," she said.

"For what?" The words accompanying a yawn.

She pulled his shirt over his head, leaving him in his dark blue boxer shorts. "The fear of losing you."

He managed a smile, but his brain couldn't string enough thoughts into words before sleep came over him. Emma's hands guided him until his head hit her pillow and then eased his legs onto the mattress. The comforter was pulled over him followed by the familiar weight of Belle hopping into bed and pressing against him. Emma's lips brushed against his temple, and he finally let go.

CHAPTER 29
LIAM

The darkness came and the voice with it.

Liam struggled to make sense of it. He squeezed his eyes shut as the sound whirled around him. High-pitched and childlike. And without joy.

Only sadness.

Anger.

Dread.

He needed to move.

To run.

His mind was alert, but his body was asleep. Numb and paralyzed. His mind told his limbs to shake his body awake. The frantic movement fired through his arms and legs, but they remained dead.

Still.

The voice grew louder, but no clearer. It filled the darkness, yet the space remained empty. Liam opened his mouth and cried for help. His voice made no sound. He screamed until his throat was hoarse and his lungs were weak. It didn't matter. The only voice he heard wasn't his.

The voice became deafening and distorted. Like microphone feedback and static on an old TV. It pierced Liam's ears and buzzed through his body. It burned like a thousand bee stings and just as he began to beg the Goddesses for Death to take him away, the light came.

The blinding light pushed back the darkness of the void until the voice once again became a whisper. Relief washed over him, and he bathed in the light.

But soon, the darkness returned, and the torture began again.

CHAPTER 30
DIARY OF SARA CORTESE

The Valley of Asters, late summer circa 1620

As I write, I gaze upon a different view. Gone is the sight of my children whilst they work and practice magic among the trees and tiny streams. I no longer see the comings and goings of those that live near or hear the chatter of friends and the squeals of their children.

Those comforting sounds of my community have been replaced with the quiet of an endless, unfamiliar forest.

It seemed as though our village was experiencing a reprieve from the most concerning news. It was believed that the most radical of the Commarasi have gone into hiding or quieted their message. Villagers remain fearful but not hostile. The small factions that had formed remain, but bartering and trading has resumed as usual. We were once again sharing our abundance instead of hoarding it.

With some peace falling over the village, I argued for Bethany's release. Her symptoms worsened and hastened her decline. Having grown tired of my pleas during official business, the Council of Nine stripped me of my title. Without a successor, the elders now have their discussions in darkness.

Gathered in the square among my people, the elders' aide announced Bethany's fate. She would be sentenced to a cleansing execution to be performed at the next full moon. Some cried, others shouted their objections. Some walked away with heads bowed so as to not show their true emotions.

I failed her. Stephen cradled me as I wept.

Paralyzed by grief, I was unaware Stephen and others began making plans for Bethany's escape. Under the cover of a rainy night, Piper arrived to take me away. I was given only enough time to kiss the foreheads of my grown babes. Stephen embraced me but wouldn't say goodbye. He claimed I'd return with our village's healer because only I possess the sheer will, stubborn determination, and magical ability to do so.

Piper and I traversed through the rain to Belhaven's north sea. The land on the other side sits further than Willow Ridge to our south. The open waters are often treacherous during summer storms and that night would be no different. But with Stephen's blessing and a promise that our children would be safe with our trusted friends, there was nothing that could stop me from this journey.

In the dim lamplight, I saw Bethany waiting on the dock with Catrina Boudin. Her heavy cloak swallowed her frail body. My time for tears and weakness was over, and I felt renewed strength for us both. She collapsed in my arms and kissed me weakly. Her face and lips ice cold despite the hot summer rain. I yearned for her warm embrace and promised her I would bring heat back to her touch.

Three nights and days of travel aided by faceless guides brought us to a modest cottage not far from the largest of our sacred libraries, Sanctum Celestia. I have no doubt that this was intentional and have prepared to make the short journey when the sun rises. I hope that I'm not a fool to put all my faith in this endeavor.

CHAPTER 31
EMMA

It was still dark when Emma staggered out of her bed, no longer able to sleep with Liam tossing and turning next to her. She brewed him a heavy sedative the night before, but while it gave him his most restful night's sleep in almost two weeks, it was far from restful for anyone sharing his bed. Even when Liam's nightmares didn't cause him to scream and thrash in his sleep, his skin radiated cold like an air conditioner.

Emma stripped off her flannel pajamas and swapped them out for something more comfortable for the summer heat. Belle hopped onto the bed next to Liam, doing her part of their ongoing rotation to comfort him when he woke up in a cold sweat. Emma shuffled into the kitchen, Luna following silently behind save for the bell that jingled from around her neck. It rang like church bells in the quiet of Emma's little shotgun house.

She went through the motions of making coffee and when it was done, she sat at the kitchen table, carefully leafing through the last of her grandmother's spell books. Everything Emma tried gave Liam a few days of moderate relief, but nothing permanent. And everything seemed to work less and less as time wore on. Regan was the only one that knew everything that was going on, but Emma was starting to consider tapping into her trusted network of Belhaven's remaining Amora.

Her stomach growled, and she answered with a frustrated groan. Emma hadn't been food shopping in a few days, and her pantry was empty of her usual breakfast foods. Driving to Peyton's deli would have been faster, but Emma needed to walk. She needed to move and breathe the fresh air. She needed the sun on her skin.

Luna walked swiftly beside Emma as they followed the sidewalk through the neighborhood. On days like this—the ones when Emma set aside her own needs to care for someone else's—Luna followed her closely, her presence always feeling more human than feline.

As Emma neared the deli, Luna slinked off into a narrow space between the storefronts. A well-trained dog was expected. A well-trained cat raised eyebrows. Emma pulled the door open, and a bell rang overhead. The person behind the counter didn't look up from the meat slicer, but Emma recognized them anyway.

Peyton grew up in Covendale, a small mountain town in the northwest of Valen, but their roots ran deep in Belhaven Island despite being a generation removed. They were helping a lone customer standing at the counter.

While she waited, Emma scanned the flyers that adorned the community bulletin board. The colorful and friendly advertisements were a stark contrast to the government-mandated posters beside them. The ones that Peyton was legally required to have in their shop. The ones that outlined the laws prohibiting magic. The ones that warned of the penalties and provided the process to report your neighbors if you witness them using magic or in possession of magical items.

The barely legible fine print reminded citizens that false reports were also illegal. It was a fairly new law, put in place after a handful of wives desperate to leave their toxic marriages began reporting their husbands for using magic. With divorce applications seldom granted, men had been using the tactic for generations. Then the tables started to turn and Ascaria's leaders wouldn't be having any of that.

Emma was scanning a new government flier when she heard Peyton call her name. "It's good to see you open again."

Peyton's untamable dark curls escaped their Doolittle's Deli baseball cap, and their apron was spotted with flour dust. "I'm happy to be open again. The loss of business isn't even the biggest expense; it's the food waste. I gave away what I could, but I still had to replace it all outside of my usual shipments."

"Regan brought over a few containers of macaroni salad. It might be a while before I pick up any more."

Peyton's eyes sparkled at the sound of Regan's name. "I won't hold it against you."

Peyton took Emma's order and started bustling around behind the counter.

"Listen," Peyton said as they finished packing Emma's bagels and cream cheese. "I didn't hear this directly, but it comes from a reliable source. He said the Belhaven museum will be audited soon. Supposedly there was some pressure to move it up to the top of the list."

"Fucking hell." Emma knew that some pressure could be traced back to Kyle Nolan and their run-in at the gala a month ago. She pulled some folded bills from her back pocket and slid them across the counter. "Thank you for telling me."

"Any extra time we can get, right?"

Emma dumped her change into the tip jar. "I'll take every bit of it."

The bells over the door chimed, announcing the arrival of a few young lifeguards looking for caffeine before their shift and ending Emma and Peyton's conversation.

Emma spotted Luna sitting in a narrow alley, barely visible in the shadows. Emma set her bag down to free a hand and lifted the nimble cat onto her shoulders. On any other day, it would have been too hot to be Luna's perch, but the soft purring against Emma's neck soothed her nerves.

The confrontation with Kyle felt so long ago and after a month, Emma started to think that his threats didn't have any bite. She was making a mental list of ways to prepare for the impending audit when she walked through the back door and into her kitchen. The flood of sunshine and cool breeze off the water couldn't break through the gloom that followed Liam when he walked into the space shortly after. The vibrant energy that surrounded him was gone, leaving something heavy in its place. It made her sad. And lonely.

"You're up early," he said.

Emma sifted through the bag until she found the perfect egg bagel. "Yeah. I couldn't sleep."

Liam came up behind her, the chill of his body reaching through her clothes and grazing her skin. She tried not to flinch.

"Because of me?"

Emma focused on preparing her breakfast. "It was a rough night."

"I'm sorry. Last night was probably one of my better nights' sleep too."

"That's good. I'll brew some more of that elixir after work."

"Since we're both up early..." Liam kissed her neck softly. Sweetly. In the exact way that Emma liked. The way that made her putty in his hands to mold and shape at his will.

But everything felt wrong and uncomfortable.

"Liam, stop." Emma shook him off, then froze, the knife in her hand still covered in cream cheese.

Liam backed off without a word.

She was relieved and grateful that he immediately honored her demand, but she couldn't look at him. "I'm sorry. I can't explain it, but your skin is like ice, and I just..."

"It's okay," he said quietly. "I'll see you at work."

She stood in the kitchen, shredding her bagel into pieces, and forced herself to eat. The front door opened and slammed shut, leaving her feeling truly alone.

Emma slipped out of her clothes and stepped into the shower, wanting the hot water to burn her skin until it felt numb. She'd never felt so physically exhausted and emotionally drained.

The water brought to the surface every raw emotion in a tangled mess, and she started to unravel. Her chest tightened, and she put her face under the stream so she wouldn't have to acknowledge the tears that were beginning to blur her vision. Exhaling a slow breath, Emma let herself slide down to the shower floor and cried.

CHAPTER 32

LIAM

Liam's mouth gaped for only a moment before uttering a string of foul language that could make a trucker blush.

Liam, I don't see the budget analysis that was due on Wednesday. Please touch base with me this morning about its status. Thanks, Judy

Liam never missed a deadline. An email for an overdue budget analysis never should have popped into his inbox.

His fingers tightened around his coffee mug. Rage rolled in his belly. It boiled over, filling his chest and neck and to release the pressure, he hurled his coffee mug at the brick wall behind him.

Belle scrambled from her bed and voiced her own displeasure with a few short barks.

"Oh you're fine," Liam spat. "You were nowhere near that wall."

"Liam?" Emma's disembodied voice echoed through his office.

"What!"

Emma's soft footsteps padded through the hallway and stopped at the office entrance. Liam knew he should have felt remorse for being nasty to Belle and Emma, but anger and frustration consumed him.

"What's going on, Lee?" Emma asked gently.

He stood up from his chair and reached for a broom. "It's nothing," he said, but shame started to settle in. "I... I missed a really important budget deadline."

He prepared himself for a barrage of follow-up questions. Emma always had follow-up questions. They were well intentioned, but rarely helpful, and Liam wasn't confident he'd be able to hide his annoyance this time.

Instead, though, she let out a quiet, "Oh."

She stood at the edge of the room, giving him a wide berth as he swept up the bits of broken ceramic.

"How can I help?" she asked finally.

He let out an annoyed groan. "I don't know, Emma."

He should have stopped there, but words tumbled from his mouth like he had no control. "Right now, I just need to get this proposal finished and math isn't exactly your best subject."

Liam didn't want to look at her, but he did. Emma pushed herself off the wall, her arms crossed tightly, and a look of absolute fire on her face.

"Wow." That was all she said. And that was all she needed to say. Liam knew a thousand emotions were tied to that one word.

He put down the broom and sat down on the edge of his cluttered desk. He pressed the heels of his hands into his eyes until he saw little clouds of color.

That was the first time he heard the voice of his nightmares while wide awake.

She's tired of you.

It was so quiet, but so clear.

"I'm so sorry, Em. I know you're tired of me."

Her body softened. Her features twisted in confusion.

"I'm not tired of you, Liam." She pointed at him for emphasis. "But I am tired of being your emotional punching bag."

"I know." Liam whispered. His anger was gone, leaving only shame. "I'm sorry."

"Get your work done. I'll see you at lunch." Emma turned on her heel and left, slamming the door shut behind her.

Feeling restless, Liam needed to move. He was exhausted, but he needed to exhaust himself. He shot off a half-assed reply to Judy. He might take a professional hit for the delay, but he'd work better without the restlessness that coursed through him.

He found tree limbs that needed trimming, flower beds that could use covering, and walking paths that needed another layer of wood chips. He worked through the body pains and the headaches. He worked through fatigue and exhaustion. He worked until he heard a command and needed to comply.

Get Emma away from the door.
She must not go near it.

CHAPTER 33

EMMA

Maybe he's fine and just an asshole, Emma thought as she stomped through the museum lobby on the way to her office.

She would rather that than whatever the alternative happened to be. It would be easier to cut ties with Liam if that were the case. It would be easier to tell him to fuck off forever. She could move on from that. That was pain she could get over. It's why she wanted to keep him at arm's length in the first place.

Mabel was sitting in everyone's favorite overstuffed armchair when Emma huffed into her office.

"Rough morning?" Mabel asked breezily.

"You could say that." Emma tossed her stuff onto her desk and collapsed into her chair.

Mabel lobbed a plastic container onto Emma's desk. "I made these last night. My gut told me you'd need them. Seems like I was right."

Emma opened the container and inhaled the sweet scent of Mabel's chocolate chip cookies. Just the smell brought Emma's blood pressure down a few notches. A whole cookie would be just the tranquilizer she needed.

"Oh you're a goddess. Thank you." She took a bite of the delightfully undercooked cookie.

"You're welcome. I know that sometimes, the fights aren't worth the make-up sex."

Unprepared for Mabel's salacious commentary so early in the morning, Emma gagged on her half-chewed baked good. She sputtered and coughed while Mabel sat there looking far too pleased with herself. She finally slid Emma's water bottle within reach, and Emma cleansed her palate until she could breathe easily again.

"How do you know about that?" Emma choked out, her voice still hoarse from coughing.

"What? That you and Liam are sleeping together?" Mabel's brown eyes sparkled with glee, but she rolled them to emphasize her point.

"I don't know who you think you're fooling, but you two have been looking at each other with passion and fire in your eyes since the day you met."

Not to be deterred by her near-death experience, Emma took a bite into another cookie, giving her at least thirty more seconds to avoid responding.

"Until a few weeks ago," Mabel continued. "Now all I see is hurt, sadness, worry. And Liam has been so unlike himself. Instead of a friendly golden retriever, he's like a chihuahua with an ax to grind."

Emma decided it was time to confide in Mabel. She told Mabel about Liam's mysterious collapse, how Luna guided her to make a protection spell, and how Liam had been suffering from painful migraines making him uncharacteristically unkind and impatient. She recounted all the spells she used and how they'd work for a little while, but never long enough.

"Liam always had this effect on my magic," Emma said. "Like it wants to reach out and suck him in. It's really similar to what Regan and I share, but it's exponentially stronger. And... sexually charged."

Mabel's face relaxed into a soft smile. "Sounds like you two are bound souls."

"Soulmates?" Emma thought so, but she could never bring herself to say the words out loud.

"More than soulmates." Mabel's broad smile deepened the wrinkles around her eyes.

Too shocked to swallow the bite of her cookie, Emma asked her question with a mouth full, "There's something stronger than soulmates?"

"Indeed. Soulmates are people whose spirits are connected and create an even stronger connection. Like you and Regan. Me and..."

Mabel trailed off, her excitement replaced by a look of maudlin sadness. Her curiosity piqued, Emma needed to know everything about this mystery person.

"Anyway," Mabel continued. "Bound souls are entwined spirits that are more powerful when they're together. Their souls are like two halves of one piece. Their magic doesn't just complement each other, it's amplified by the other. The magic that brings bound souls together is extremely powerful. They were rare even before the Commarasi came to power and weakened our magic."

Emma chewed on this new information, wishing it was a tactile thing that she could roll in her hands. She really needed a large glass of wine at this point, but another cookie would have to do.

"That's how it felt, but now my magic is repulsed by his. It pushes him away like he's dangerous, but only so far. And this bound soul shit makes this feel a fuck-ton worse."

"That it does." Mabel agreed thoughtfully.

They sat together in reflective silence for a few minutes until Mabel checked her watch and stood up to prepare for an upcoming museum tour. "I'll check my library for something that might be useful. I wish you would have told me this sooner. Remember, magic wasn't meant to be done alone. There's a reason why our people lived in community with each other."

Emma nodded, feeling a bit guilty she didn't confide in Mable sooner. Though their relationship grew once Emma came to work at the museum, Mabel had always been part of Emma's life. Back then, there were more Amora on Belhaven Island, and they stayed close to those they considered part of their village. Emma always credited her grandmother for raising her as a child, but it was Mabel who guided her as an adult.

"Secrets are safer," Emma said finally.

"It often feels that way." Mabel rubbed Emma's back for a moment, then quietly walked away.

With the announcement of an audit looming, Emma pushed away the cookie container. She wrapped her headphones over her ears and picked her most energetic playlist that still allowed her to focus. Hitting play, she turned the volume up to a deafening level, giving her tired brain the stimulation it needed.

Moving through her checklist, she accomplished one task after another. The pop-punk and hip-hop from her youth blasted in her ears, temporarily silencing not only the world around her but the constant strumming of her worries.

It was mid-morning when she heard her name being called over the music. "Yeah?" she called, turning around to face the open office door.

She pulled her headphones off her ears and the quiet hum of cool air coming from the vents hit her senses like a baseball bat. Emma was alone in the room, the only voices coming from her headphones.

She stuck them back over her ears with a sigh and an eye roll and continued working. The call of Emma's name became more persistent. It played under the music like a hidden track. She tried to ignore it, convinced it was the lack of sleep messing with her head. But she was compelled to listen when her magic began vibrating in her chest. Emma felt it more than she could hear it.

She stopped the music. The call continued. She took off her headphones and placed them on her desk.

She heard it all around her, but the urgent call was within her. She didn't fear it, but it was far from comforting.

The edges of her vision grew hazy. She followed the pull in her chest as it guided her out of her office and through the unusually silent hallways of the museum. The elevator doors opened as she approached, but no one stepped out.

The doors opened to a basement flooded in heavy darkness. The light from the elevator disappeared over the threshold, failing to illuminate even a few feet of distance. She took a step into the darkness and the overhead light above her flickered on.

"Thank you, Goddess," she said in whispered reverence.

She took a few steps forward and the next overhead light flickered on, the one behind her dimming until the path behind her darkened.

She continued forward into the vacuum of light and sound, the lamps above illuminating just enough space under her feet to provide a clear path. She moved with confident purpose, unafraid despite the unusual circumstances. She was protected by the darkness and whatever force pulled her deeper into the basement to reach the last steps in the last hallway.

Shimmering in a golden light, Emma saw every detail of the ancient wooden door. Every sliver of wood breathed with magic. She felt it in every cell of her body, giving her a burst of clarity she'd never experienced. Without any hesitation this time, she wrapped her hand around the tarnished silver knob, turning it effortlessly. The door should have squeaked or groaned from lack of use, but any sound it made was pulled into the darkness.

Beyond her were primitive tunnels made of stone and clay. Emma's eyes quickly adjusted to the darkness with feline clarity. Stone artwork adorned the space, which may have once held the bodies of her ancestors as the village prepared for their resting ceremonies.

She whispered a forgotten prayer and took another step further into the tunnel.

A tight hand gripped her forearm, ripping her from the vacuum of light and sound in which she'd been immersed.

A blinding light flooded into the tunnels. Emma covered her eyes with her free hand, but she couldn't escape the overwhelming feeling of being in a place too bright. The ambient noise rang in her ears. Her own breath thundered. Where she was once safe and protected, she was now afraid and vulnerable.

Hunted.

The instant change in sensation knocked her off-balance, and she swayed towards the ground. The firm grip on her arm yanked her back to her feet, and she cried out in pain.

A distorted voice said her name, and she struggled to make sense of it. "What are you doing down here?"

She looked up. Her eyes focused. Her head began to clear.

"Liam?" The weakness in her voice surprised her.

"You shouldn't be here."

Liam's tone set her on edge. He was angry. With the light at his back, his normally bright eyes looked dark. Cold. They stared down at her without a touch of concern or worry.

She stood up straight. "You're hurting me!" She jerked her arm from his grip.

He put his hands on his hips like a disappointed parent. "What are you doing?"

"I work down here! What are you doing here?"

He rolled his eyes. "You were late for lunch again. And since you were down here last time, I figured you were down here again."

Emma swallowed and fought back tears. It was too much. The sensory overload, the lack of compassion in Liam's voice, the physical pain he caused when he grabbed her. Everything was just too much.

"I forgot." She tried desperately to keep her voice steady, but a lump in her chest encouraged her to release the tears she'd been holding back for weeks.

"You forget a lot of things."

The lump in Emma's chest exploded into pure rage.

"I get that whatever you're going through is making you fucking miserable, but that doesn't mean I have to tolerate you acting like an asshole! I'm almost forty fucking years old, and I'm well beyond letting people treat me like shit and making me feel stupid. So get your shit together, Liam, or just fuck off forever."

She pushed past him through the old door, and into the damp, cool basement, now lit by the humming overhead lights. Seething, she stomped through the space, her anger building with every moment that passed without hearing Liam begging her for forgiveness.

Emma passed the elevator and threw open the door to the stairwell. Three flights of stairs later, she was still no calmer when she entered her office. It quickly became apparent that she was too amped up to get back in her chair so she grabbed her bag and left.

CHAPTER 34

LIAM

The sharp pain at the base of Liam's skull worsened anytime he tried to focus on a screen. He rubbed the back of his neck as he struggled through an important email from Judy. He got the gist though. There would be a mandatory staff meeting to discuss an audit by the state's historical oversight department. An audit that got pushed up by almost six months with far less time to prepare than usual because Liam needed to stroke his ego by taking Emma to a very public event.

She blames you for ruining her life.

"She wouldn't be wrong," he mumbled.

Liam deserved all the vitriol she spewed at him less than a week ago. He couldn't remember how he ended up in the basement. One minute he was spreading wood chips over a muddy section of walking trail, and the next he was in a dark tunnel forcibly holding Emma by the arm and demanding to know why she was there. The hurt on her face destroyed him and all he could do was watch like a prisoner in his own body, fully conscious but without any control.

Emma screamed at him with a ferocity he didn't know she was capable of, and he deserved every syllable. After she left, he stood there in the darkness until the thrumming in his chest became so unbearable he had to leave.

Without a word to anyone else, he left work and drove himself to Belhaven Medical Clinic. The clinic might be one of the least corrupt in this part of the region, but money still talks. Liam gave them a number—every penny in his savings—and told doctors to find the cause of his suffering: the migraines, the insomnia, the nightmares, the fatigue, all of it.

The results dripped in and by Wednesday morning, Liam had his answer:

Nothing.

On paper, Liam was a perfectly healthy thirty-seven-year-old man. Which, considering how much destruction he inflicted on his body in his twenties and early thirties, should have been cause for celebration.

He picked up his phone and began tapping another text to Emma. He'd started and deleted dozens since Friday and this one would be no different.

Liam rushed into the conference room, breathing through the pain that radiated through his body. He slid into a seat across from Emma and acknowledged her sad eyes with a tired smile.

"Liam, did you run here?" Judy asked when she took her seat. "Why are you out of breath?"

"I, uh, yeah," he stuttered. "I'm sorry. I lost track of time."

Judy began the meeting with a commanding yet sympathetic voice.

"Thanks for being here on such short notice, everyone. I know your daily routines are important, and I appreciate your flexibility." She took a long sip of her coffee before continuing.

"As a museum, we are subject to periodic review by the federation's Historical Facilities Oversight Commission. I have received word that our review will be happening next week. For a few of you, this might be the first time you've prepared for something like this, which is why I wanted to have this meeting. The museum will be closed to the public for at least the next two weeks to prepare for the audit and implement any necessary changes."

Liam had never been part of an audit, but much of his old job involved moving money around so that it wouldn't get flagged when one of his clients came under review. His financial records were clean, but he used this insight to his advantage.

"I suspect they're going to focus on the landscaping renovation since it's the biggest expense the museum has had in the past few years. Liam, please hang around after so we can talk."

Liam nodded. Judy's choice of words gave him the impression she wanted to talk about more than just the renovation.

"Auditors will be looking for any positive associations or sympathetic references to Belhaven's Amoran history. The exhibitions team will have to take a look through everything and adjust any wording as best as you can on such short notice. I know we try to handle this before an exhibit goes up, but sometimes, things slip through the cracks."

Liam saw Emma slide down into her seat as she often did when she was tired or stressed.

"A few years ago," Emma's voice cracked when she began to speak, "we had to tear down an entire exhibit about early Belhaven architecture because the auditor deemed it too sympathetic to people who'd lost their homes. One passing line was all it took to destroy three months of work and put us on a list for more strict oversight of our finances."

People around the room nodded, either in understanding or recollection.

Judy turned her attention to Hector. "They'll also be looking for evidence of organized rituals or magic lessons happening here at the museum. I'd like the programmers to go through the class schedule and the room rental calendar and cancel anything that looks even slightly mystical."

For the next hour, Judy outlined the museum's plan for the impending visit. Liam's attention began to wander just as the meeting was wrapping up. He tried to give Emma a signal that he wanted to speak to her later, but she continued to avert his gaze. Subtle signals during staff meetings had been one of their most favorite games and being ignored wrecked him.

He remained in his seat while everyone else filed out, taking their heaviness and stress with them. When Judy returned from the bathroom, she closed the door and was on Liam before reaching her seat.

"Liam. What the hell is going on with you? You've been a mess for weeks, and I'm at the point that I can't let it go anymore."

She can't be trusted.
She'll use your magic against you.

Liam squeezed his eyes shut and tried to shake away the persistent voice echoing in his head. Every day it grew louder and his own grew softer. Every day it seemed to consume and control more of his thoughts.

"I'm just not good right now," he choked out.

Judy sat forward in her seat, her deep brown eyes forcing him to meet her gaze. "Liam, I need you to be good, because I need you to be the point person on this. Your family name has much higher standing than mine or anyone else's here.

It's not why I hired you, but it's a perk I'm willing to exploit if it keeps my museum open."

She's lying.
It's exactly why she hired you.

"Liam. What do you need to be good?"

Liam opened his mouth, but something held them back and the words refused to come.

Emma

If not for Mabel, the day would have been an absolute waste. Emma wanted to curl up under her desk and hide from the world, but Mabel was there to prod her through their exhibit review.

The emergency staff meeting was the first time Emma had seen Liam since their fight; the physical and emotional distance between them shattered her into a million pieces. Emma floated on an ocean of anger, resentment, fear, worry, sadness, longing, and heartbreak. She took offense to Regan's unwillingness to join her in egging Liam's apartment.

With vandalism off the table, Emma brewed the last untested spell in her books. The elixir to help him sleep had to be used sparingly; too much increased the risk of permanent sleep, and her books seemed to be missing the antidote for a coma.

She was staring at the calm blue water below her office window when she was startled by a quiet knock at the door.

Hector didn't wait for the okay to come in and join her by the window. He put an arm around Emma's shoulders and pulled her into his side. The comforting affection was almost too much and threatened to send Emma crumbling.

"What's going on with Liam?" He asked gently.

Emma inhaled a deep breath and exhaled it slowly to steel herself for this conversation.

"I thought he was off at the staff meeting, but I chalked it up to a bad day until Jake told me he's been kind of a dick lately. He said if Liam keeps it up, he's going to punch him in the face."

Emma sighed a laugh. "Yeah, well, Jake can get in line."

Hector squeezed her a bit tighter.

Emma considered how much to divulge to Hector. She trusted him, but trust was only one part of the equation. Safety was always the other. Lies of omission were an accepted part of the closest friendships.

"I don't know exactly what Liam is going through, just that it's something not completely within his control."

"You're sure about that?" Hector sounded skeptical, and Emma didn't blame him. She'd been having trouble believing it herself lately.

"Something is pushing me away. Like the poles of the magnetic force that brought us together have flipped and it's trying to drive us even further apart for my own safety. But something even stronger than that is keeping me from giving up on him."

Hector sighed and rested his head on top of Emma's. She had to change the subject before the heaviness in her chest exploded into uncontrollable sobs.

"So you're hanging out with Jake, huh?"

Hector laughed. "You know I'm looking for love. Jake ain't it, but he's fun."

"What makes you say that?"

"On the surface, he just wants someone to have a good time with. Secretly, he wants intimacy and companionship, but he's not going to let someone get that close. Someone is meant to break down those walls, but it's not me."

Emma let Hector's answer sit with her for a beat. "Sounds like me and Jake have a lot more in common than just the urge to deck Liam."

"That you do."

CHAPTER 35

EMMA

Parked outside Liam's building, Emma readied herself for a hurtful dismissal or another fight. She knocked on his apartment door in her usual rhythm. Over Belle's excited barking, she heard Liam yell to come in.

Emma poked her head inside and scanned the room. It was flooded with light from the evening summer sun, but Liam slumped low in the darkest spot on the couch, still in his work clothes. Usually by now, he would have showered and changed, but the musty smell made her wonder when he last did laundry.

She crossed the room and sat on the opposite end of the couch. Belle sprawled between them with her head on Liam's lap.

"I made this for you." She pulled a small vial out of her bag and placed it on the coffee table in front of him. "You have to be really careful with the dosage. If you take too much, you won't wake up."

Liam laughed through his nose. "Not a bad idea, actually."

Emma's heart splintered like tempered glass and the pieces threatened to escape through the heavy sobs building up in her chest.

When Liam's eyes finally met hers, she was struck by their dullness. The crisp blue had become muted, like a layer of clouds covering the sky.

"I'm sorry," he said gently. "I'm so angry all the time. I wake up pissed off and wanting to set the world on fire. And if I'm not feeling full of rage, I'm feeling guilty or ashamed for turning all that on you. It's impossible to be happy right now."

Emma slumped into the couch. She couldn't excuse Liam's behavior, but she could empathize with it. It took decades to stop making her loved ones the regular target of her explosive emotions. She seldom let people get that close to her anymore.

"And the intrusive thoughts are so much worse," he continued. "They're more like my own voice. They're so much harder to shake off. My brain will tell my body to do something and then I'm just watching it happen like I have no control over it."

This new revelation worried Emma and added another symptom to the list.

"Your words really hurt me," she said softly, but firmly. "I can accept your struggles as a reason, but it's not permission for you to do it without consequences."

"You're right. I just don't know how to feel better."

Belle moved to the floor, giving Emma space to move next to Liam. Fighting through his frosty touch and her magic's resistance, Emma wrapped her arms around him. A few of Liam's tears fell into the crook of her neck. She pulled him closer, as though doing so could mold their bodies together, enabling her to share his pain.

When his body and his grip relaxed, she did the same and used her thumbs to wipe the tears from his cheeks. "Mabel is looking in her library for something that will help. I hate that it's taking so long."

Liam took a breath and let it out slowly. "I know. I trust you."

"Go take a shower. I'll make dinner, and we can try this new spell."

Based on the science experiments living in his empty refrigerator, Emma assumed that Liam hadn't eaten anything at home in more than a week. A pizza arrived just as he emerged from the bathroom in fresh clothes.

They ate at the kitchen island in an uncomfortable quiet that was so unlike meals they've shared before.

"I wanted to tell Judy," Liam said in between bites. "I couldn't though. Something wouldn't let me."

Emma nodded like his statement was completely ordinary, but it made the hairs on the back of her neck stand on end. "I can talk to her."

"I think I'm ready to try that spell."

She put down her pizza and followed him to the couch. "You sure you don't want to sleep in your bed?"

He stuffed a soft blanket under his head. "Yeah, I want you to have a comfortable place to sleep if you stay."

Emma watched two drops of the clear liquid fall onto Liam's tongue. "I'll stay."

Liam fell asleep almost immediately and once she felt confident that he wouldn't stop breathing, she returned to her dinner.

She grabbed the newspaper that sat on the corner of the counter. Turning the pages while she ate, she stopped when a pair of stunning blue eyes caught her attention.

"Oh shit," she muttered.

She knew this face. It belonged to the woman Liam and Mabel were talking to after the first time Liam found her wandering in the basement. She remembered her face, but it was the way the woman made Emma feel that remained embedded in her memory. The anxiety and discomfort and the dread. So much unhappiness.

The color picture of this beautiful young woman with a lively smile accompanied the most heartbreaking of headlines.

Husband Cleared in Investigation of Wife's Mysterious Death

Belhaven Island resident Jeremy Menken has been cleared in the initial investigation into the mysterious death of his wife, Nora Menken. District officials, however, have requested a more in-depth investigation from the Valen Regional Criminal Necromancy Review Board.

Jeremy Menken denies responsibility for any mystical element to his wife's deadly illness.

"We hope that the results of this investigation will clear any doubt that Nora's death was nothing more than the result of a tragic illness that took her much too soon," Menken said in a statement through his attorney. "With the investigation closed, we can finally grieve."

The Menken family is considered in good standing and does not have any additional open investigations.

Nora Menken, 34, died on July 5, after a short battle with an undiagnosed illness that her family says caused severe migraines, fatigue, weight loss, and insomnia. Nora Menken sought treatment on May 12 following a collapse in her home. The district medical investigations board began reviewing Nora Menken's case as a possible necromancy-related crime when her condition worsened despite having no obvious health conditions.

Goosebumps erupted across Emma's flesh. Her chest grew tight. Like a broken dam holding back the ocean, words flooded her memory.

... her conditions worsened despite having no obvious health conditions...

... collapse in her home...

... migraines. fatigue. insomnia...

... Piper's father, John, collapsed in his stables...

... Vivid nightmares keep him from a restful sleep...

... mood has been most unpleasant...

... only seem to be slowing his worsening symptoms...

... she woke with no memory of how she came to be sprawled on John's floor...

... her face and lips ice cold despite the hot summer rain...

"I fucking missed it," Emma whispered. "I had the answers the whole time."

CHAPTER 36

EMMA

The magic pulse of the wooden door beat in time with Emma's racing heart. She'd been drawn there, and nothing would stop her from reaching her unknown destination. The stone and earthen walls absorbed the light from her lantern and muffled the sound of her steps and harried breath.

Invisible wisps of magic weaved around her, guiding Emma through the low, narrow tunnels that ran like veins under the museum. They nudged her forward anytime she stopped to admire a dusty tapestry or intricate carving embedded in the stone. The niches in the walls held a trove of art and leather-bound books, and she wanted to examine them all. Every piece must have a story. An intention. Those stories would be heard another day. She was a moth in search of a flame.

The dusty path beneath her became slick with streaks of mud that formed from drips of water above. A few falls sent her to the ground, caking her hands in dirt. She brushed them on her jeans knowing she'd have to come up with a way to explain herself to Liam later.

Emma slowed her pace knowing she was nearing the end of her journey. The same hands that moved her now stopped her. The tunnel continued, but she'd reached her destination. She turned in slow circles. The lantern light grew brighter, illuminating the darkest corners and erasing every shadow.

Her eyes adjusted to the light and focused on an overturned wooden trunk. She flipped it back onto its footing with a thud and the broken lid opened with a groan. Though it was nearly identical to the one that held Sara's diaries, the contents hadn't been as securely packed. She lifted a heavy iron urn out of the trunk and into the light. The latch closure holding the lid in place had cracked, breaking its airtight seal.

She set it down and pulled out a backpack-size leather satchel. Her heart raced as she untied its bindings to free the stories inside.

CHAPTER 37
DIARY OF SARA CORTESE

The Valley of Asters, late summer circa 1620

The air was crisp this morning, and I can feel the change in the earth that arrives with the coming autumnal equinox. The mossy ground under my feet is warm, but the first fallen leaves have begun knitting their winter blanket. On the second day of our stay in The Valley of Asters, I collected all that the forest could spare for my potions and elixirs. If rationed well, my pantry should last through winter, though I hope that we will be home in Belhaven before then.

The sharp pains in her temples and disrupted sleep have taken their toll, leaving Bethany temperamental and weak. Holding her in my arms as she rests does not keep the nightmares at bay but offers her immediate comfort when she wakes in terror.

I wake each morning to the call of the crows singing for the dawn light. As I ready my mare Zephyr for my journey to the Sanctum Celestia, I'm greeted by the family of red wolves that stand guard around our home. I offer them our dinner scraps and fresh water in appreciation of their patrol.

The crows are my escort, flying just ahead to guide us through the dense forest. They follow the calls of the chickadees, leading us on the safest path. I always sigh a breath of relief once I pass under the sanctuary's stone archway. I've heard stories of this place, but the magnificent cathedral exceeds everything that I've ever imagined. I long to spend days among the collection of works that fill the domed space, but my needs are very specific, and I vowed to Bethany that I would always return by dusk.

I'm aided each day by a wise and compassionate librarian named Isolde who fills my arms with spell books, scrolls, and storybooks written by fellow scribes. Although they offer no source or cure, in these works I've found a number of spells that have gifted Bethany a modicum of relief. Some ease her pain while others offer her a more restful sleep.

This evening, I returned to our cottage just as the moon was beginning to rise. Bethany grinned when she greeted me with hot stew and a loaf of fresh bread. Although her eyes remained dark and her shoulders hunched, to hear her laugh after so long set fire to my soul.

CHAPTER 38

DIARY OF SARA CORTESE

The Valley of Asters, early fall circa 1620

The air is cold, but the Valley of Asters is a riot of warm color that I've never before seen. From the towering heights, leaves rain down around us with every soft breeze or shake from a squirrel's hurried climb.

Bethany and I honored the Goddesses during the autumnal equinox with traditional offerings, but it was a somber celebration. We miss the vibrance of our village and the love of our community. I have no regrets over my decision to leave them in order to give Bethany a chance to survive, but she struggles to believe I will find something that will free her from her presumed fate.

In a late-night confession, she told me about the voice that lives inside her. It has grown louder, and she fears that soon she will be unable to tell the difference between it and her own thoughts and desires. It sometimes speaks for her, using her body to utter its lies. John Dawson heard the voice too, she said. It verbalized his deepest fears, his worries, and resentments, destroying his heart and mind while his body withered.

I'm frustrated with Bethany for this omission. I could have narrowed my search instead of exhausting myself and wasting precious time behind a pile of useless books. My anger burns, but I refuse to feed it. Bethany needs my love, and I need the hope that this revelation will lead to a cure.

CHAPTER 39
DIARY OF SARA CORTESE

The Valley of Asters, early fall circa 1620

Tonight, I write with a weariness in my body and the last bits of hope in my soul. I hear Bethany muttering in her sleep. Another nightmare from which she can't wake. I sit under a dome of stars bathed in the light of the full moon. I look to the sky as though the stars will send me a sign that all will be well soon.

With insufficient rest, I woke before the call of the crows, and the wolves eyed me with curiosity as I began my ride to the library before dawn's first light. Expecting my arrival, Isolde stood firm and tall at the entrance.

I jumped off my horse, speaking swiftly as I scrambled towards the door. Surely with this new information, the librarian could better target her knowledge.

"They sent warning of you," she said.

I asked Isolde what she meant.

She said the elders of Belhaven sent warning that a dangerous prisoner escaped, aided by an herbal alchemist intent on curing what cannot be healed. A chill carried in her voice, but her deep brown eyes remained warm and sympathetic.

I told them of their plan to let Bethany die. To sentence her to a cleansing execution not to save her spirit, but to absolve their own. I shook with conviction. The woman, not much older than myself, deserved my grace and respect, but I am tired. And angry. "I will not let her die until I have tried everything in this realm and others to keep her alive!"

I feared my outburst may have signaled the guards and slowly placed a hand on the hilt of the dagger strapped to my hip.

Isolde remained silent for several moments. When she finally spoke, she said, "We are entering into a very fragile time, my dear. Those we love may have to be sacrificed to maintain our ways."

Her words filled me with rage and hot tears streamed down my cheeks. But she spoke again before I could once again plead my case.

"Even if I wanted to help you and your beloved, I have no way of doing so. I believe you will need a spell that comes from Teremedi found in the Cipher of Stellara. This anthology is protected in the lowest vault of this sanctuary. Only those it deems worthy may access it. I am unable to descend into that part of the library, and I assure you I am not worthy. Rest as long as you like before your journey home, but I will not be speaking to you again should your elders question if you came through my halls."

She left then, leaving the entrance unguarded. I thanked the Goddesses for sending me Isolde's assistance and rushed through the grand temple to the staircase hidden deep within its corners. I moved swiftly into the darkness of the library's lowest levels. Only a few torches lit the way, but I wouldn't have needed them. The force that pulled me forward did so with divine strength, and I knew exactly where I was going and that I would be protected on my way.

The stale air buzzed with lethal magic, and my own vibrated in reply. Perhaps I should have hesitated or considered the consequences of my impulses. Instead, with my eyes settled on the pearlescent leather-bound book, I stepped into the archway allowing the spell to burn my skin on its way to judge my soul. I refused to scream as I walked through the invisible fire but released a primal cry when I emerged within arm's reach of the sacred book.

There was no time to reflect on that moment and what it meant to be deemed worthy to wield the most powerful of magic. I grasped the book and hugged it to my chest as I ran for an eternity. I didn't stop until I reached my mare and begged the Goddesses to allow her to get us home quickly and safely.

At the edge of the forest where the sun shone bright, I collapsed to my knees and cried tears of relief.

Tears of joy.

Tears of frustration.

Tears of fear.

I finally had the key to saving Bethany.

CHAPTER 40
DIARY OF SARA CORTESE

The Valley of Asters, mid fall circa 1620

Bethany is the mortal host to an Orostori Demon. We have not seen their kind in several hundred years, as they can only move freely in the middle realm and require a mortal body should they wish to walk among us. I can only presume this generation of Orostori Demons are inclined to have more power and have been on this side of the rift feeding on the lifeforce of mortals.

From dawn to dusk I make preparations for the expulsion spell that must take place at the height of the full moon. During that time, the Orostori Demon grew stronger and more resistant to my spells to build Bethany's strength or limit its control. Where she would once have a day or so of peace, she may only have a few hours.

Bethany's body grows frail, but her words are daggers thrown at my heart. Though I know it isn't Bethany speaking these hurtful lies, every day it becomes harder to care for her while the demon uses her voice to spout its vitriol. It manipulates Bethany's memories to create fabrications that trigger my guilt and worries. My heart is able to separate the two, but my mind has begun to see them as one. Sometimes, I fear her and that causes me more grief than hating her.

Orostori Demon

An often-malevolent spirit with moderate power that moves freely within Teremedi.

Has <u>no corporal body</u> of its own and cannot survive long in Tereprima without a mortal host.

<u>P</u><small>ARASITIC</small> >>> Feeds on the spirit and life force of its host. Prefers sadness, anger, and fear. Will control its host's thoughts to create the environment on which it feeds.

It can control a host's thoughts, words, and actions. I<small>TS FINAL FORM WILL ALLOW IT TO CONTROL A HOST WITHOUT KILLING THEM.</small>

When the host is weak, the demon will seek out another host and force a transfer.

<u>D<small>EATH OF THE PREVIOUS HOST IS LIKELY</small>.</u>

Demon is weak after its transfer but grows stronger with each host.

Should the host perish before another suitable host is found >>> <u>Orostori will invade the nearest mortal.</u>

Without a host, it will return to Teremedi. It is believed that the <u>Orostori retains its host's memories</u>.

Expulsion spell

A soulmate of the host MUST perform the spell. SOULMATE MAGIC REQUIRED TO EXPEL AND TRAP TO PREVENT REINFECTION.

Can be trapped in iron vessel made by Amora metalworker.

DESTRUCTION REQUIRES THE STRENGTH OF BONDED MAGIC BETWEEN HOST AND SPELLCASTER.

Risk

DEATH

Host and mage must have compatible magic

Chapter 41
Emma

Magic hummed in the air and vibrated through Emma's body like a familiar sentient being. The pearlescent white book remained in the satchel. After all this time, its protective spell continued to keep its secrets. Emma wasn't ready to find out if she was worthy of its power.

Sitting cross-legged on the hard lid of the antique trunk, Emma read Sara's diary for a third time. Sara's emotions were engraved in every word; each one floated from the page creating a picture so clear Emma could have lived every moment. Emma felt Sara's fear and her worry. Sara's anger and her heartbreak. Emma became consumed by Sara's unyielding determination to not let Bethany die without a fight.

Emma finally closed the book and held it close to her chest, wiping away her tears before they landed on the delicate leather. The existence of these books and this broken vessel meant that Sara saved Bethany. The spell saved Bethany's life and banished the Orostori Demon to the urn.

The urn and its protective box toppled off its ledge and cracked just enough to allow the demon to escape.

"I guess Sara didn't anticipate this shit getting tossed around during a sewer pipe replacement," Emma said to herself.

Emma knew that performing Sara's spell was the only way to save Liam, but she didn't have Sara's confidence or Sara's knowledge. Sara was allowed to practice magic freely and learn from those before her. She practiced openly without fear that she would be arrested and jailed.

It was clear to Emma now that she and Sara shared the same family tree. But Emma was living an entirely different existence. This wasn't a balm that cured a headache or an elixir that helped her focus. It was a very literal exorcism of a demon from a living person and banishing it to a canister.

Emma set down the book and stood up, suddenly aware of the tightness of the space. She gripped her hair at the roots. Claustrophobia and aggravation were building, and she released the pressure with a wail. Like Sara had done generations before her, Emma fell to her knees onto the muddy ground and sobbed.

When Emma emerged from the museum, the dark sky welcomed her with a blanket of stars. The comforting roll of the tide hitting the shore below eased her back from two emotional journeys. Leaving the golf cart behind, she walked through the darkness to Liam's apartment.

Bits of Liam surrounded her. He was in the early summer blooms and evergreen shrubs that lined the path and the young trees that filled in the spaces between. His magic wasn't weak. It was just unaccessed. It always tangled with hers when she and Liam were together, but now she felt it everywhere he'd been. It flowed through the roots and stems of the plants that he placed into the ground with care and intention. Even as he crumbled, the bits of nature he touched continued to thrive.

She sat at the picnic table in front of Liam's building and pulled out her phone.

Regan's alarmed voice came through on the second ring. "Are you okay? What's wrong?"

Emma heard Regan's frantic shuffling like she was getting ready to run out the door. "I'm safe, but I know what's going on with Liam. Can you come to his place? I don't want to talk about it over the phone."

"Fuck. Calling instead of texting and wanting to talk in person? I'll be right there."

Regan didn't wait for Emma to respond before hanging up, abruptly returning Emma to the quiet night.

Regan made the fifteen-minute drive to the museum in under ten, but Emma didn't have the energy to scold her friend for reckless driving.

Emma sank into Regan's open arms, encased in the warm, familiar magic that Regan radiated.

"You said you knew what happened to Liam. What's going on?"

Emma rehashed it all. From reading Nora's obituary to the spell book in her backpack. Regan crossed her arms tighter and tighter as Emma spoke. When she was done, she gave Regan a moment to process all that she heard, but the silence between them was a painful torture.

Regan began to pace, and Emma released a slow breath. Regan always paced when she was working out a problem and right now, Emma needed Regan's beautifully analytical mind. Regan would figure this out.

Regan stopped pacing and looked at the ground. "Every option sucks."

"There has to be something that sucks the least!" Emma's frantic voice rose several octaves.

"You have two options to get this demon out of Liam: You can isolate him and let him die."

"Regan!" Emma stared at her. Horrified not only at the suggestion, but the quickest of seconds in which Emma considered it. "Liam dying isn't an option!"

Regan grabbed Emma's shoulders and shook her. "Stop it! Listen to me."

Untethered from reality, Emma found a lifeline in Regan's firm grip and assertive tone.

"If Liam dies, the demon will jump into another body, or it will take what it knows to the middle realm. Or you can attempt this spell. If you attempt the spell, and you're successful, you'll trap or destroy the demon. If you attempt the spell and you fail, you'll both die, and the end result for the demon is the same."

"So there is a less shitty option," Emma said, her tone more harsh than she intended.

Regan loosened her grip on Emma's shoulders and a weak smile formed on her face. "I wouldn't call potentially losing my best friend the less shitty option, but yes. Since you and Liam are soulmates, you're the only one who can perform the spell. I can't let you do it without knowing all the options and the consequences."

Emma nodded and sighed heavily. "I'd do it for you."

"I know. And I'd do the same for you." Regan looked up at the sky. "Okay. The full moon is next Friday, so we have a week and a half to get everything we need."

"The audit is happening Wednesday," Emma added. "We have to get Liam through that without attracting attention. I think I have what I need to try that spell Sara used to give Bethany a boost of energy."

Regan nodded in agreement and offered to procure what Emma needed so she could focus on the audit. From her car, Regan retrieved a notebook and her camera.

"We need to keep discussions about this in person. Don't use your phone. We need to make copies of the spells and the ingredients so we can keep these books hidden."

In the dim lantern light, they took a picture of each page as insurance before copying it by hand, just as Sara had done before. As Emma's hand began to cramp, she thought of Sara and how much more effort this process must have taken before the invention of ballpoint pens. Sara had taken a risk copying these spells for those the book would consider unworthy of the knowledge inside.

Emma heard the cantor of an animal nearby. Belle stopped at Emma's feet and gave her an urgent whine.

"Listen to me," Regan said with enough force that compelled Emma to meet her deep evergreen eyes.

"We will save Liam, but you can't tell him about this spell. Tell him what's inside of him, but don't tell him how or what we know about how to get rid of it. Otherwise, it will jump the minute it's strong enough."

"Emma! What's going on?"

CHAPTER 42
LIAM

Emma and Regan sat next to each other at the picnic table outside his office. A lantern between them and pens flying across a page.

When Emma saw him, she stood up slowly.

You can't give her what she wants, but Regan can.

"Is that why Regan is here at 11:45 at night?"

"What was that, Liam?" Emma asked. Her voice was firm but cautious.

Regan's concerned gaze flicked between him and Emma while she gathered some books and shoved them into a ratty looking bag.

Liam didn't mean to ask the question out loud, but now he wanted the answer. "Why is Regan here at 11:45 at night?"

Belle followed Emma closely as she neared and took a protective stance between them. The floodlight beaming from the garage cast a shadow on one side of Emma's face. The illuminated side looked red and puffy like she'd been crying.

"She brought me a book she found in her family's library."

She's lying.

"But why now? Why in the middle of the night?"

"She's an astronomer, Liam. Over the summer, most of her workday happens at night."

Liam eyed Regan skeptically, and he recognized a flash of hurt that lasted only a blink. The logic was sound, but he had trouble believing Emma. These were his old lines. He'd lost count how many times he'd gotten caught snuggling up to someone else and spun a story that sounded just plausible enough to be true.

"Liam." Emma reached for his hand. "We know what's wrong with you."

He didn't reach back, but he didn't pull away when she tentatively knotted her fingers with his. He stood in a daze as she talked about magic and realms and demons. He didn't know if Emma was telling him the full story or just the highlights. Either way, it was too much. It was so foreign and surreal. And he wouldn't have believed her if the voice inside his head hadn't confirmed every word she said with maniacal glee.

"So this is why I've been feeling like shit? Because there's a demon inside me that wants to use my body to take over the world?"

"That's the gist of it," Regan answered. She hovered closer to Emma, the bag now gone from his sight.

"That's also why it's so hard for me to touch you," Emma said. "It's not just because your skin feels like ice. My magic senses danger, and it's trying to keep me safe."

Liam started to laugh. He barely survived his last major depressive episode, and it took nearly five years of medication, therapy, daily sunshine, and exercise to get to a functional level of mental illness.

"And what am I supposed to do? Recite positive affirmations? Write in a gratitude journal? Meditate for good vibes?"

"We'll figure it out. You just have to trust me for as long as you can."

He looked into Emma's tired, pleading eyes. Eyes that used to look at him with fire and lust, but now only showed deep sadness and worry. "I do trust you. I'll think happy thoughts for you. I'll hold on as long as I can."

Because I love you, he tried to scream.

But she'll never hear you say it.

CHAPTER 43

LIAM

Liam absentmindedly swirled his coffee cup while he reviewed the museum's financial records for the thousandth time.

A foul-smelling tonic mixed into his coffee subdued the Orostori Demon enough to give him a day or so of relative normalcy. The voice quieted and the headaches lightened. He felt less angry and depressed. It gave him the physical energy to be outside and move his body in ways that made him feel alive instead of so close to death.

She's doing this to you.
She wants you sick and weak so she can control you.
She's the real reason why you're feeling this way.

But as the demon grew in strength, the tonic became less potent. Emma said it just had to get him through Audit Day and that day had finally arrived. He didn't know what Emma had planned for him after this; sometimes, he wanted it to be death, but he knew she'd never willingly go that far.

He restructured the financial report to hide spending and income that might flag further review and now he sat at Blair's computer checking her work.

Blair was an amazing financial director.

Liam was better at creative accounting.

"This looks great," Liam said. "I'm sending copies to everyone's printer."

Blair was sitting in a soft leather chair across from her desk. One long leg was crossed over the other, her foot bouncing gently. "And you're sure this isn't illegal? Because illegal means different things depending on who you are."

Liam stood up and grabbed the stack of papers on the printer behind him. "The money is all accounted for, they just have to do a little more work to find it." Liam handed one copy to Blair and stuffed the other in a folder and tucked it under his arm. "The math is mathing and that's all they care about during these things."

Blair scanned the pages with discerning eyes. "I better be careful. Judy might promote you to financial director."

"I'd rather die than do this full time again." Liam smiled to compensate for the impulsive seriousness in his tone. "But after this audit, I'm happy to give a workshop on questionably legal financial practices."

You won't be alive that long.

Liam downed more of his coffee, hoping the liquid would quiet the voice just a little bit longer.

He left Blair's office and shuffled down the hall to Emma's. She was sitting at her desk, her eyes trained on her screen. She fiddled with the high neck of her flowy, long-sleeve blouse. Liam thought she looked like absolute perfection, but it was obvious that she was painfully uncomfortable.

"I like the low-cut shirts more too." He smiled and fell into the armchair near her desk.

Her mouth curled into a rare smile. "Modesty is always better with these guys, but I brought a change of clothes for after they leave."

Emma got up and pulled a thermos out of a nearby cabinet. She poured him a fresh cup of coffee and handed it to him with another vial of the demon-suppressing tonic.

She kissed the top of his head, and Liam leaned into her touch. He craved the feeling of her skin against his and the softness of her wet lips. Her avoidance fed the demon more than any words it could hurl at him.

She was physically close, but emotionally distant. He missed her. He missed her laugh and her snarky retorts.

Emma took on a new level of stoicism since finding out he'd become the owner of his very own parasitic demon from another dimension. She endured his hostility and his sleepless nights with a grace he didn't think he deserved. A light layer of makeup did little to hide the dark circles under her eyes. The silvery white strands in her hair seemed to multiply overnight; the waves hung limp without care.

He knew Emma was silently struggling, and it made his heart ache. She brushed off all his attempts to put the focus on her.

"How are you feeling about the visit today?" Emma asked.

Liam tried to smile. "Super. What could go wrong? Donnie Demon decides to out me somehow and I get thrown in some kind of hole never to be seen again? That wouldn't exactly work in its favor."

"Oh, Donnie is a good one. I like that better than Dominic."

Naming Liam's pet parasite was a new coping strategy that seemed to work for them both.

Emma slid back into her seat. "If Donnie is going to throw anyone under the bus, it's going to be me."

Liam sighed, knowing that she was right.

Liam stood outside Judy's office, anxiously flipping through the binder he'd prepared. A dull pain radiated from his temples, making it hard to focus on the numbers, but he did it anyway.

Judy arrived escorting two stern men and stopped to introduce Liam before stepping into her office.

"Liam Doran is our property manager, and he will be assisting me with the review."

The inspectors looked nearly identical in their dark blue suits, red ties, and similarly receding hairlines. Their pale white skin even seemed to wrinkle in the same way.

Judy sat behind her desk and motioned for the men to sit. The museum's best office chairs were reserved for the pair, but they ignored her and opted to stand.

Speaking directly to Liam, Inspector One began without so much as an introduction, launching right into the purpose of the day with a tone that implied he was ready to shut the entire place down just for the fun of it.

"It's very important that we ensure Belhaven's history highlights how the Commarasi have allowed the people of Ascaria to thrive," he said. "Necromancy did nothing but keep the common man from finding his own success. We don't want to confuse people. Doing so could threaten our country's very existence."

"Speaking of path," Judy interjected with a broad grin.

Liam was familiar with it. She used the same overly friendly smile when dealing with high-dollar donors she didn't like.

"It is such a beautiful morning that I would suggest you take a tour of the park that has been created using our most recent influx of funding."

Liam stood up straight and took a few steps further into the room.

She'll turn on you the moment they discover you used magic. She'll say you enchanted her and forced her to hire you, and everyone will believe her.

Trying desperately not to react, Liam pressed his eyes shut. When he opened them, Judy and both inspectors were staring at him.

"What do you think, Liam?" Judy asked with a bit of urgency in her voice.

The demon had stolen his attention at the same moment his boss asked for it. He turned on as much charm as he could muster. "I apologize, gentlemen. Over five years of working with loud equipment has impacted my hearing. I'd love to show you what my team and I have done on the grounds. I also have copies of the museum's financial reports if you'd like to review them while I show you around."

He opened his binder and pulled out two stapled copies of the reports. Inspector Two looked particularly irritated with Liam's recovery but held out his hand and motioned for Liam to pass the reports forward. Inspectors One and Two quickly leafed through the pages before shoving them into a portfolio they carried.

"Well, let's get on with it, Mr. Doran." Inspector One walked toward the door, Inspector Two following close at his heels.

Liam cleared his throat and motioned to a golf cart parked in front of the door. "Gentlemen, I can start by showing you some of the improvements we've made to the parking lot, and I'd be happy to answer any general questions on the way to the nature classroom at the far end of the property."

With a few grunts and several huffs, they climbed into the cart, which Liam took to mean they were happy with his suggestion. He drove them to a shady spot in the parking lot where he anticipated explaining the merits of expensive cobblestone pavers instead of asphalt, but Inspector Two wanted to get right down to business. Holding a copy of the financial report on his lap he began asking Liam to explain budget items in rapid fire succession.

The smug look on Inspector One's face slowly morphed into reluctant approval as Liam reviewed each line item in great detail using every bit of financial jargon he picked up over a decade. Their follow-up questions were met with equal knowledge. Their bullshit questions were torn apart using their own logic and the numbers in their hands. Liam was good with numbers, but it was his ability to back them up without a breath of hesitation that once made him rich.

When a silence finally fell between them, Liam put his hands back on the steering wheel and said, "Why don't I take you around now?"

You're too cocky.
They're surely onto you now.

Liam stifled a sigh. As exhilarating as it was to destroy Inspectors One and Two, doing so used more energy than he expected. His shoulders began to ache and the dull pain in his temples spread across his forehead.

Liam parked the golf cart near the nature classroom and prepared for another round of questioning. The old men seemed satisfied with his finances, but Liam could tell he had not earned their favor yet. "This is an outdoor classroom that I designed with the help of ecology professors at Willow Ridge University," he said as he led them into the space.

"What kinds of classes are taught here, Mr. Doran?" Inspector One eyed some young shrubs that had started to bloom. Though it was early in their lifecycle, it wasn't entirely uncommon.

"The space only recently became available, so we've had some kids' nature classes and backyard gardening classes for adults." Liam flashed him a smile and Inspector One turned around to take a closer look at some of the other plants surrounding the space.

"You're Joe Doran's oldest?" Inspector One asked casually.

For the briefest of moments, Liam considered lying, but it wouldn't do anyone any good. This is why Judy had him leading this tour alone and why he'd be by her side the rest of the visit.

"Second oldest, sir."

"Right. The one that worked for Phalax Capital Management."

Liam nodded but remained quiet. They had enough information on him. He didn't need to do them any favors by filling in the blanks.

After a few beats, Inspector One said, "How did Joe Doran's second-oldest son go from a partner-track position with Phalax Capital Management to museum caretaker?"

They know what you are.

Liam didn't need his demon friend to spell it out. He heard the subtext.

"My dad always taught us that you can make a real impact when you work from the inside." Liam knew that Inspector One would take that in a way that would fit his agenda.

Inspector One nodded his head and wrote something down in his portfolio and snapped it shut as Inspector Two walked up beside him. They exchanged a look, but Liam couldn't read it.

"The earthquake that happened on April 14. There was an excavation going on, correct?" Inspector Two asked.

Liam sucked in a breath. "Yes, sir. Some sewer pipes were being replaced."

"We'd like to see that," Inspector One said.

They know there is magic in the ground. They'll burn it down with Emma inside and salt the earth as a reminder of what you did.

"Well?" Inspector Two urged when Liam didn't answer.

"Sure. I can show you that area."

They rode in silence to the excavation site, which now showed little sign that a major earthquake had threatened to destroy the entire property. Plenty of scientists came around to study the area, but they all had the same inconclusive results.

"I've included the pipe replacement project in the financial records, but Director Baudin would be the best source for more detailed information," said Liam as they climbed out of the golf cart. "All the planning and funding for it was approved before I came on board."

"You do manage the property," said Inspector One. "Because you are the property manager, aren't you?"

Liam clenched his jaw. "I am. And I'll answer any questions you have to the best of my ability."

Inspector One walked off, leaving Inspector Two with Liam. "So, what was going on when the earthquake began?"

Liam's chest tightened. "We had contracted a crew to replace some old sewer pipes at the same time other excavation work was being done around the property."

Inspector Two jotted down some notes on a blank page of his portfolio. "I'd like you to be more specific."

Liam's head started to throb. "The excavation team was digging in this area and stopped when the earthquake began."

"Hmm." Inspector Two added more notes to the page. "Did they hit anything unusual leading up to the earthquake?"

Liam clenched his fists. "I wasn't there when it happened. I wasn't required to physically oversee the excavation, so I went into the museum to use the bathroom and ask our social media manager if she wanted to take pictures of the site. I was in her office when the earthquake began."

"And your social media manager is?"

"Emma DiMarco."

"Right. Miss DiMarco." More notes. "Do you spend a lot of time with Miss DiMarco? You weren't listed as one of her known associates on her most recent survey."

"I don't do serious relationships anymore because the person I'm with is targeted."

Emma's words rang through Liam's ears. He'd always believed her, but he was unprepared to experience it in real time.

"We work together on a number of projects that promote the renovation and the new facilities as they are available."

"Do you work together outside of work?"

Tell them all about the magic she does for you. Tell them about her hidden spell books and the medication she gives her friends.

Anger flooded Liam's body. His chest burned, and his hands began to sweat. He fought the demon's compulsion to confess it all.

"We see each other outside of work," he choked out. "It is a small island."

"Are you aware that a member of the crew died shortly after the earthquake?"

"Yes. Sadly, I am."

Inspector Two flipped a few pages in his portfolio. "Did Miss DiMarco have any contact with the excavation crew?"

"No. I was the only one that had contact with the crew before and directly after the earthquake." Liam shifted on his feet attempting to diffuse the pulsing energy that flowed through his limbs. He needed this line of questioning to end so he could get back to his office and punch a hole in a wall, throw something heavy at a window, or anything else that would satisfy the desire to snap the man's neck.

Inspector One walked up and only then did Liam realize he had no idea where the man had been snooping. He hoped now that the pair was reunited he could finally be done with the tour.

"Why don't I show you the way back inside? I'm sure Director Baudin is ready to show you the indoor exhibits."

They shared another nondescript look, and Liam found the silence unnerving.

He led them back to Judy's office and excused himself to go to the bathroom where he locked himself in a stall. He put his head in his cold hands, hoping the chill would ease the sharp pain that had returned to his head. He felt the energy draining from his body. He reached into his pocket and pulled out the vial. The liquid landed on his tongue and sizzled without his coffee to soften the blow.

His day was so far from over.

CHAPTER 44
EMMA

The inspectors exited through the museum's glass doors sometime after six. Once they were out of view, Emma slid down the wall she was leaning against and tucked her knees into her chest. The grueling review zapped every bit of her reserve energy, leaving her an empty shell that needed to be refilled with copious amounts of wine, ice cream, and sex. She'd be satisfied with any two out of the three.

She wasn't sure how long she'd been sitting there when Judy threatened to throw her out. "Go check on Liam," Judy said. "He barely made it through that last review."

Emma sucked in a breath and exhaled it slowly. One crisis was over. One more left to go.

"But before you do," Judy began.

Too tired to accurately read Judy's energy or body language, Emma braced herself for the worst.

"Emma, I don't want you to give me any details. I have an entire team to keep safe, and I can't do that if I know too much. But I do want you to answer truthfully because I can't keep you safe if you lie to me." Judy's voice was quiet, but she spoke clearly and slowly, drawing Emma's attention to every word. "Are you sure you're the only one who can help L iam?"

Emma kept the circle small, but those little circles of knowledge often had circles of their own. Where Judy got her information, Emma couldn't be sure. "Yes. I'm positive."

"If you attempt this, you could die."

"But if I don't, he definitely will."

Judy enveloped Emma in a hug. A sigh escaped her with the pressure from Judy's embrace. Judy often used her tall stature to command a room the moment she entered. But Emma also knew the warmth in those features. Judy curled over her like a protective shell, wrapping her long arms around Emma and holding firm while Emma fought back the tide of her emotions.

"Bring that man back to us. He's too beautiful to die."

"I know, right?" Emma shook with laughter that allowed her to feel the glorious effects of a surge of oxytocin and serotonin. There had been so little laughter lately and somehow, Judy knew that Emma needed that more than any words of encouragement.

Emma loosened her grip, and Judy stepped back. She gave Emma a gentle smile and walked back to her office.

The crows that blanketed the trees surrounding Liam's building should have set Emma on edge. But it was seeing Belle standing guard at the front door that filled her with dread. Even when Liam was at his worst, Belle rarely left his side.

"Where is he, Belle?"

Emma followed the retriever into the building and up the stairs. Belle whined and Emma cringed. The magic that flowed through her became a taut resistance band trying to pull Emma away. Emma worked to summon it to her body's depths.

By the time Sara did the spell to save Bethany, the demon had full control of Bethany's thoughts and her voice.

Bethany's body was too weak to manipulate, but the demon did plenty of damage to Sara anyway. Emma gripped the knob of Liam's apartment door and steeled herself for the worst.

The curtains were drawn shut, blocking out the early evening sun. The air conditioner pumped cold air into the small space, sending a chill down Emma's neck. She found Liam sprawled across his bed.

"Em?"

She forced herself to cross the room and take his frozen hand. "Hey. How are you doing?"

He ignored her question and with a raspy voice asked one of his own. "How did the rest of the audit go? Did we get caught?"

"I don't think so."

Liam let out a weak chuckle. "That's too bad. The anger from forcing you two apart could have fed me for months."

Emma released Liam's hand, and it fell to the side of the bed like dead weight. She backed away.

It wasn't Liam, but it had his face and his voice, though neither were quite right. Emma expected that once the Orostori Demon grew strong enough to control Liam's body, he'd be nothing but a frail skeleton wrapped in his skin. Liam still had quite a bit of muscle mass, but his face lost its vibrance, and his hair had thinned and grayed.

"I was going to use your body next," Liam's mouth rasped. "Your magic is so much stronger, and you have so much more anger. But I'd rather use his hands to kill you. It'll be one of the last things he remembers before he dies."

Emma backed up against the wall but shook off her shock and fear to make a big show of rolling her eyes. "What do you even expect to accomplish here? It's not the same world. And you suck a person dry before you even have the opportunity to do anything worthwhile with your new body."

It laughed weakly.

"Though it is a process that requires patience, I grow stronger with every soul I consume. And when I have that strength, I will no longer need to feed off my host. We will live as one. Nothing has changed, my dear. Men still desire power and those are the men that I seek."

CHAPTER 45
EMMA

Emma stepped onto her porch, letting the storm door slam shut behind her. She was pissed at the weather for having the audacity to be gorgeous while the rest of her life felt so shitty. It reminded her that while she prepared to perform a dangerous ritual using magic she was not qualified to wield, the rest of Belhaven would be moving about their day in presumably more normal ways.

She sat down in her rocker and pulled a cigarette out of a fresh pack. She lit one and took a long drag, feeling the heat of the smoke fill her lungs. She looked up when she heard the door across the street loudly squeal open. Regan pursed her lips when she made eye contact with Emma taking another drag.

"You're fucking smoking again?" Regan scolded as she crossed the street with an oversized plastic tub.

"I'm fucking stressed!" Emma ashed the cigarette in a mug of water.

Regan put the tub on the floor in front of Emma. "It's still disgusting."

Emma looked away. "I probably won't be around long enough for it to turn into a habit. Again."

She heard Regan sigh heavily but couldn't bring herself to look up. Smoking was Emma's longest-running self-destructive behavior, and it only reared its ugly head when she was about to crash and burn.

"This is the last of it." Regan tapped the bin with her foot for emphasis. "Everything on the list in Sara's spell book. I was able to have the vessel repaired, but I don't think you'll need it."

Using both hands, Emma picked up the small iron urn, no larger than the water bottle she carried with her everywhere. The iron latches were fixed and the container closed and locked with ease.

Emma didn't know any metalworkers in Belhaven but that didn't mean they weren't around. "Who worked on this?"

"I know a guy."

Emma knew that was all she'd get out of Regan. She put the urn back in the bin. Emma wanted to light another cigarette. But she wouldn't. She couldn't handle the additional look of worry in Regan's eyes.

"Thank you," Emma said quietly.

Regan gave her a gentle smile. "I'm going to put this in your car and then make us some tea. Stop smoking."

"There better be whiskey in it."

Regan didn't put whiskey in their tea, and Emma was undecided if that made Regan a good or bad friend. They each held up their cup, offered each other a quick blessing of good health, and took a sip. It was a ritual as old as their friendship.

From Emma's front porch, they'd watch the sun set behind Regan's house and count the bats as their little silhouettes fluttered across the pink and purple sky. Sometimes they spent the evening in silence, just being in the company of each other while they watched the movement of nature. Other times, their vibrant voices filled the street, their laughter carried on the wind that rushed off the water.

"What happened to Bethany and Sara?" Regan asked, still staring ahead at the sinking sun. "Aside from the diaries and vessel being left in the catacombs, I mean."

"I'm not sure." Luna jumped into Emma's lap, and she scratched her behind the ears until she curled into a tight ball. "There are more entries, but I couldn't bring myself to read them. We know she saved Bethany from the demon, and if I'm going to die tonight, that's the only knowledge I want floating around in my head."

Regan rolled her eyes. She was clearly irritated and over Emma's shit.

"I'm not trying to dismiss the very real danger that comes with the magic you're going to be doing tonight, but for fuck's sake, Emma."

Regan sat up and pointed at Belle lying underneath the table between them. "His dog. His gift sent from the Goddesses themselves is here with you. And connected to you just as she's connected to him. That can't happen if you two aren't bound souls."

Emma opened her mouth to protest but shut it when she couldn't find the right words.

She sighed and stared into the amber liquid in her hand. By the time she was in her mid-thirties, she had made so much progress finding herself and her self-worth, but she realized she still had so much work to do.

"You know I need to hear it. Even with everything I've seen and felt and witnessed, I just won't be able to believe it until I hear it."

Regan took a sip of her tea. "I love you. I'm so fucking annoyed with you right now, but I love you."

Emma smiled. "I love you too."

They enjoyed their tea for a bit longer, but the sun was getting low, and Emma knew it was time.

"I will be at Liam's by 2:45 am, unless I hear otherwise." Regan picked up Luna and cradled her like an infant.

Emma nodded and scratched Luna behind the ears. She was leaving her feline guide behind, and while Emma knew it's what was needed, she was sad nonetheless.

"I'll see you both tomorrow morning," Emma said with as much conviction as she could muster.

"Yes." Regan kissed Emma's cheek and smiled. "You will."

CHAPTER 46
EMMA

Emma pulled up to the back entrance of the museum. In the dwindling daylight, the crows stood guard on the stone wall that traced the perimeter of the property. Emma drove forward, seeing more perched in the trees along the road. They followed her as she drove slowly along the dirt and gravel path. A few flew ahead, landing on low limbs waiting for her to pass. Her avian escorts took her to Liam's building, but didn't leave once she arrived. They perched in the nearby trees.

However, the crows weren't watching Emma. Their black marble eyes were trained on the windows of Liam's apartment. The sight rang through her like an alarm bell. She decided to keep her precious materials in her car until she knew they could be handled safely.

Taking only what she needed for the first part of her plan, she and Belle slowly and quietly made their way to Liam's door. It was much like she left it a few days before. All the curtains in Liam's apartment had been drawn shut, encasing the space in shadow. Belle stepped ahead of Emma and growled. Emma's eyes quickly adjusted to the darkness, and she quietly stepped into the living room, Belle remaining close to her side.

"She's finally returned!" A harsh voice called out from Liam's bedroom. Belle growled loudly. "You left me here all alone."

"Well, you're not as fun as you used to be," Emma replied, opening the nearest window. The floodlights cast a few beams into the room.

Belle's hackles were up, and her lips receded to show her sharp teeth. Belle's eyes were trained on the bedroom doorway where Liam's body stood, gripping the frame for support.

His eyes were so dark. So black. So void of life.

"You moved on quickly. He always thought you would. Once he knew he was going to die."

"Liam isn't jealous of Regan, so if you're looking to play mind games, you'll have to pick something else." Emma crossed the room and opened another window, allowing just a bit more light into the space.

"No, I suppose he didn't have a reason to be because she wants someone of equal brilliance. She was never a threat because you were never a serious option."

Liam's body took a few steps forward but remained in the darkest corners of the room. Belle stayed close and continued to growl and bear her teeth.

Bethany had been much weaker. Sara wrote of a struggle to bind her hands and feet, but Bethany was already confined to her bed. Emma didn't anticipate Liam being strong enough to move around. She needed to sedate him and expected that he'd be easier to subdue.

"I can see it all, you know. Liam's memories. All the times he was disgusted by your clutter and annoyed with your forgetfulness. He thought you were so fragile, unable to make the easiest of decisions without dissolving into tears. Pathetic."

Emma froze, momentarily stunned by the verbal blow. Weeks of him poking at the fragments of her insecurities left her more damaged than she realized. He started to speak again, his voice harsh and scratchy, but Emma didn't hear the words. She needed to maintain control.

"Ugh, yes. I get it. Just shut the fuck up already." Emma started to move closer to him, her hand wrapped around a syringe in her vest pocket. Belle slinked forward, creeping low and ready to strike.

Liam's body lunged at her with impossible swiftness. Emma barely dodged his outstretched arms. He stumbled forward but kept his balance and quickly recovered. Emma shoved the coffee table in between them and cursed when he easily stepped up and over it.

He taunted her. "I told you I'd get stronger, Emma."

She backed up into the fireplace and reached for a poker. He stalked towards her. She threw a piece of firewood at him, giving her a chance to get away from the wall and back into the open living room.

"He can see everything, Emma. He can feel it all too. He sees how terrified you are. Even if you succeed, he knows you'll always be afraid of him."

She swung the poker at his legs. He stepped just out of reach but forced her into a corner. She reeled the weapon with all her might. He caught the poker in his hand, just missing its pointed hook. He tore it from her grasp and raised it over his head.

With a snarl of terrifying aggression, Belle launched herself at Liam's body, catching his lifted arm in her razor-sharp teeth and strong jaw. He dropped the poker, and Emma kicked it across the room. Belle brought him down to the ground, twisting his arm to keep herself out of reach.

Emma jammed the syringe into Liam's exposed thigh, sending a cocktail of drugs into his system. Emma crawled to the other side of the room. She fought back tears as he thrashed against Belle's grasp until he passed out.

Belle let go, leaving him with several fresh puncture wounds. She padded over to Emma and licked the sweat from her brow. Emma tried to wipe the blood from Belle's muzzle, but the crimson stain remained on her bright white fur.

Emma hadn't prepared for a physical fight, but she used the rush of adrenaline to her advantage, pushing the furniture out of the way and clearing a path to the nearest wall. She pulled Liam across the room until his hands could reach the solid metal radiator. The blood oozing from Liam's arm had slowed. It was thick like motor oil and smelled like rotting meat.

"If you fucking die of a dog bite after I save you from a fucking demon, I will be so fucking pissed."

Emma poured rubbing alcohol on the wounds and watched Liam's face for a reaction, relaxing just a bit when he remained unconscious. She cleaned his injuries quickly, then wrapped his arm in a heavy layer of clean gauze, not caring that she left little for herself should she need it later. Then she secured Liam's wrists to the radiator.

"We're usually having a lot more fun when we do this," she muttered.

She knotted the rope at his ankles before rolling him onto his side. Emma checked his pulse and his breathing, and both were a bit too weak for her liking. As far as she knew, Liam didn't have to be conscious for the ritual, just alive.

She cupped the side of his face and ran her thumb across his forehead. His skin was clammy but cold as ice. She brushed his shaggy hair out of his face, gently combing through the new gray around his hairline.

The fuel that kept her going no longer pumped through her and fatigue was setting in. She pushed through to gather her supplies for the rest of the night ahead.

The memory of Liam lunging at her flashed in her mind, and her chest grew tight. "We're going to need so much therapy."

She choked out a heavy sob, but she couldn't succumb to her sadness. She checked her watch and peeked out the window. The sun had dipped well below the horizon and the moon started to make its climb.

It was time.

CHAPTER 47
EMMA

Emma stared at the Cipher of Stellara sitting on Liam's kitchen table. It remained in its case and beckoned to her, offering to share its knowledge. Sara would have copied the spell accurately, but Emma knew it wouldn't work unless the book first judged her worthy. To be judged worthy, she first had to believe it.

She slid the book out of its protective case, but her hand floated just over its cover, unable to let it rest.

Belle urgently nudged Emma's other hand with her wet nose. Emma laughed wearily as tears threatened to fall. "Be the person your pet thinks you are, right Belle?"

Emma dropped her hand on the pearlescent cover. It burned her skin with an invisible flame that sank through the layers of fat and muscle down into the marrow of her bones.

Emma gritted her teeth and refused to scream.

It stopped as abruptly as it started.

"Okay, then," Emma said through heaving breaths. "Let's fucking go."

Turning Liam's kitchen into a laboratory, Emma measured and mixed and chanted long-forgotten ancient words. She may have been physically alone, but the room was filled with the spirits of Amora that came before her. Drawn there by Emma's magic, their presence vibrated through the space. Carefully, she poured the thick, sweet-smelling liquid into a large glass vial. She sealed it with a cork and set it on the kitchen table next to a black tourmaline bowl and a fur-lined leather scabbard.

In the candlelit darkness of Liam's bathroom, Emma fished through a small toiletry bag for the ointment she needed for the cleansing ritual. She used a cotton washcloth to soak her skin with herb-infused water that bathed in the light of the last full moon. Every brush of the cloth released a familiar earthy aroma.

Both Sara's diary and the Cipher of Stellara were silent on what a spellcaster wears when attempting to eject a parasitic demon from the love of their life. She hoped her most comfortable workout clothes would be sufficient.

Emma moved through the darkness, lighting candles around the edges of the living room. She would have been more worried had the building not been made of rock and stone.

Liam started to mumble and twitch. He'd wake up soon. Belle sat by his side, her body tense as she watched for danger.

"You feel him in there, don't you?" Emma said. Belle's ears only flickered in response. "I feel him too. Faintly. But I do."

The dog sighed heavily, and Emma felt Belle's sadness. Low moans from Liam kicked Emma back to work. Pulling the cork out with her teeth, a third of the vial's contents was poured into the heavy, black bowl.

She pulled a long dagger from the scabbard. Her grandmother died before she could explain its importance or its use. She knew little about it other than it being in her family for generations. When the spell called for a blade adorned with quartz, she suspected this one would do.

The stones embedded in the hilt glinted in the firelight. In a memory so clear it could have been own, she saw Sara using the blade when she was forced to perform this spell.

Emma spilled some alcohol on the blade and rubbed it down with a clean gauze pad. She also refused to die of an infection. The disinfectant was barely dry when she sliced open her middle finger, allowing a steady trickle of blood to escape.

Emma sucked in a breath and movement caught her eye. Belle was standing up now. Alert. And watching Emma closely. She dipped her bloodied finger into the bowl and the tepid substance came alive with heat. It bubbled but didn't burn. It smoked but didn't scald.

She took the bowl and walked to the north wall. Removing her finger, she used the heavy liquid to painstakingly draw three symbols. Fearing she would forget each stroke, she used a permanent marker to draw them on her opposite forearm. But she didn't need the guide. The symbols came to her with vivid clarity. The movement of each stroke was woven into her muscle memory.

When she was finished, she crossed the room to repeat the process on the south wall. She'd almost finished the eastern wall when Belle began a low growl. She continued her work with one ear listening to Liam shift and struggle until he rolled onto his back, muttering obscenities in a variety of languages.

"How was your nap, sunshine?" Emma called over her shoulder. "Sedatives have come a long way in 400 years. I didn't even use magic for that."

It laughed Liam's laugh, and Emma's heart fell into the pit of her stomach. She used her sadness and her anger to push her throbbing hand to finish the final stroke.

"It won't work." It sighed. "Your magic isn't strong enough. Sara was more powerful than she realized and only the strongest Amora can perform these spells. Your kind has become so weak without your magic."

By the time she stood in front of the final wall, blood from her swollen finger trailed down her hand, leaving crusty red rivers on her forearm. Nonetheless, she dipped it into the bowl, the liquid thickened with her blood. The metallic odor overpowered all others.

"You're right. We have become weak." Emma scraped her battered finger along the stone that made up the western wall. "But you know Liam and I have enough power to trap you in that urn."

"Only if he believes it. And he doesn't." It laughed. Hoarse and cold.

Sara failed to mention that part.

Pulsing with rage, Emma finished the final strokes. Nothing motivated her more than the pettiness of proving someone—or some *thing*—wrong.

"Well, I'm sure you had a great time living it up in the twenty-first century, but we have enough issues going on right now so you're going to need to go."

"This is just the beginning for me. Do you truly believe I'm the only one of my kind here?"

Emma didn't answer. She stomped to the kitchen table where the urn sat next to a bowl of infused water. Lifting the heavy urn with her uninjured hand, she scrawled three more bloody marks on its side. When she finished, she dunked her hand into the bowl of water, watching the purple mixture swirl with her fresh blood.

"Many of us were already walking among humans when the Commarasi began their rise to power."

It was trying to get into her head. Distract her from finishing the ritual before the moon reached its highest point. After that, the opportunity would be lost until the next full moon. Liam didn't have that kind of time. Liam and Emma would walk away from this building of their own volition or not at all.

"Imagine the power they hold if they've survived this long." The excitement in its voice made Emma seethe. How many more lives have the Orostori taken since Sara banished this one to its container?

Emma crudely wrapped her finger in clean gauze and medical tape. "And the Orostori as a whole are just as weak as the remaining Amora." She slammed the tape roll against the table. She picked up everything she needed for the worst part of the ritual and placed it on the nearby coffee table.

She stood over Liam.

Liam's body.

And stared into the black pools of Liam's eyes. "The rift is closed."

"Is it?"

The question did exactly as intended. It pulled Emma away from the task at hand, and her mind began to spin. It distracted her only for a moment, but it was long enough for Liam to shift his bound legs.

He kicked her legs out from under her. She slammed her head on the corner of the coffee table. Her vision turned hazy. Her head pounded. The dizziness made it nearly impossible to find her bearings in the darkness.

Emma crawled across the room and leaned against the wall. She needed to breathe. Belle moved between Liam and Emma, snarling as Emma's protector.

"Backing off so soon?" It taunted her in Liam's perfect voice. "I knew you were an easy quitter, Emma, but I figured saving your soul mate would put more fight in you."

It carried on, calling her worthless and stupid for ever thinking she could take on a mystical being. It repeated every vulnerable admission she ever shared with Liam and used it against her. Emma squeezed her eyes shut and covered her ears so she couldn't hear the words that echoed through the room. Words that she knew were lies being used to hurt her. To weaken her. To paralyze her and stall until it was too late.

The seconds passed like hours. Emma knew she had to keep going, but her head pounded. A gust of air rushed by her. She opened her eyes. A hazy silhouette glided across the room and into the bathroom. It returned a moment later, swooping over Emma. A heavy object landed in her lap. Picking it up forced her to uncover her ears, but Liam's heckling now sounded like whispers on the wind.

Sara's necklace. A gift of love from Bethany. A sign of a love so strong, they banished a demon into a cage for 400 years and lived long enough to tell Emma how to do the same.

She slid the necklace over her head. In sync with her heartbeat, the stone pulsed against her skin. Emma's magic reached out and found Sara's and Bethany's magic radiating from the stone. They fused together, sending heavy waves from her chest to every cell in her body. The pounding in her head ceased, and there was only this new rush of magic.

Tucking the necklace under her top, Emma stood up and scanned the room for the items that had fallen off the table.

Liam's body stopped laughing. It stopped speaking. Emma felt its eyes on her as she stalked around the room.

"Em?" It was Liam's voice now, but Emma knew not to trust it.

She pushed the table further away and on top, she dropped the iron urn with a heavy thud.

"Em, don't do this. You'll kill me."

She opened the vial and refilled the heavy tourmaline bowl. She slipped the corked bottle into her pocket. She dropped onto her knees, straddling Liam's hips, his skin cold between her thighs. Without a word, she used the blade to slice open another finger and dipped it into the still-bubbling liquid. Its heat filled her body, renewing her strength.

"Emma, Deryn will be heartbroken if you kill me. She's already lost so much. You're going to take me away from her too." He continued to plead with her, but she remained silent and focused while she drew marks on his chest.

"Shhhh," Emma hushed. She set aside the bowl and picked up the knife.

Despite his blackened eyes, Liam's face only showed fear and desperation. Emma sucked in a breath as she dragged the edge of the blade along her left wrist. She dropped the knife beside her and pulled the vial out of her pocket.

"Think of the power we could have together. I clearly underestimated your strength. With your magic and my army of Orostori, we could take down the Commarasi together."

Blood streaming down her arm, she stared directly into Liam's eyes, searching for the bits of him that were left and sending out mycelium threads of her magic.

"Liam, I know you're in there somewhere. For this to work, you have to believe our souls are bonded by magic. And if you don't, we'll both die."

She poured the rest of the vial over her cut wrist, the liquid mixing with her blood. "So, no pressure."

Emma forced her wrist into Liam's mouth, pressing down on his jaw and smothering a scream. The bloody mixture coated his lips and tongue. He thrashed to throw her off, but Emma squeezed her thighs against his chest. His teeth sank down into the tender flesh of her wrist. Emma screamed in pain and held his nose until he released her.

Gusts of icy air circled them like they were in the eye of a hurricane. The candles grew brighter, illuminating the room in a daylight glow.

"Belle, get outta here!"

Belle ran for the open door and slid out just as it slammed shut. The icy wind grew stronger, and Liam stopped fighting. Emma eased up and removed her wrist from Liam's mouth. His body was now limp and caked in blood.

She couldn't see the Orostori Demon, but she felt the wrath and sadness in the air. The demon swirled around the room, its screams like the brakes of a freight train. Emma curled over Liam, shielding his chest and head with her body. The walls shook with the demon's deafening wails. A blast of blinding light erupted around them, blowing out the widows, cracking the doors off their hinges, and extinguishing the candles.

Within seconds, everything was still once again.

The room smelled of iron and embers.

Emma cut the ropes to free Liam's wrists, then laid her ear on his chest. His skin was gloriously warm against her cheek. She held her breath so she could feel his own. Tears collected in the corners of her eyes when she saw the slight rise and fall of his chest and felt the quiet beating of his heart.

"Emma."

She lifted her head at the sound of Liam's voice—his real voice—whispering her name.

In the dim glow of the moonlight, she saw the icy calcite blue of his eyes.

Chapter 48
Liam

Liam's body hurt, but it was a blissfully human pain. His shoulders ached from being bound over his head, and his wrists burned from fighting against the rope. His mind was foggy, but his thoughts were quiet.

He brushed Emma's hair away from her face, renewing the flowery scent that soaked her skin. He pressed his lips to her forehead and instead of flinching, she sighed deeply into him. Silent tears collected in the corner of her eyes and dripped onto his chest.

He used a gentle finger to lift her chin until her glassy eyes met his. "I love you," he whispered.

His lips found hers for a tender kiss before she could reply. He needed this connection with Emma like he needed air to breathe and water to drink. He wanted to kiss her for hours to make up for all the times she recoiled from his touch.

He pulled away only to wipe more tears from her face.

"I love you too." She smiled, but her voice was hoarse and tired. It was time to take care of her.

He couldn't carry her gingerly to a romantic four-poster bed. Not with a dog bite that burned through his forearm. But he could help Emma onto the couch and lay her head on a dusty pillow. He shuffled to the kitchen, finding the first aid supplies Emma used to bandage his arm. He would have gladly been mauled by his dog if it meant protecting Emma.

He called for Belle while he filled a bowl with clean water. She appeared by his side moments later, her excitement looking no different than if he came home after a long day at work. He kneeled and rested his head on hers, feeling her soft fur against his skin.

"You did it, BeeBee," Liam whispered. "You protected her when I couldn't. I love you. Thank you."

With the first aid supplies in hand, he returned to Emma on the couch. Liam silently cleaned her wounds. The demon used his voice to cause her pain and not saying anything for a bit felt like the right thing to do.

An alarm sounded from Emma's phone. Liam finished wrapping her wrist in a clean bandage and headed toward the noise. He found her phone in the bathroom.

"Too late," he read the alarm out loud, then turned off the sound.

The demon knew Emma's window to perform the spell was closing. It vowed not to make the same mistake again. In those final moments, Liam watched helplessly as the demon stalled for time.

Emma saved him with ten minutes to spare.

CHAPTER 49
DIARY OF SARA CORTESE

Belhaven Island, late fall circa 1621

In the span of a life lived, one year is hardly remarkable. But in the year that Bethany and I have shared together, so much has happened. So much has changed.

After banishing the Orostori Demon to a temporary vessel, and Bethany recovering to good health, I sent word to Stephen so that he could share the news with our children. Fearing for our safety, I requested that he only reach out should they be in danger. Though I desired nothing more than to hear from them, their constant silence meant all was well.

Our status as dangerous fugitives made for a difficult year. Without the kinship of our community, Bethany and I had only each other on which to rely for our survival each day. We were not meant for this sort of solitary life.

The winter brought with it the most horrific of storms. Our cabin barely survived the wind and heavy snow. We rebuilt the structure of our home and our partnership with the warmth of the spring. Our passion grew with the heat of the summer.

As we prepared for another harsh winter in the Valley of Asters, we were blessed with a visit from Piper Dawson.

Many on the Isle of Belhaven perished during the harsh winter months, including several of our elders. After their deaths, the truth of the Orostori Demon came to light along with the elders' desire to manipulate their people to remain in power.

New village leaders were chosen. These leaders are the same allies that helped Bethany and I escape. Once trust was restored, they sent Piper to bring us home.

The village looked different but felt the same. The bonds among the people were stronger after having gone through such a harrowing ordeal. The winter storms had taught them well and when they rebuilt, they heeded their lessons.

Bethany was welcomed back into the arms of the community with nothing less than affection. She had cared for so many during their darkest hours, providing comfort when it seemed lost. The village now wanted to care for her, and by extension, us.

My children are nothing if not resilient. My absence caused them pain, but they directed their anger at the elders who forced us to flee. Stephen finished his cottage, and the children were free to move between their family homes as they wish. But everyone finds their way to our kitchen each day to dine. Bethany lovingly feeds them all and anyone else that happens upon our door in time for a meal.

The Orostori Demon remains contained in its vessel, which has been placed in our sacred resting space under our village temple. Perhaps one day, the Goddesses will send us bound souls with the power to destroy the demon without losing a mortal life.

Our village is still rebuilding and there is little time for study. Many villages on Arcanos were destroyed during the winter storms, providing ample opportunities for power-hungry men.

The new elders offered me the role of village scribe and story keeper, and I claimed it under the condition that I would be able to write freely without influence from those in power. They readily agreed to my terms. I fear that the ways of the Amora are threatened, and should our people fall, I pray that the Goddesses lead another scribe to these ledgers so that they may use them to fight and rebuild.

CHAPTER 50

LIAM

Nothing on earth could reasonably prepare Liam for the days after a demon exorcism. Nothing about his life the past two months was normal, but the days following the expulsion ritual were as close to normal as he could ask for.

Arriving when she promised Emma she would, Regan found them wrapped in each other's arms; alive, but fragile. Regan took them to Emma's house where a healer named Lily was waiting. Like Bethany, Lily's magic used her energy to hasten their healing. Emma said she didn't know Lily well, but they shared Mabel as a mentor and that's all the women needed to earn each other's trust.

It was almost dawn when Mabel arrived with a pot of soup that she warmed on the stove. She handed them both bowls and put the rest in the refrigerator. She cared for Luna and Belle and changed the sheets on Emma's bed. Morning and night, she came by to check on them. She warmed up a meal and changed their bandages. Mabel said little, but her serene energy set Liam at ease.

Liam and Emma slept, mostly. They spoke little. Liam had so many apologies, but no words to express them. He struggled to convince himself that he was worthy of her forgiveness.

On the rare occasion that sleep was slow to come, he wondered how Bethany and Sara moved on after a similar ordeal. Without soup and drugs and therapy. And living during a time when demon possessions were a risk of just existing.

On the fifth day, Judy came by. She brought them bagels and salted meats and tubs of cream cheese and their favorite coffees. They sat around Emma's patio table, Emma on the side with the shade of a redbud tree, while Judy and Liam basked in the sun. Luna curled on Liam's lap. Maybe Luna liked him after all. Belle relished Judy's long nails scratching behind her ears.

Judy used her free hand to pull an envelope out of the large purse next to her. She handed it to Liam, and he narrowed his eyes at it curiously.

"It's a get well soon card for you both." She picked up her bagel and took a bite.

Liam tore open the seal and opened the brightly glittered greeting card without reading the front. "Sorry about your chicken pox?" He read.

Emma laughed and began to gag on the half-chewed bagel still in her mouth. She drank several mouthfuls of water and regained her composure. "I guess chicken pox works," Emma said and reached for the card.

Judy took a sip of her coffee. "It's a good way to keep people out of your hair for a couple of weeks, which is the absolute minimum I want you two to take off. You can let me know then how much more time you need."

Emma looked up from the card and quietly thanked her.

Judy turned her attention to Liam, but his mouth and his brain couldn't come together to agree on a way to express his gratitude.

"Liam, I wouldn't blame you if you wanted to move out of your apartment. You were never required to live there to begin with. It's been scrubbed and painted so there is no physical evidence of what you endured there. But the memory of your experience is forever enshrined in those walls."

Liam glanced at Emma, but he couldn't read her expression. The moving-in-together conversation would be comparably easy next to all the others they had yet to have.

"Either way, you'll be the last occupant." Judy took a sip of her coffee and waved her hand. "We'll set it on fire or something."

"Thank you, Judy." Liam didn't think the three words were hardly sufficient, but it was a start.

Emma pulled apart her bagel.

"I don't know if Donnie Demon was just fucking with me or," she trailed off. Emma took a breath before continuing. "But it said the rift is open. Or a rift. Somewhere."

In the little they'd spoken, neither Liam nor Emma broached the topic of the Orostori Demon or its plans. Liam would have talked about it had she asked, but he wasn't ready to begin that conversation.

Judy leaned back in her chair. Her face was serious but unreadable. "Do you believe it?"

"I do," Liam answered before Emma could.

Judy picked up the bag beside her and slung it on her shoulder, then picked up her plate and napkins from the table. "You two need to heal. Your injuries won't last forever, but neither will this." She waved her finger at Liam and Emma, her implication clear. "If you two don't heal. Got me?"

Liam and Emma nodded silently. Judy bent down and kissed them both on the cheek, threw her trash in the nearby garbage can, and left out the back gate.

Luna jumped off Liam's lap, allowing him to stand up and walk over to Emma. He pulled a chair close, and she turned to face him.

"Talk to me, Em." He entwined his fingers with hers.

"It's not over," she sighed. "I think this is the beginning of something."

She didn't have to say any more. He understood because he felt it too.

"I know." He pulled her from her chair and into his lap. "Whatever happens next, we'll handle it together. But Judy's right. We need to heal us first."

With light fingers on her chin, he guided her mouth to his. The sweet and tender kisses rocked him just as hard as those filled with lust and passion.

Emma pulled away and rested her forehead against his. "So, you're moving in, right?"

"Oh abso-fucking-lutely."

"I love you." Emma threaded her fingers through his hair, a peaceful smile on her face.

"I love you too." Every gentle touch sparked the magic inside him. He felt it now. The ribbons of their magic knotted and flowed, and he finally felt whole.

BOUND BY INK: A SCIONS OF BELHAVEN NOVELLA

Four centuries after they were penned, Emma DiMarco discovers a collection of diaries recording a world where magic was woven into the fabric of the community.

The diaries were written by Amora scribe and herbal alchemist Sara Cortese while she found love with healer Bethany Clement in the shadow of violent uprisings and attacks by malevolent creatures from another realm.

Though Sara's writings provided a window to Amora culture before the rise of the Commarasi, they only told part of the story.

Going beyond the pages of her diaries, *Bound by Ink* is a *Scions of Belhaven* novella that brings to life Sara and Bethany's love story.

buy.bookfunnel.com/iinkfqsw8
z

AFTERWORD

Roots in Ink is about many things, but at its core, it's a story about storytellers, and how history, culture, and familial connection is kept alive when powerful people want it erased. While this novel can touch on these themes, at best it's a starting point for further learning and reflection.

Here are a few resources to get you started:

PEN America pen.org

PEN America stands at the intersection of literature and human rights to protect free expression in the United States and worldwide. We champion the freedom to write, recognizing the power of the word to transform the world.

ALA Office for Intellectual Freedom ala.org

Established December 1, 1967, the Office for Intellectual Freedom is charged with implementing ALA policies concerning the concept of intellectual freedom as embodied in the Library Bill of Rights, the Association's basic policy on free access to libraries and library materials. The goal of the office is to educate librarians and the general public about the nature and importance of intellectual freedom in libraries.

Drag Story Hour dragstoryhour.org

Drag Story Hour celebrates storytelling through the dynamic art of drag performance. Our network creates programming where audiences are invited to express their authentic selves and become bright lights of change.

The 1619 Project 1619books.com

The 1619 Project is The New York Times Magazine's award-winning reframing of American history that placed slavery and its continuing legacy at the center of our national narrative. The project, which was initially launched in August of 2019, offered a revealing new origin story for the United States, one that helped explain not only the persistence of anti-Black racism and inequality in American life today, but also the roots of so much of what makes the country unique.

African American Cultural Heritage Action Fund savingplaces.org/

In November 2017, the National Trust for Historic Preservation launched its African American Cultural Heritage Action Fund, a program that makes an important and lasting contribution to the American landscape by preserving sites of African American activism, achievement, and resilience. Through this preservation effort—the largest ever undertaken in support of African American historic sites—we work to expand the American story.

SaveHistory.org savehistory.org

Theft, vandalism, and grave robbing degrade Tribal sovereignty and senses of place, community, and security. Our mission is to end archaeological resource crime on Tribal lands and raise public awareness of the importance of heritage sites.

Association of Tribal Archives, Libraries and Museums atalm.org

ATALM is an international non-profit organization that maintains a network of support for Indigenous programs, provides culturally relevant programming and services, encourages collaboration among tribal and non-tribal cultural institutions, and articulates contemporary issues related to developing and sustaining the cultural sovereignty of Native Nations.

Asian & Pacific Islander Americans in Historic Preservation apiahip.org

APIAHiP is the only national organization dedicated to protecting historic places and cultural resources significant to Asian and Pacific Islander Americans.

Mental Illness and Intimate Partner Violence

If you're struggling with depression, emotional distress, alcohol or drug use, or just need to talk to someone, please reach out to the suicide and crisis lifeline at 988 or 988lifeline.org.

You deserve to be in a healthy relationship. If you aren't and you need assistance, contact the National Domestic Violence Hotline at 1.800.799.SAFE (7233) or visit thehotline.org/get-help

These resources and more can be found on my website at ariellamonti.com/resources.

ACKNOWLEDGEMENTS

I've always been a writer. And when you're a writer there are always people telling you to write a book. I always laughed and said I'd stick with journalism. I wasn't creative enough to write a novel. That took skill and imagination that I absolutely didn't possess. I was right about the skill part, but I was wrong about the creativity and imagination. I'm thankful to all the people that saw that in me before I d id.

This book wouldn't have been completed if not for my first set of readers. A rag tag group of friends who volunteered to read the roughest rough draft in order to tell me if it was even worth finishing with the intent to publish. Some of them went on to beta read the completed draft and in a full circle moment signed up for an advance reader copy.

To my book coach Meghan Clancy who guided me to a finished manuscript and gave me a crash course in narrative writing. The learning curve switching from journalism to prose was steeper than I anticipated so she had her work cut out for her.

To all my beta readers whose feedback helped to shape this story. I learned so much about storytelling from that process and this book wouldn't be what it is without you.

To the members of my critique group, Roots in Ink would have remained a MILF if it weren't for your support, advice, creativity, and all around awesomeness.

To Ruthie Bowles for sharing with me your knowledge, expertise, and experience that helped me write an inclusive story that represents the diversity of Emma and Liam's world.

To Amanda Hawkins for the cover you plucked from my mind and made real. You're a brilliant artist.

To Jenny Sliger, without you this book would be downright unreadable. I am truly thankful for your skills.

To mom and dad for always pushing me toward my writing career instead of pulling me away from it. I've never taken for granted your emotional support and belief in my dreams. I'm extremely grateful for the financial support you've provided to make this book a reality.

To Chuck, my real life hockey romance, and Killian, my epilogue baby, thank you for being a part of this happily ever after.

Special shout outs to:

The Merriam-Webster thesaurus and Laurel Clarke's Sexy Thesaurus for adding some variety to my writing.

Dark Side Divas Chris and Stef for their hilarious and insightful script analysis of the entire Marvel Cinematic Universe. The Marvelous Divas podcast was the college-level writing course I wish I had in undergrad.

ABOUT ARIELLA

Ariella is a former journalist, but uses "former" loosely. Her curiosity for all things is insatiable and research is her favorite part of any project.She writes cozy contemporary and high stakes fantasy romances. Her work is swoony and open door absolutely not intended for readers who are under 18.

Someone once told her to write what you know so all her millennial protagonists are bisexual, neurodivergent, and live with chronic mental illness. They mostly have their life together and Ariella chronicles their coming-of-middle-age stories.

When she's not writing, she teaches yoga and falls behind on laundry. She lives in the suburbs of Raleigh, North Carolina with her husband, child, a collection of aging pets, and a flock of chickens that won't stop tearing up the new plants in her flower garden.

Visit my website to read my blog or buy your next book.

Subscribe to my newsletter for book updates and bonus content.

WEBSITE
BLOG
SHOP
ariellamonti.com

NEWSLETTER

free short stories
bonus scenes
exclusive content

subscribepage.io/6AzoIL

MORE BOOKS BY ARIELLA

Contemporary Romance

Let it Rain
Radio Romance
Chasing Ember

Fantasy Romance

Roots in Ink, Scions of Belhaven, Book 1
Bound by Ink, Scions of Belhaven Novella

 **SWEET MAGNOLIA SHOP**

signed paperbacks
special editions
ebooks you own

ariellamonti.com/shop

TWO WEEKS LATER

Emma reached for the cup of tea on her coffee table and hissed a few four-letter words before switching to the other hand. Her wrist ached, and her fingers were stiff, but it was the sudden sharp pains that caused her the most grief. They reminded her the most of how it felt to pierce her skin with the blade of a knife.

The panic came next, bringing with it a tightening of her chest and a racing heartbeat. Emma covered her eyes with her bandaged hand and squeezed them tight as she tried to keep her breathing calm and even. In the darkness of her anxiety, Emma felt Luna's paws padding silently over her thighs and belly, easing Emma back against the couch until Luna could rest her vibrating body on Emma's chest.

The doorbell rang. Emma exhaled a breath and took another one slowly before yelling, "Door's open, Lily!"

Emma's magic was stronger now, and she felt it in ways she hadn't before. Lily's magic was different from the others. Healing magic always was. But she felt Lily's presence the moment she stepped onto Emma's porch.

Lily frowned when she stepped through the door. "Another panic attack?"

She crossed the room and sat next to Emma. Emma's magic reached out for Lily's like tree branches seeking sunlight.

"Luna caught it before it got too bad," Emma replied.

"The Goddesses gave you a beautiful gift." Lily smiled, but while there was genuine warmth in it, her golden amber eyes were always detached and distant. "Can I touch your hand?"

Emma nodded, and Lily took Emma's hand in hers and carefully unwrapped the bandage. Sitting so closely, Emma could smell the sunscreen and salt water on Lily's sun-darkened light skin. Her long black hair was still damp and twisted in a braid over her shoulder.

Emma didn't know the details of Lily's life before Belhaven, only that she was in a place where her feet never touched the sea. Since arriving on the island two years earlier, Lily spent much of her free time on the water.

"How's the water today?" Emma looked away while Lily examined the cut that ran across her palm.

"A little rough. I got tired pretty quickly and didn't swim as long as usual." Lily adjusted her position next to Emma until she could cup the injured hand in both of hers and rest her thumbs softly on Emma's self-inflicted wound.

The hum of Lily's magic trickled through her fingertips and seeped into Emma's skin until it consumed the entire limb. Emma sighed contentedly, intoxicated by a flood of happy chemicals also triggered by Lily's magic.

She didn't know much about healing magic until she read Sara's diaries. Mabel was also a healer and taught Emma the basics. Because of her age, Mabel didn't do much healing anymore, and Emma sometimes wondered who Mabel would have mentored had the Commarasi never come to power.

Sara may have been madly in love with Bethany, but their love story made up little of the remaining diaries. Sara mostly wrote about how the women worked together to care for the people of their village.

Seeing how Lily worked to care for her and Liam, Emma began to yearn for that type of care in her world.

"I can help you with your work." The words slipped out before Emma could consider their impact but kept going. "So you're not as tired. That's how it was always meant to be done."

Lily sighed and kept her eyes on Emma's hand. "I don't heal people anymore. Special cases only."

"Right," Emma said quietly. "Mable said you're a death doula now. I can still help."

The corners of Lily's mouth almost quirked into a smile, but it disappeared as fast. Still, her eyes failed to leave Emma's hand. "I work better alone, but I do genuinely appreciate the offer."

Emma fought the impulse to ask more questions. When Lily arrived in Belhaven, Emma did everything she could to pull Lily into their little family, but she always kept her distance. It took Emma a little while to accept that Lily wanted to be on the fringes.

The pair sat in silence until the back door creaked open and slammed shut. Belle emerged from the kitchen and placed her chin on Emma's lap. In a now familiar game, Luna got up and sprinted for the kitchen looking for Liam. Their animal caretakers switched off at intervals only known to them.

Liam walked into the living room with a sports drink in one hand and Luna cradled in the other.

"I'll be back," Liam said. "I'm heading to the hardware store."

"Liam Doran," Lily said with a firm tone rivaling any mother. "If you re-injure yourself building something, you're on your own. You'll have to use non-magic healthcare."

The scolding made Liam turn red and Emma cackle.

"I know. Jake is coming with me. He'll help me get stuff loaded. I'll see you later." He bent down and pressed a long kiss to Emma's forehead. "I love you."

Emma couldn't get enough of hearing him say those three beautiful words. "I love you too."

"Who's Jake?" Lily asked after Liam left the room.

"He's a mechanic at the museum. Liam hired him, and they seem to get along really well."

Lily hummed, but Emma had a feeling something else was on her mind.

"Can I ask you something?" Lily let go of Emma's hand and sat back against the couch. "It's related to your mental health so it's kind of connected to your care. But it's also really personal so I understand if you don't want to answer."

Emma shrugged but inside, she was elated. Maybe they'd become friends after all. "Sure. I'm kinda done with secrets, honestly."

"After everything Liam said and did to you, how can you even look at him?"

Emma sighed a laugh and looked into Belle's friendly brown eyes as she scratched behind her floppy ears. "Demon Liam wasn't the worst boyfriend I've had."

Emma shrugged. "It's so hard to explain because it's something so deeply embedded in my being. When Liam was possessed, I was in this constant state of being pushed away and pulled back. My magic wanted to protect me from the demon. It was hard to be near Liam. I couldn't touch him. Because it wasn't completely him.

"But the part of my magic that's bonded and bound to Liam's kept me from drifting too far because we're meant to be in each other's lives, and I was the only one who could save him. And now that I have, I feel *him* again. Even stronger because his magic is stronger now."

Lily arched a brow slightly, and her mouth twitched as though she was trying—and failing—to hide her disbelief. If Emma's body hadn't been lulled into a state of blissful relaxation, the slight gesture would have been enough to send her into a battle to defend Liam and their relationship.

"Without the magic, all this would be so much harder," Emma said instead. "It's still hard, but Liam isn't the face of it."

Lily finished wrapping a new bandage on Emma's wrist and hand and stepped aside to put her supplies back into her medical bag. Belle filled Lily's space on the couch.

"Logically, I know you're right," Lily said thoughtfully. "Just in practice, I don't think I could forgive that easily. Even if we were soulmates."

Lily didn't say much, but it was enough for Emma to have a better understanding of why she probably kept people at a distance. "Sounds like there's someone out there that really got under your skin."

Lily laughed and picked up her bag. "Yeah, you could say that. Wherever he is, I hope he's fucking miserable."

Need More?

How about a bonus scene?

Subscribe to my newsletter for access to a bonus scene where Liam and Emma drop some clues for the setting of *Healed with Iron*, the second full novel in the Scions of Belhaven series.

Scan the QR code or follow the Bookfunnel link for access.

Current subscribers can also find the link at the bottom of each newsletter.

dl.bookfunnel.com
/3f5yxfzlt6